RISKING IT ALL

TITANS: SIN CITY BOXSET

SIERRA CARTWRIGHT

RISKING IT ALL

Copyright @ 2022 Sierra Cartwright

First E-book Publication: April 2022

Editing by Nicki Richards, What's Your Story Editorial Services

Line Editing by ELF, GG Royale, Jennifer Barker

Proofing by Bev Albin and Cassie Hess-Dean

Layout Design by Once Upon An Alpha

Cover Design by Once Upon An Alpha

Photo provided by Depositphotos.com

Promotion by Once Upon An Alpha, Shannon Hunt

All rights reserved. Except for use in a review, no part of this publication may be reproduced, distributed, or transmitted in any form, or by any means, electronic or mechanical, including photocopying, recording, or by any information storage and retrieval system, without prior written permission of the author.

This is a work of fiction. Names, characters, places, brands, media, and incidents are either the products of the author's imagination or are used fictitiously, and any resemblance to any actual persons, living or dead, is entirely coincidental.

The author acknowledges the trademarked status and trademark owners of various products referenced in this work of fiction. The publication/use of these trademarks is not authorized, associated with, or sponsored by the trademark owners.

Adult Reading Material

Disclaimer: This work of fiction is for mature (18+) audiences only and contains strong sexual content and situations.

It is a standalone with my guarantee of satisfying happily ever after.

All rights reserved.

DEDICATION

Thank you for reading!

As always, I appreciate Miss Whit, Shannon Hunt, ELF, Bad Ass Bev, Nicki Richards, GG Royale, Cassie Hess-Dean, Angie, Angela, Marianne, my ARC team, beta readers, newsletter subscribers, and the fabulous members of my reader group, Sierra's Super Stars.

I'm grateful to have a wonderful team surrounding me.

HARD HAND

TITANS: SIN CITY, BOOK ONE

HARD HAND

SIN CITY TITANS

USA TODAY BESTSELLING AUTHOR
SIERRA CARTWRIGHT

CHAPTER ONE

Cole Stewart.

Breathing in jagged hiccups, Avery glanced again at the tuxedoed gentleman. No one else was that tall and imposing, hardened by numerous tours of duty overseas, and —if rumors were correct—some sort of undercover work. He moved his head to study the stage, and the light caught the scar on his cheek. The jagged white line arrowed downward, ending dangerously close to his jugular. Her last doubt vanished. It was definitely Cole Stewart.

She curled her toes in her too-high, too-expensive designer sandals. *What is he doing here?* She'd been over the guest list for her great-aunt's eightieth birthday extravaganza dozens of times. The Sensational Miss Scarlet had been a mainstay in Las Vegas for more than six decades and had made hundreds of friends. Because she wanted everyone she cared about to attend her Saints and Sinners masquerade ball, the names of the invitees had been studied and restudied for more than a year.

A man wearing a security guard uniform emblazoned

with the Royal Sterling Hotel's logo, entered the room and stood next to Cole.

Since Avery was behind the elaborate champagne fountain wearing a fabulous ornate black mask, she was free to feast her gaze on Cole, the Dominant of her fantasies.

His dark hair was longer than she remembered. It was no longer tortured by a military buzz. Instead, strands teased the collar of his jacket. The look didn't tame him. It simply made him more roguish.

Although Cole wasn't classically handsome, he was rugged in a don't-fuck-with-me kind of way. His physique was more sumptuous than ever. Everything about him from his size to his stance promised he was capable of protecting his woman. And she knew he could make one scream from pleasure.

A memory of watching him interact with a submissive lanced through Avery, and she squirmed.

Two years prior, she'd been at a BDSM play party at the home of her friends and renowned legal eagles, Diana and Alcott Hewitt. Cole had entered with his submissive, Gia. Most times when Avery watched scenes, the partners appeared to be in sync, maybe a little in love. But Gia had goaded him. In addition to addressing him disrespectfully, she chose to ignore some of his commands. He never raised his voice or lost his temper. Instead, he'd continued to state his wishes without emotion. Gia had responded, however, to his gentle caresses.

Once he'd taken her down from the Saint Andrew's cross, he was tender, and Gia leaned into him.

Avery longed to be with a man as patient and firm as Cole.

Many times, she masturbated to thoughts of him. Once, when she'd been with another man, she pretended she was with Cole.

About six months ago, she'd seen him again at the Back Room, an upscale BDSM club. This time he was alone. He kept to himself, brooding, detached.

She'd been alone for year, and she craved a hard hand to soothe her. But the breakup with her Dominant had left her emotionally uncertain. As she watched Cole across the dungeon, she mentally rehearsed and discarded a dozen openings. Walk up to him and kneel? Meet him as an equal? Ask mutual friends for an introduction? Hope he would notice her interest?

After more than an hour of indecision, she convinced herself to say hello. But the moment she'd gotten close to him and their gazes met, she froze. Even though she was an experienced BDSM player, she'd never had a visceral reaction like she did to Cole. His eyes—charcoal and intense—pierced her submissive soul. Nerves trumped courage. She started to tremble. In the end, she couldn't force herself to take the final steps.

Ever since, she regretted that night, and she'd vowed to be braver if given a second chance.

Now that she was in the same room as him again, she understood her own cowardice. With his arms folded across his chest, legs braced apart, he was a force of nature.

Perhaps sensing scrutiny, he turned in her direction, and his powerful gaze locked on her. He scanned her body, starting at her shoes and sweeping up. Cole took so much time that her internal temperature spiked. When he reached her face, he quirked an eyebrow, as if in recognition. *That's not possible*. They'd never met, never spoken. Even if they had, she was still hidden behind a mask, and she'd traded in her long light-brown hair for shoulder-length blonde with bright-pink streaks.

Still, just like that night, she trembled.

Marie, the party planner, strode through a side door.

Electronic pad clutched in her hands, she made a direct line to where Avery stood. "Does everything look all right?"

Grateful to be jolted from the nerve-wrecking memories, Avery replied, "It's perfect." And it was. The stage was set in a retro manner, including oversize square microphones. The band members wore tuxedos. Several food stations were in place with hors d'oeuvres for the wine hour. Around the periphery of the room, tall tables were draped with black or silver tablecloths and decorated with soaring centerpieces crafted from flowers, masks, and peacock feathers. And there was dazzle everywhere—sequins and crystals strung from the ceilings, tacked to the walls—all befitting one of the country's most accomplished and scandalous burlesque dancers.

Backstage, a number of entertainers wore gold or silver body paint and nothing else. They represented sinners for the evening. Others were dressed in nuns' habits or monks' robes. A couple of women even wore halos.

"Have you tried the champagne?" Marie questioned.

"Not yet. Should I?"

"Please."

From a nearby table, Avery grabbed a flute and held it beneath a stream of the flowing pink bubbly. Of course Miss Scarlet had selected a rosé. It had been a favorite since she saw *An Affair to Remember* with Cary Grant and Deborah Kerr. Miss Scarlet said she'd once shared a glass with Cary himself. Though Avery wasn't sure about that, she didn't doubt it was possible.

She took a small drink, expecting it to be overly sweet. She was surprised by complexity. "Wow. It's fantastic."

"That's what I thought."

Seduced, Avery savored another sip before putting the glass down. "I'm betting this isn't the fifty-dollar-a-bottle stuff that I approved?"

Marie winced. "Miss Scarlet was at the tasting, and when she sampled this stuff…"

"Say no more." Even though Avery served as her great-aunt's financial advisor, Miss Scarlet controlled her own fortune. If she wanted to drop five hundred dollars a pop for the best bubbly on the planet, that was her choice.

"I'm sorry to say we didn't save any money on the dessert either."

Avery sighed. "I'm not surprised."

"You will be," she replied cryptically.

"Oh?" Avery arched her eyebrows.

"Your aunt is planning something extravagant. With a cake. Of sorts."

"You don't think I should have been warned?"

"I promised secrecy." Marie pantomimed locking her lips and tossing away the key. "But I can tell you the changes have thrown us about fifty thousand dollars over budget."

Stunned, Avery blinked. "I assume she knows that?"

"Yes."

"In that case, we should enjoy every moment."

A door closing at the back of the room made her turn around. Cole was gone. She sighed in relief, but then a stab of restlessness went through her. "Were there last-minute additions to the guest list?"

"Not that I know of."

"I saw Cole Stewart a few minutes ago."

"Who?"

The most gorgeous man on the planet. "He's the billionaire security tech genius who sold his first company to Julien Bonds." According to an article in *Scandalicious,* her favorite online gossip site, Cole's groundbreaking software package was now installed on every new Bonds device.

Marie typed the name into her pad.

"He was talking to someone I assume was with security."

Marie shook her head. "He's not on the list. No one will get in without an invitation. I'll chat with Lucy and see what's up."

"Thank you."

Lucy Pine was the Royal Sterling's head of security. The petite woman might reach five feet tall in her heeled boots, but she was badass enough to take down the hardest of criminals, all without her braid coming undone.

"Anything else?" Marie asked.

"You've done a great job. I'll go check on my aunt."

"The doors will open in about twenty minutes. Make it quick?" Marie pleaded.

"Promise." Avery headed toward the elevator that had access to the building's top floors.

Maybe because of the alcohol or her stupid-high heels—but definitely not because of Cole Stewart—she had to steady herself on a railing when the car rocketed past the spa level, then the hotel floors.

With a soft *ding*, the car arrived, and she exited into a gorgeous long hallway. She made her way to her great-aunt's condominium that had an awe-inspiring view of the Strip. Miss Scarlet said she loved lording over Las Vegas. Over the years, she'd seen a lot of changes and mostly liked them. At times, though, she sighed wistfully, still missing a particular dark and dangerous mobster she'd had a mad affair with.

Avery knocked on her great-aunt's door, and the summons was answered by none other than Mademoiselle Giselle, a New Orleans shop owner and ballerina of international renown.

"I had to see Miss Scarlet in her outfit," the woman admitted after accepting Avery's gentle embrace. "We've got a busy night, but I couldn't resist bringing her some flowers."

There were at least a dozen more bouquets than there had been earlier this afternoon. "Are you dancing tonight?"

"Oui. It's my honor."

Mademoiselle and Miss Scarlet had been friends for at least half a century and shared secrets that would only be revealed in a posthumous memoir.

Once Mademoiselle said goodbye, Avery made her way to the living room.

Miss Scarlet was standing on a platform where a seamstress was making final alterations to her costume. A headdress sat off to the side, waiting to be affixed.

Even at eighty, she was a bombshell, with a radiant smile, a fit body, and long legs shown off by slits that ran up the sides of her skirt, almost to her buttocks. A number of feathers had been applied in strategic locations, and a pair of long black gloves were draped over the cheval mirror.

As she'd done almost every night for decades, Miss Scarlet had applied false eyelashes and glittery stage makeup. She completed her ensemble with an artistically placed beauty mark.

Avery leaned in to kiss her great-aunt on the cheek. "Happy birthday."

"I never get tired of hearing that! In fact, I think I should have two birthdays a year now. I love the attention." She batted her eyes. "And the gifts."

Avery grinned.

"Move over there, into the light where I can see you," Scarlet ordered.

Though Avery shook her head from mild embarrassment, she did as she was told. She spun around then offered a little curtsy.

"Bravo! As I imagined, your dress is perfect, and you are magnificent."

Avery struggled with the compliment. When she opened the gift from Miss Scarlet, Avery had stared in shock. She'd never seen anything like the gorgeous clingy black gown. It was cut asymmetrically across her chest and had only one strap. The open back plunged to the base of her spine, leaving her exposed. Since the dress was tighter than most of her clothing, she'd promised herself that she would lose five pounds before the event. Those plans were dashed when the Royal Sterling installed a cupcake-dispensing machine in the hotel's lobby. Willpower had been defeated by a single swipe of her credit card. Still, she was glad she'd worn the dress. It gave her confidence and made her feel sexy.

"Did you try the champagne, darling girl?" In the mirror, Scarlet's gaze found Avery's.

"It's amazing."

"Isn't it? Highly recommended. An online review says it has an evocative finish."

Avery wasn't quite sure what that meant. "I'll take your word for it."

"Don't worry about the budget."

"Aunt Scarlet, it's your money. You should spend it on anything you want."

"That's not what I meant at all." She waved a hand. "I'm going to get Rafe Sterling to pay for it."

"Are you?" Avery had met the CEO of Sterling Worldwide on a couple of occasions. Though he was an excellent businessman, he wasn't involved in the day-to-day operations of each property. "How are you going to manage that?"

"I pack this hotel every night that I perform. And I'm sure he'd like me to sign another contract. All part of the negotiation strategy, my dear." Miss Scarlet winked, and her eyelash twinkled from the glitter dabbed on it. "I won't squander your inheritance on rosé, no matter how good it is."

"You've worked hard every day of your life." The familiar refrain made Avery sigh. "It's you I love, and I want to enjoy your company. That's the only thing that matters."

"Good thing, since I intend to live another forty years."

With no plans of ever retiring. Not only did Miss Scarlet own a studio where she taught dance and exercise classes, she'd recently opened a museum for cabaret memorabilia. Even now, she was choreographing a new burlesque show to debut in the fall.

"Get the party started, will you?" Miss Scarlet suggested. "I'll be down just as soon as I can."

"Marie mentioned a surprise. Anything I should know?"

Miss Scarlet's sculptured eyebrows arched higher. "I've no idea what you're talking about, darling girl."

"That was what I was afraid you'd say." She shook her head. "I saw Cole Stewart downstairs."

"Delicious, isn't he?"

"Is he your guest?"

"He's consulting with hotel security." She hesitated. "He's a...VIP."

"A..." Avery's heart plunged.

"Yes."

Why am I not surprised? Though she was an ordinary person living a very ordinary life, her aunt had found a place in the upper echelons.

Avery had learned about the Zeta Society early on when she'd picked up an owl from her great-aunt's shelf. For years, the statue with its emerald-green eyes had fascinated her, but it wasn't until she was a teenager that Avery questioned its meaning.

Scarlet swore Avery to secrecy about the Zetas—whose members were known as Titans. Politicians belonged, as did royalty, entrepreneurs, writers, Hollywood A-listers, scientists, prize winners in every field, and even members of the Mafia. Initiation fees were astronomical, and yearly dues were equally onerous. Still, the wait list to join was several years long.

"You'll have Marie add his name to the guest list?"

She sighed. "Of course." After giving her great-aunt another quick kiss, she made her way back downstairs. One of the security guards opened the ballroom door for her. She was grateful that Cole wasn't there. Part of her wondered if she'd conjured him from a very vivid imagination. Or maybe an unstated need. It had been forever since she played with a Dom, years since she'd been in a committed relationship.

The banquet captain stood in the middle of a circle of hotel employees, issuing final instructions. Marie was speaking with the head of security, and Avery joined them.

"Marie tells me you were asking about Cole Stewart," Lucy said.

"Miss Scarlet filled me in. Thank you."

"Good. Then it's not a problem if he checks in from time to time?"

Only to my libido. "He's an invited guest."

"Let me know if there's anything you need." With a curt nod, Lucy excused herself.

When they were alone, Marie tapped her electronic pad. "Everything's checked off. Ready?"

"Yes." Avery straightened her mask. "Let's get this party started."

Marie signaled to the band, and they began their instrumental rendition of Frank Sinatra's *Luck Be a Lady* while servers moved into position. A couple of the painted entertainers stood still, appearing to be statues. One perched on the grand piano while another linked arms with a nun in a stunning juxtaposition.

When Marie nodded toward the security guard, he signaled to have the doors opened, and the guests began to file in.

Some headed for the bar, others to turn up chairs and lay claim to tables, and a few made their way toward the food.

For the next thirty minutes, Avery greeted guests while

wondering what was keeping her great-aunt. Part of the surprise?

The moment Cole entered the ballroom, she knew it, even without seeing him.

Wisps of hair rose on her nape as the recognition of his power over her danced down her spine.

Avery desperately wanted to turn and look at him, but she held off, continuing to smile and talk with attendees, pretending an interest she suddenly didn't have.

A tall, thin, gorgeous Black singer stepped onto the stage in a catsuit and started to belt out the words to *Fever*.

Avery watched, entranced as the performer strutted down the stairs to lean against the grand piano. At least a dozen men, snapping their fingers, emerged from behind the curtain to add to the seductive chorus.

She had to admit, Miss Scarlet had done a spectacular job with the music and entertainment selections.

Drawn by the pulse of primal energy in the room, Avery could no longer resist. She glanced over her shoulder to where she instinctively knew Cole was standing.

That familiar spark of fear snaked through her, leaving her rooted to the spot, even though she wanted to go to him.

A waiter passed by, and she snagged a flute. As she sipped, bubbles tickled her nose and heightened her senses. Avery watched the band and performers, trying to shut out thoughts of Cole.

But the harder she tried, the more he occupied her mind.

Every part of her yearned for a Dom. And tonight, not just any Dom. Cole.

So, what am I going to do? The longer she thought about it, the more adrenaline flooded her body, making her jittery.

He could have a girlfriend or submissive at home. Even if he didn't, he could still reject her, but since he wouldn't know who she was, her ego would remain intact.

Since her hand was shaking, she crossed the room to put down her mostly untouched glass.

This was her moment. If she deliberated too long, she might lose her opportunity.

Her stomach dancing with butterflies, she traced the curlicue outline of her mask, drawing courage and reassurance from its anonymity. For tonight, if never again, she wanted to be the woman she was in her dreams.

Avery chatted with some of the guests as she made her way across the room. She smiled until she thought her makeup might crack, all the while keeping an eye on him.

Eventually—too soon and simultaneously not soon enough—she reached him.

For a moment, her words lodged in her throat.

The passage of time had only made him more attractive. The cut of his expensive tailored tuxedo should have made him look civilized. It didn't.

Her nerves doubled.

"Evening." His voice was like the finest liqueur, rich and deep with a hint of sweetness laced through the danger.

Rockets of arousal shot through her. She forced herself to pretend she didn't know who he was and that she wasn't a bundle of apprehension. "Glad to have you at Miss Scarlet's birthday party."

"Cole Stewart."

"A pleasure to meet you. I'm—" She thought for a moment through the onslaught of apprehension. Finally, she seized on a name. "Layla."

He extended his hand, and his ring caught the light. An owl, with inset emeralds for eyes.

Avery slid her palm against his much larger one, and her knees buckled. Instantly, she caught herself, but she was stunned by the strength of her instinct to kneel for him. No doubt, even women who weren't into BDSM would recognize his authority.

"Layla," he echoed with a slight mocking smile, as if he didn't believe her.

He continued to hold her, and his grip was as powerful as she'd expected. It wasn't crushing, however. Cole clearly knew his strength and harnessed it.

"And what do you do?"

"I'm a project accountant for a construction firm. Not very glamorous, but I enjoy it."

"You like having everything neat and tidy?"

"I've never looked at it that way." She shrugged. Even without knowing her, he'd made an accurate guess, not that she was surprised.

"But?"

"You're right. Math is absolute. And I do enjoy chasing down discrepancies so that the numbers add up." How much was he willing to reveal in return? "And you, Mr. Stewart?"

"At the moment, I work as a consultant to Hawkeye Security."

"I've heard of them."

He inclined his head to one side. "Have you?"

"The company I work for has just signed an agreement with them." Curiosity drove her next question. "Are you in Las Vegas permanently?"

"I have a home here, but I don't spend much time in it. As you said about your job, it's not very glamorous. I make recommendations that people don't want to follow." He gave a wry grin, and then the conversation hit a natural lull.

What the hell should she say next? *I can't help but notice how commanding you appear. Are you a Dominant?*

"Which are you?"

Perplexed, she frowned. It was as if he'd read her mind. "I'm sorry?"

"It's a saints or sinners masquerade." He traced a finger around the corner of her mask. For a heart-stopping moment, she thought he might try to take it off her. "I'd say a saint?" He swept his gaze over her. "But in that dress?"

"Ah—"

"There's something innocent about you, but you didn't answer immediately to tell me you were a saint. So that makes me wonder."

This was her chance. He'd offered the opening she hungered for, but her boldness wavered.

Cole leaned forward, indicating his interest in her answer.

Then abruptly, the music ended. Shocked, she turned toward the stage. Whatever was happening wasn't on the program she'd approved a few days ago.

In true gentlemanly form, Cole steadied her by placing his hand on the bare skin of her back. Electricity arced up her spine to settle at her nape. If she had this kind of reaction to his touch, what would it be like to submit?

A spotlight hit the stage, and the band struck up a fun version of *Happy Birthday*.

As she watched with Cole's hand still firmly on her spine, four men in skintight clothing wheeled out a gigantic cake. The thing had numerous layers and a great big candle on the top.

Cole leaned closer, his breath warm on her ear. "Where's Miss Scarlet?"

"No idea," she whispered back.

A chorus line of women in feathers and little else began to sing as the band launched a second run-through of the song.

When they reached the *happy birthday, Miss Scarlet* part, the top of the cake exploded open, and Miss Scarlet emerged.

The crowd cheered. Avery clapped wildly. She should

have suspected her great-aunt would dazzle, but Avery had never guessed she'd make such a stunning entrance.

The song ended, and Miss Scarlet blew kisses as she waved. A hundred cell phones were pulled out, and guests snapped pictures.

Men, in their gold paint, lined up in front of her. Then, in the silence, she dived forward.

Stunned gasps rippled through the guests as she hung suspended in midair, her chin cupped seductively in her palm and her knees bent in a way that made her gown billow about her.

As one, the men undulated, reaching to guide her down, and a spotlight reflected off the silver wire Avery hadn't noticed until now.

As she'd been doing for more than half a century, Miss Scarlet commanded the room while wearing a towering headdress and elaborate costume.

"Isn't she fabulous?" Avery asked Cole.

"She is indeed."

Rather than leaving the stage, Miss Scarlet took a place in front of the chorus line.

A song Avery didn't immediately remember began to play, and a man in a top hat sauntered onto the stage. He stood there, appearing mysterious as a woman strolled in front of him.

Several seconds in, Avery recognized the tune, *I'm a Good Girl*, in which the performer was anything but.

Toward the end of the song, Miss Scarlet was plucked from the stage. In her glittery stilettos, she wrapped herself around the guidewire and made a sensual writhing motion before turning to shake her backside at the crowd.

Several dozen more female cast members exploded onto the scene, wriggling their feathered rears while the male performers raised their eyebrows as well as their top hats.

The full-on burlesque number rocked the room.

Cole said something, and Avery leaned in to hear him.

"She's amazing," he repeated.

"Every day she wows me," Avery confessed.

As the song segued into a new one, a spotlight hit the stage, and a curtain was pulled back. A showstopping rocking horse dominated the scene, at least ten feet tall and ungelded. On his back was a woman dressed in a corset and tulle skirt. As the stallion moved back and forth, the woman undulated her hips provocatively.

Avery watched, shocked and riveted, aware of the way Cole was still touching her and the heat that was flowing through her. It wasn't just from him, but from the raw sex oozing from the cabaret show.

"What do you think?" Cole asked against her ear.

A tremor splashed through her. This was the opening she'd wanted.

Avery turned slightly, grateful she was incognito and could be someone she wasn't, even if it was just for this moment. This time, she prayed courage didn't desert her.

CHAPTER TWO

Cole narrowed his eyes and wondered what the hell game Avery was playing.

No matter how clever she thought she'd been in not using her real name and hiding behind a mask, he would know the beauty anywhere.

Her eyes were wide and luminous, innocent yet provocative. She'd cut her hair, changed from brown to blonde, and added streaks of color.

And none of that mattered.

Her curves were the kind he remembered. His reaction to her was visceral, the same as it had been six months ago when he'd seen her at the Back Room.

He'd thought she might approach him that night. Instead, she vanished.

The next day, he asked mutual friends about her. He learned she was single and that she'd had a bad experience with a Dominant.

This evening, her attempt at casual conversation had charmed him. She'd been seeking out information about his job and where he lived. He didn't need a background as an operative to figure out she was interested in him.

Cole glanced at her ring finger. Bare. But her necklace intrigued him. It was bold, made from interlocking pieces of silver that snuggled against the base of her throat. It didn't appear to be a collar, though it was close enough that he couldn't be certain. Of course, no one who wasn't in the lifestyle would even question the piece of jewelry.

The song ended, and another began, the routine something like the world-famous Rockettes would perform, with high, exciting kicks and energy.

The adorably submissive Avery shifted her weight from one foot to the other, radiating her discomfort. If his guess was correct, she wanted to be on her knees with his hand tangled in her hair, awaiting his command. Right now, if he had a choice, that command would be to suck his cock.

The burlesque show ended, and the performers received a standing ovation.

As the stage was cleared, the band segued into another Frank Sinatra signature song, making it a bit easier to talk. A few couples wandered onto the dance floor, and he had no intention of letting her vanish a second time. "Shall we?" he invited.

Her mouth parted slightly, and he was tempted to kiss away her hesitation.

Where the hell did that thought come from? The tender impulse shocked him. He was not a man given to romance. To distract himself, he held out a hand.

A few seconds later, she accepted.

It was the first step toward dominating her.

On the parquet dance floor, he led to the slow beat, and she followed in flawless moves. Her skin felt luxurious. No matter what he asked for with his body, she responded.

Would she behave the same way in private? Suddenly, he was anxious to get her out of that dress.

The tune ended.

By unspoken accord, they crossed the room to stand near a group of people flocked around Miss Scarlet. She held an open black fan emblazoned with a sequined kitten, and as she spoke, she waved the thing around.

Avery remained close to him, as if they were a couple. It surprised him how much he welcomed that idea.

A waiter passed by with champagne, and Cole asked if she would like one.

"Thank you. No." She shook her head. "I think I've had enough."

"Good." He wanted her sober enough to play with him later. "Tell me about your jewelry," he invited.

"Sorry?"

"Your necklace."

Behind the mask, her eyes widened. She fingered one of the links, probably without being aware of the act.

"Does it have any significance?"

"Something I bought myself recently at an art festival downtown."

"Intriguing," he said.

"How so?"

He was done allowing her to hide. "I wondered if it might indicate an interest in bondage."

"Bondage." She dropped her hand. "Is that something you're into, Mr. Stewart?"

"I generally don't discuss my personal life in a public setting."

"But you're the one who brought it up."

He wondered if she had any idea how breathless her voice was. "So I did. And the answer is yes. Do you know anything about it?"

She was saved from an answer when Miss Scarlet breezed over in a cloud of perfume.

"You were marvelous," Avery enthused.

The woman's smile dazzled, and it encompassed Cole. "You are more handsome every time I see you."

She offered her gloved hand, and he raised it to his lips.

"Always a pleasure, Miss Scarlet. Your entrance was spectacular."

"I do enjoy leaping into the arms of strong young men. I'll be doing that for my ninetieth as well."

"I believe it."

Her attention was claimed by admirers wearing old-fashioned black-and-white-striped prison garb. Sinners, no doubt.

"If you'll excuse me?" Miss Scarlet didn't wait for an answer before flipping open the kitty fan and moving off, leaving him alone again with Avery.

"Where were we?" He figured he'd give her the opportunity to pursue or avoid the question he'd asked her earlier.

"We were talking about bondage." Despite her comment about the necklace not being a collar, she absently touched it again. Then, as if realizing that she was fidgeting, she stilled and lowered her hand. "And yes, I'm familiar with it."

"You're a submissive."

"What?"

Cole often worked undercover, and he was skilled at blending in. He could adapt to any environment, appear to be anyone. But a one-on-one relationship was different. After the emotional turmoil left behind when Gia moved out for the third time in a fit of hysteria, he wanted honesty, even if it was uncomfortable and ugly.

For this moment, he'd let her shield her identity, but his tolerance wouldn't last. "You've ascertained I'm a Dom."

"I…" She licked her upper lip.

"Admit it." He leaned in a little closer to her, not enough to intimidate her but enough to let her know that, to him, there were no other people in the room. "Something in you responds to me intuitively, female to male. You won't deny that."

Avery lowered her gaze before shaking her head and looking back up at him.

"What color is your thong?" he asked.

She choked. "Excuse me?"

Avery—*Layla*—lifted a glass of champagne from a passing waiter's tray, but Cole took it from her. "You said you'd had enough. If you'd like this conversation to go any further, you need to drink something nonalcoholic. Your choice."

For a moment, she was contemplative. In her eyes, her struggle played out. She clearly wanted to go forward, and she seemed to be fighting for nerve to say so. When she answered, her voice was barely discernible over the band. "Sparkling water."

"Lime?"

"Yes. Please."

He left her long enough to head to the bar and fetch her a drink. When he returned, she hadn't moved, and she was again tracing the interlocking links on her necklace. He offered her the glass. "I'm waiting for your answer."

"How do you know I'm wearing a thong?"

"No panty lines. And you don't strike me as a woman who would skip her foundation garments unless her Dom told her to." He grinned. "How was my guess?"

She traced the rim of her glass before meeting his gaze. "It's black."

"Lacy." It wasn't a question.

"Yes."

"Take it off."

She blinked.

"You can do it here, or you may excuse yourself to the ladies' room."

"I didn't bring a purse down with me." She blinked, then took a deep drink.

"Do you need me to problem solve this for you?" He fought to suppress a smile. There was no doubt he'd shocked her. But she hadn't refused him. He let his question hang for a few seconds before adding, "Or are you going to do as you're told?"

Avery hesitated for a moment, opening and then closing her mouth.

"I'll go with you," he decided.

"That won't be necessary."

"On the contrary."

He saw the question in her gaze. Then he noticed the way she glanced around the ballroom, seeking out her great-aunt.

When she saw that Miss Scarlet was occupied, Avery nodded.

They left the party to make their way down a long, almost deserted hallway. When she placed a hand on the restroom door, he snagged her wrist to guide her toward a different one, intended for families. He followed her inside, then turned the lock with a decisive *click*. She gasped but didn't protest. Part of him was pissed that she'd come in here with him. "Leaving with a man without telling anyone could be damn dangerous, Layla."

Avery met his gaze with trust he didn't deserve.

Cole longed to rip off her damn mask and have no pretenses between them. "Don't do anything this stupid ever again." Why it bothered him so much, he didn't know. This need to protect her stunned him. "What's your safe word?" His tone had a bite, and that didn't seem to scare her either.

"Red. And I use slow, rather than yellow."

"What's on your limits list?"

"The usual. Permanent markings. Well, I mean, unless there was a long-term relationship in place. Then it might be open to negotiation." She paused. "No breaking my skin. Or humiliation."

"Agreed. There are condoms in my room. If we get that far, it will be completely your choice, and we'll be practicing safe sex."

She nodded. "I'd like that."

His cock was heavy with arousal.

Without him needing to prompt her, she removed her thong. A deep red stained her cheeks when she held out the material toward him.

"Put it in your mouth," he said, rather than accepting it.

She gasped, and the room pulsed with her fear-induced excitement.

With any other woman, he'd go slower. But he was unaccountably annoyed with her pretense. "When I give you an order, sub"—he took a step toward her—"you will obey."

She shivered.

"Unless you need to use a safe word, your acceptable replies are 'yes, Sir,' or 'yes, Cole.'" He dropped his voice. "Master works fine too." That, he wanted to hear.

"I..."

"Do you understand?"

"Yes, Cole."

"From here on, hesitations will be dealt with appropriately. Questions?"

She stuffed her panties into her mouth.

Blood rushed to his dick. She was perfect. He hadn't realized how much he'd missed playing with a sub. "Now I want you spread-eagle, hands on the wall."

Slowly she pivoted and followed his instructions.

"Is your pussy wet?"

Her mumble was hard to hear, but absolutely delightful. "Yes, Sir."

"Do you like it when you're told what to do? When to do it? Do you like being naughty, wondering who saw you walk in here? Are you anxious about what might happen?" He came up behind her, close enough that he inhaled the sharp and unmistakable scent of her arousal. "You should be."

She spread her fingers farther apart.

"I'm going to check to see if you're wet. Am I going to be disappointed?" With the back of his hand, he brushed hair away from her neck. "Or is your slit going to be so damp that I'm pleased?" Her arms trembled. "What will I do if you're not properly responsive? Pinch your thigh?" Through the dress, he did.

She swallowed deep but didn't protest.

"Perhaps I'll lift your dress and spank your bare ass just because I want to."

Avery whimpered, the sound soft and pleading—everything he wanted.

"Perhaps I'll just put one finger in your pussy and another in your ass."

The little sub squirmed.

"I'm not known for my kindness. You should understand that."

In silent challenge, she stuck her ass out a little.

Enchanting, if reckless. "You're much more of a sinner than a saint, aren't you, Layla?" He grabbed a fistful of her gown and yanked it up to her waist. "That's it—push your butt out toward me even more. Give it to me for a spanking."

She didn't hesitate. Instead, she braced herself on the wall, then thrust back, a woman desperate to receive what he was desperate to give.

"Has it been a while?" he asked.

"Yes, Sir." A second later, she confessed, "Too long." The

words were garbled by her makeshift gag, but her response was clear, her plea impossible to deny.

"What do you want?"

"Spank me, Sir."

Rather than delivering what she requested, he worked his hand between her legs to find her hot cunt.

She moaned and let her forehead rest against the elegant wallpaper.

He rubbed three fingers across her shaved pussy, using her dampness to prevent friction. He stroked her clit quicker and quicker, making her legs shake, driving her toward an orgasm before pulling his hand away.

Then because she was so wet, he put one finger against her rear entrance. "Do you like it dirty?" he asked against her ear.

"Yes. Yes, Sir." She groaned.

He loved that she'd shown no hesitation when he'd bared her, toyed with her, pressed a finger to her anus.

When he saw her at the play party, she'd been so much more restrained. Now he realized that was more a result of the man she was with. "Whatever you want," he promised. "Whatever it is. I'll be sure you get it." He eased his finger into her a little.

She inhaled and allowed the wall to support more of her weight. *So fucking hot.*

He pushed past her sphincter and breached her anally. It wasn't as comfortable as if he'd used lube, he knew, but she didn't protest.

Cole worked his finger all the way in, then brought his other hand around to play with her pussy for a couple of seconds. "I'm going to enjoy fucking you later, when your ass is so sore that the sheets hurt your skin."

While holding her still, he spanked her left ass cheek hard.

She went rigid.

"More than you expected?"

"Yes, Sir." Avery turned her head to the side, and he saw that her bright-green eyes were wide, unblinking.

"Less than you can take?"

She squeezed her eyes closed and nodded.

"Less than you hoped for?"

He saw her fingers curl.

"Yes, Sir," she admitted around the lacy fabric.

With his finger still in her ass, Cole spanked her again and again until she tapped her heels on the marble floor.

She was getting hotter, wetter. And that was the time to stop, when she was frustrated, his to command.

Cole fisted her hair and pulled back her head, forcing her to look at him. "Any doubt who's in charge, sub?"

"You." Her voice caught in a sob. "You are, Sir."

"Correct." Cole slowly extracted his finger, then flipped down her dress.

While he washed his hands, he left her there, frowning but not questioning. At this point, he wouldn't have been surprised if she was furious or puzzled. But one thing was certain—she knew he would control the scene, and she also knew she was safe with him. He'd read her responses, left her wanting.

He dried his hands on one of the cotton towels, then wadded it and tossed it in a wicker basket. "Put your thong in the inside pocket of my jacket."

She pushed away from the wall, then faced him. He offered an arm for her to brace herself on while she rebalanced on the strappy fuck-me sandals.

Slowly she pulled the fabric from her mouth. She locked her gaze on his face, never severing eye contact as she pulled back his lapel, then skimmed her fingers across the fabric, searching for the opening in the lining.

A few seconds later, she tucked her underwear inside. She allowed her palm to linger on his chest.

"Bold move for a sub who didn't have permission to touch her Dominant." He captured her wrist, even though he liked what she did.

"Yes, Master Cole."

"And brave, looking me in the eye."

She didn't take the hint to glance away.

"No apology?"

She didn't respond.

"Are you a brat, Layla?" He flattened his hand on hers. "With me, you don't have to be. I told you I will ensure you get what you need. You can tell me. Talk to me." Again, Cole was tempted to rip off that damn mask. "Be real with me. Trust me with your secrets."

"Thank you for the offer. I appreciate it." Her cheeks were captivatingly pink. But she hesitated before going on. "And thank you for the spanking, Sir."

He sighed. *One step at a time.* "More to come." He released his grip, then straightened his cuff as she dropped her hand. "We should get back."

"What?"

"The food here—even banquet food—is five-star. You need energy for the night ahead."

"What? We just…" She drew her eyebrows together. "You want to eat?"

"Absolutely. I understand steak and lobster is on the menu." He offered his arm.

He watched the war, the frustration in her eyes. She wanted to protest, but she'd heard him, and she'd agreed to obey him.

Even though she pursed her lips, she composed herself, then placed her hand on his arm as they left the restroom together.

CHAPTER THREE

It was the longest, most nerve-racking meal of Avery's life.

She'd hit on Master Cole, and he'd humbled her in the family restroom, driving her to the edge, proving his dominance, leaving her panting for an orgasm.

She'd expected him to take her up to his room, not back to the party. Sitting here, her pussy damp, her underwear in his jacket, was unbearable.

"Is your filet all right?" he asked, putting down his fork after watching her pick at it for a while.

"It's wonderful." The problem wasn't with the steak—it was with Cole's insistence on her revealing her true identity.

Servers cleared the plates. Then the hotel's pastry chef and several helpers wheeled in a stunning cupcake assortment.

The display resembled the staging that had been set up. Each cupcake was topped with a mask or feathers crafted from fondant. On the top tier was a cake fashioned to resemble Miss Scarlet in a burlesque costume.

The star of the hour took to the stage for a few minutes to

thank everyone for coming. "Please enjoy the music and dancing. And indulge in some free champagne, courtesy of Mr. Sterling himself." She lifted an imaginary glass toward someone in the back of the room. "Thank you, darling!"

By the time Avery turned her head, the doorway was vacant. If the hotelier had been there at all, he wasn't there now.

The musicians struck up again, and the waitstaff went to work, offering cupcakes.

She wrinkled her nose and sighed wistfully when a chocolate one with mile-high frosting was offered to her.

"She'll take it," Cole told the waiter, accepting the plate and a fork.

"But—"

"If you want it, eat it. Or have a bite."

She sighed, never taking her eyes off the confection. "It's my weakness."

"We all have one."

"The calories in that thing," she protested, looking at him.

He had a wide, indulgent smile. "What about them?"

"I need to lose a few pounds."

"Do you?"

"I don't?"

"Only if you think so. I like spanking your delectable ass."

She gave the dessert another couple of glances before meeting his steel-gray eyes. When she saw his approval of her, she picked up her fork.

The cupcake machine in the hotel was wonderful, but this...

"I gather you like it?"

"To die for." She dabbed her mouth with a napkin. "Or certainly worth extra exercise for. Maybe I did die and go to heaven. Did I die and go to heaven?"

"Not yet. But soon."

The reminder of what he had planned made her stomach plummet. Nerves getting to her, she pushed the plate away.

Once they'd had coffee, he said, "It's too early for us to leave. How about another dance?"

She loved being in his arms, so she nodded. So much a gentleman, he stood, pulled back her chair, then offered his elbow and led her to the parquet floor. She loved being publicly claimed by this Dom.

Like earlier, she placed a hand on his shoulder. This time, however, his touch wasn't polite. He placed his palm against her back and brought her in close.

Her step faltered, and he tightened his grip to compensate and help her recover. She gave him a smile of gratitude. His lead was competent as he gave her slight nudges that provided unmistakable cues to follow. His skill as a Dominant extended to the dance floor.

When the final notes trailed off, he released her and gave a slight bow.

For the next hour, they danced, conversed with people, watched circus performers and a burlesque preview—including a teaser of the new show Miss Scarlet was debuting next month.

Cole was patient and polite but maddeningly hands-off. Because of the way he'd behaved earlier, she anticipated a constant stream of commands, but he acted as if they were on a casual date while tension built deep inside her.

When the first guests trickled out of the doors, he looked at her with purpose. "Ready to make our escape?"

His words shot nerves through her. "Yes."

He stood, and this time, his grip wasn't just tight—it was possessive. She liked it more than she would have imagined.

It took a few minutes for them to make it to the front of the admirers lined up to talk to Miss Scarlet.

"The party will be going on until the wee hours." She cast

a glance between them. "In case you want to rejoin us once you've worn yourselves out." With a grin, she waved her fan in front of her face.

A gentleman less than half Miss Scarlet's age pinched her bottom. She squealed and turned around.

Avery couldn't hide her laugh.

"She seems to be having a good time."

"She's inspiring."

Cole held out a hand to indicate Avery should go ahead of him. "Did I understand that you have a room here?"

"Yes. Even though I live not too far from here, I splurged." An evening at the Royal Sterling was a rare treat. With its spas, pools, workout room, and unbelievable food, it was a mini-vacation.

"Which of our rooms do you prefer?"

"Yours." So she could make her escape when she was ready. "But I'd like to collect my purse, maybe freshen up a bit. If it suits you, I can meet you in about fifteen minutes."

"No. That doesn't suit me at all," he replied. "We'll go together."

Nerves that had been at a manageable level flooded through her.

When they were alone in the elevator car, he faced her. "We know spankings are on your approved activities list."

"Yes, Sir." She shifted her weight to her right foot.

"Flogging?"

"Yes." The word emerged as a sigh.

"Cane?"

Avery twisted her hands together. "That can fucking hurt. Sir."

"It can," he agreed. "And for the right sub, it can be sublime."

At his words, hunger unfurled. There was nothing she liked more than the exquisite dance of pain so rich it caused a flash of unbridled pleasure. In the wrong hands, the cane was miserable. But Cole was right. There had been one time when she'd found it sublime. "Yes, Sir."

"Is that a yes to the cane?"

"It takes trust. But..." She licked her lips. "It's something I like." There was nothing like its unyielding, expansive sear.

"All in good time," he agreed. "I'll suggest it again later."

Avery nearly melted at his feet, and no doubt he was astute enough to know that. She looked away from him, trying to diminish the influence he had over her.

"Trust goes two ways." He paused. *"Layla."*

It's as if he knows. She sucked in a breath. "Master Cole, please..."

"Why so secretive?"

She watched the numbers for the various floors fly past. "Can we have tonight?" *Let me be bold, someone I'm not. Let me be the sub I dream of. Tonight, just tonight, allow me to be brave.*

The elevator glided to a stop.

"Tonight," he agreed. "Don't count on anything more. I don't like masquerades—literal or figurative. I despise subterfuge."

"Fair enough, Sir." Her breath was shaky as she exhaled in gratitude.

With the heat of his gaze on her rear, she walked down the hallway to her room.

Avery pressed her thumbprint to the scanner to open the door. She sighed. If only she'd been less scattered before leaving. The bed was strewn with clothes, lingerie, purses she'd considered taking, even a new pair of shoes she'd purchased on a whim at one of the hotel's numerous ground-floor shops.

"Do you have any toys with you?"

"An egg-type vibrator. It has a remote control." The expensive Swedish thing had cost a small fortune, and it had been worth every penny. It worked well whether she was teasing her clit or using it internally.

"Excellent. Bring it with you."

She dug both pieces from the bottom of her suitcase and tucked the toy into her clutch. "Can you excuse me for a moment?"

He went to stand by the window, and she headed into the bathroom.

With the door closed behind her, she removed her mask. For a moment, she hardly recognized the bold person staring back at her. This Avery had gotten spanked in the restroom of the Royal Sterling Hotel, had Master Cole's finger up her ass, and was prepared to go back to his room with him—all things she might never have ordinarily done.

"Two minutes, sub. Don't make me come in there."

"Yes, Sir!" Quickly she brushed her hair. Then, stalling in an attempt to steady her nerves, she applied a fresh coat of mascara. After painting her lips a vixen-red color, she replaced the mask.

All that done, she rejoined him.

He stood near the minibar, a small glass bottle of mineral water in hand. "You are worth any wait."

She sucked in a breath.

Cole perused her, eyes deep with appreciation. In that moment, she believed what he said. "You're very kind, Sir."

"I've warned you that kind isn't a word associated with me. Remember that."

Trepidation danced down her spine. How well *did* she know him?

"Ready?"

She curled her hand into a fist in a futile effort to stop her hand from shaking, then dropped the mascara and lipstick into her clutch. For a moment she debated adding other toiletries, then decided against it. No doubt she would be back in her own room in a couple of hours. She closed the flap on her purse and gave him a tight nod.

In the hallway, he said, "Please walk in front of me."

Her insides lurched.

Everything this man did spoke to his understanding and mastery of a sub.

He instructed her to precede him onto the elevator, then from it when they arrived at his floor.

With his burning gaze on her, Avery had never been more aware of her femininity.

Once they were sealed inside his suite and she'd placed her belongings on his desk, he offered her a drink of the mineral water.

Since there was no way to hide her trembling hand, she shook her head.

Cole pressed a button on his docking station. Within a few seconds, smooth instrumental jazz wove a sensual atmosphere.

Avery looked around. Though they had the same luxurious linens on their beds, he had a couple of additional pieces of furniture, higher ceilings, a wet bar, and an additional window. "You have a lot more space than I do." She just hoped that when she returned to her room there would be chocolate-covered strawberries on her nightstand as well.

"I have a house about thirty minutes from here, but when Sterling offered me a room for the duration of the project, I decided to skip the daily commute." He shrugged. "The fitness center is world class."

"I sometimes think I shouldn't stay here. Going home afterward is always a letdown. Don't get me wrong, my apartment is nice. But it's small. It's not on the Strip. And it doesn't have a cupcake machine." If that wasn't enough to convince her, the twenty-four-hour room service and someone to do her laundry certainly was.

"That should be remedied."

"I've suggested it to management numerous times."

He grinned. "We should enjoy as many of Sterling's amenities as we can. The armoire is unlocked. Have a look inside." His statement was flat, with no inflection. It wasn't a suggestion.

Her legs felt wobbly in a way that had nothing to do with her heels.

She crossed the room to open the doors of the piece of furniture, then stared in wide-eyed shock. He had every impact device imaginable, from floggers to paddles, carpet beaters to crops and canes. Even a single-tail hung curled from a hook.

"This is some collection."

"The Royal Sterling caters to every need."

"So… These aren't yours?"

"Some are. The cane for example." He joined her. "And the short red flogger."

She wanted it on her skin.

"You asked for tonight," he reminded her. "In return, I will demand your total honesty in every other way."

She faced him. "I'm not sure I understand."

"When I ask a question, I want an answer. I've told you that you'll get what you want from me, but you need to be clear about what it is. I expect you to be completely honest."

Avery squared her shoulders, drawing from the strength that anonymity gave her.

"Good." He took a seat in an easy chair, then propped an ankle on the opposite knee. "Please remove your dress."

Taking off her clothes in front of a man for the first time always made her heart careen.

He pressed his hands together and looked at her. There was only a tiny zipper near the base of her spine, and she grabbed the pull tab to slowly lower it.

She brushed the one strap from her shoulder, then allowed the bodice to drop.

She was braless, and his gaze lingered on her breasts. Because of the cool air, her nipples hardened instantly. Or at least that was what she told herself, rather than believing it happened because of the way he watched her.

Without further encouragement, she pulled off her dress. She draped the material across the foot of the bed. "What about the shoes?"

"I like them. But it's up to you. If they're comfortable enough, leave them on. If you feel more like my little sub when you're naked and barefoot, take them off."

"I'll keep them on." Uncertain, she waited for his next instruction.

"Do whatever feels natural."

She clutched her necklace for inner strength. Thoughts tumbled through her, and she took a breath. Deep down, she knew what he expected. A moment later, she knelt.

"Yes," he whispered.

She spread her knees wide and placed her hands behind her neck before tipping back her head and closing her eyes.

"Very nice."

He allowed time to drag and stretch. She forced herself not to fidget. A full minute or so later, she realized—*fuck it*—that he was waiting on her. "Please, Sir, will you touch me?"

"I'm sorry?"

"Will you please touch your sub?" she amended.

"I'd be happy to. In what way?"

If she were Avery Fisher rather than a brave incognito woman, she would never be able to continue this way—asking, taking. But tonight, she could be the sub she dreamed of being. "Will you inspect your sub, Sir?"

"Very well done."

She opened her eyes to see him walking toward her.

Within seconds, he stood over her, deliciously imposing. Slowly, he circled her.

"I like you on your knees, sub."

"Thank you, Sir."

He yanked her hair back, exposing her neck, making her open her mouth. God, this was everything she imagined.

He put his finger on her lips.

"Please may I suck it, Sir?" It stunned her to realize just how much she actually wanted to.

"You may."

As if it were his cock, she circled his finger with her tongue, then drew his finger into her mouth, sucking, licking, adoring.

"Show me your breasts."

Since he hadn't pulled away, she continued to suck while she pushed them together.

He extracted his finger. "What are you thinking?"

"That I'd like you to fuck them, Sir—my breasts—maybe come on them."

"You are a sexy woman, Layla." He placed his hands on hers, forcing her breasts even closer together.

She moaned a little.

"What else needs inspection?"

"My cunt, Sir." Then instantly, she corrected, "Your sub's cunt, Sir."

"You were reminded once, earlier. Weren't you?"

Her pulse stuttered. "Yes, Sir."

"I think the lapse should be punished."

"Please, Sir." *Please, please, yes.*

"Slap your cunt."

"Sir?"

"You seem to think it belongs to you. Therefore you should be the one to punish it."

Stunned by the order, she looked at him. He wasn't going to do it for her?

"Are you waiting for something?" He took a step back to give her some space.

Despite the chill in the room, her body was hot. Having no other choice, she slapped her pussy. The pain surprised her.

"You might have better access if your legs were spread farther apart." His words sounded like a suggestion, and she knew they were anything but.

"Yes, Sir." She followed his order and gave herself a second slap, then a third. "How many, Sir?"

He shrugged. "How many would you like?"

They were playing a sinful game she could never win. "As many as you say, Sir."

"Ah." He smiled.

This man tested everything she knew about BDSM.

Because he hadn't said she could stop, she kept going—two more, three, four... *It damn well stings.*

Her pussy became inflamed. And because she was submissive and there was nothing hotter than having a powerful Dom looming over her, commanding her actions, she started to get wet.

She lost track. All she knew was that her pussy was unbelievably sensitive.

"If it were my pussy, it would get a different kind of attention."

She frowned at him. "Sir?"

He continued to regard her, and she continued to spank until fresh realization dawned. "Show me," she invited. "Show your sub how you would treat your pussy, Sir."

"Fuck."

For a moment, she thought he might use her real name, but that wasn't possible.

"Please stand and put your hands behind you."

Her motions weren't as graceful as they might have been if she'd recently had a Dom and routinely knelt. But he didn't complain. In fact, he smiled as though he approved of her actions.

He took a step in her direction, and she sucked in a breath. She was hyperaware of him. His stance communicated power and command.

"Wet my fingers." He held his hand in front of her face, and she licked them as she continued to meet his gaze.

He slid his hand between her legs and teased her, slipping his fingers in and out of her pussy, driving her mad.

She closed her eyes. The soft pumping of his fingers coupled with the sharp smacks she'd given herself made her delirious.

Tremors shook her as she imagined what she looked like, naked except for her gorgeous mask, the necklace, and high-heeled sandals, breasts thrust out, shoulder blades drawn together, hands behind her neck, legs spread. Surrendered to his mercy.

He removed his hand and she moaned.

But then he slapped her cunt so hard that she screamed, lost her balance, and pitched forward.

He caught her. "Back into position."

She couldn't. "The pain..." She squeezed her thighs together, desperate to escape the burning sensation. "Damn. Damn. *Fuck.*"

"*That's* how I would treat my pussy."

Avery gulped, but shockingly once the searing pain receded, pleasure flooded her. She'd never been more sexually aroused than she was at that moment. God. It wasn't enough. Avery thrust her hips forward, seeking his hand and the release an orgasm would bring.

"Back into position," he repeated.

She realized she was gripping his forearms and that he'd leaned in to offer his body as support. Without her being aware of it, he'd been there for her. "Thank you," she whispered.

Slowly, she righted herself. Momentarily she closed her eyes to reenter the submissive mindset.

"Now show me…show me how you should spank it next time I ask."

He expects me to do that to myself? There was no way she could bear it. For a wild second, she considered using her safe word. But then… She knew she might never have another night like this one or a second chance to play with Master Cole.

"I'm waiting."

"Yes, Sir." Harder than she could have imagined, she did as he said.

On top of the pain she'd already experienced, this was stunning. Before she could sort through the emotional ramifications, he was there, an arm around her waist, stroking her labia, easing a finger inside her.

She gulped for air, feeling as if she were drowning. "Sir!"

"Come anytime you want," he said against her ear, the words gruff and simultaneously promising.

He slipped a second finger inside her. The sensation was hot, fucking hot. Then he inserted a third and spread them apart, fucking her hard and deep. Her pussy blazed in response to his sensual assault.

She wrapped her arms around his neck so she could stay upright. Seconds later, a climax shot through her, its intensity shocking.

Avery's body went limp, and he picked her up. Without her being fully conscious of what was happening, he carried her to the chair where he sat and drew her against him.

She curled up, accepting his comfort, heedless that she was naked.

This Dom understood her, what she needed, maybe even on a level she didn't quite comprehend herself. "That was…" She sought for the right description, but words failed her. "Sexy."

"You like it hard."

"Yes." Something inside her blossomed. Allowing herself to be honest was liberating.

"When you're ready, I want you on your knees."

She remained where she was for another minute or two, soothed by the sound of his pounding heart, the strength of his arms, the masculine scent of him.

Being with him was so natural, easy in a way she'd never experienced with anyone else. Eventually she was able to rouse herself enough to slide from his lap to kneel on the floor.

"Undress me. Except for my pants."

Anticipation flooded her. Not that things hadn't been real before now, but this command magnified his power.

Avery started with his shoes, untying the laces of each of expensive wingtip. This part of BDSM helped her center herself. She enjoyed simple tasks that she could treat reverently. In a way, it was meditative.

Once she'd removed his shoes and tucked the socks inside, he stood, again towering over her, making her deliciously aware of her submissive pose.

His eyes were lighter than they'd been earlier, molten. Intimacy whispered around them.

"I'm waiting." He offered his hand and helped her up.

She moved behind him to take his jacket. As he shrugged from it, she noticed that her thong peeked out from one of his pockets, and she absently wondered if he had any intention of returning it.

Not that it mattered. Part of her hoped he'd want to keep it.

"There's a wooden hanger in the closet."

She hung the jacket, then smoothed imaginary wrinkles from it. That done, she returned to unfasten his bowtie.

The image of him with the ends loose against the snowy-white shirt would remain with her for years.

Avery removed his studs, then his cufflinks, noting the owl on each of them. Finally, she unfastened the remaining two buttons on his tuxedo shirt.

Again she went behind him to help him from the shirt.

His back, with honed muscles and a couple of badly healed scars, took her breath away. She had labeled him a secret-agent man, and of course there was his military background. How much didn't she know? Judging by the fact that he was consulting for the Royal Sterling, there was no doubt Cole didn't sit at a desk all day.

She hung the shirt next to his jacket in the closet and tucked his tie into the same pocket as her underwear; then she looked at him, drinking in the sight of his lean stomach and slender waist. His chest had a smattering of hair, and she couldn't stop staring at his biceps.

Even though a smile toyed with his mouth, his tone was stern. "Hurry up, sub. Unless you want to be chastised for tarrying?"

Damn, she loved being with a Dominant who made it easy for her to be the sub she wanted to be.

"What does intuition tell you to do now?" he asked.

With any other Dom, she might respond as expected, with the perfect, *"Whatever you say, Sir."* But tonight was different. Tonight she was asking for what she wanted. "If it pleases you, Sir…I'd like to suck your dick."

He inclined his head a little. "There are condoms in the

nightstand." With his thumb, he indicated the piece of furniture. "Crawl to it and bring one to me."

Avery found quite a selection, all of the shiny packages emblazoned with the Sterling's crown logo. She dug through the small bowl they were in until she located one without spermicide.

She started to crawl to him, but his words stopped her.

"Put it in your mouth."

It was uncomfortable, and she wanted to spit it out, but she didn't dare. Her eyes watered as she made her way toward him, and she fought her gag reflex while she unfastened his belt.

"Think about what you're doing and not about your discomfort," he encouraged. "Get out of your own head."

She tugged on the thin, supple strip of leather, pulling it from around his waist.

After coiling it, she set it aside.

Then she unfastened the single button and lowered the zipper on his pants.

For a moment, she held her breath, wondering if he was commando. But he wasn't. Cole wore tight dark boxer briefs. His cock jutted against them. Even though he was confined, there was no doubt he was well-endowed. Maybe *too* well-endowed. What had she been thinking when she'd offered to suck him off?

She lowered his pants, and once he'd stepped free of them, she picked them up and folded them, then offered them to him.

"You've either had some good training or you have remarkably good instincts."

She nodded.

"Which is it? The training?"

The condom package made her choke, preventing speech.

"Mostly instinct, then, hmm? I prefer that. I like to train my women to my preferences."

The idea of being his woman, his sub, made her heart race. What would that be like? Not to simply have a scene on the weekends, but to live the lifestyle more often, even daily? To have her days filled with little acts of service to her man? To have him demand dirty things from her, to compel her obedience? Avery forced away the exhilarating questions. They had tonight and no more.

He took the pants from her, then hung them on the back of the chair, undoing her careful work.

She hooked her fingers inside the waistband of his underwear and pulled down the material. His cock sprang free, jutting toward her face. He was magnificent and definitely on the large side. But the fact that he was already hard sent a flash of pleasure through her.

She finished undressing him, appreciating the way he'd trimmed his pubic hair and shaved his balls. Everything about him signaled his awareness of his sexuality. If the condom package hadn't been stuck in her mouth, she would have been tempted to start sucking now.

"I love the sight of a woman who's helpless to me. Put the condom on me."

Nerves crawled through her, forcing her to concentrate hard on what she was doing. Being this close to him—drinking in his masculinity—overwhelmed her. She couldn't resist touching his testicles and sucking his cock deep into her throat.

Cole fisted her hair. "Do as you're told."

She wanted *this*. He tightened his grip, forcing her compliance. "Yes, Sir." Avery ripped open the package and sheathed him.

"You did that well."

"Thank you, Sir."

"But you took liberties without asking permission."

Her pulse lurched.

"You know better, I presume?"

"Uhm." The temperature of the room dropped by ten chilling degrees. "I…"

"Do you?" He raised an eyebrow.

"Sir…"

"Do you?" His voice whiplashed through her.

"Yes, Sir!" She glanced away. "I do."

"And you're supposed to be asking tonight, talking to me about your desires."

Also true.

"Fetch the flogger."

Oh God. Prior to him, she had never been punished in a BDSM scene.

But then, she'd never been with a man as uncompromising and stern as Master Cole. Fuck. *Yes.* This. This was what she'd always wanted. But that didn't stop sudden terror from seizing her.

"Do I need to repeat my order?"

If it became too much, she had a safe word. Her movements were sluggish as she crawled to the armoire. She stood, then opened the doors and selected the flogger. Again, on her knees, she returned to him, sat back on her heels, then offered the implement to him.

He was so imposing with his throbbing erection that it was difficult to think.

"Anything you want to say?"

This was so real, so raw. "I'm sorry, Sir." She peeked through the curtain of her unfamiliar blonde hair. "No—" Avery cleared her throat so she could speak. "That's not true. You want honesty? I should have asked, waited for your command. But I'm not sorry I touched you."

"Thank you for being truthful." His voice was rich, like a fine red wine, and just as potent. "That will help you some."

Some?

"Go back to the armoire and stand in front of it, facing it. Put your hands on the top and spread your legs as wide as you can." He paused. "I recommend you be quick about it."

CHAPTER FOUR

Captivated, Cole watched Avery follow his order. Her motions were graceful, innately so. Her touch and her mouth were exquisite. Part of him ached to make love to her. But that wasn't what she wanted.

Typically, he didn't flog women when he had a raging hard-on. Then again, he'd never had an evening like this.

He allowed her tension to build for a couple of minutes before going to her. The moment he was close, she drew in a short, frantic breath. He trailed his fingers across her shoulders, down her spine, over her shapely buttocks. "You've got the most spankable ass of any woman I've ever known."

"It's the cupcakes, Sir."

"Then I shall hire us a pastry chef."

She glanced over her shoulder.

"You're divine," he said. "And don't think that means I won't make you too sore to sit down."

She moaned a little as she faced forward again.

He scooped her hair to one side. "I want you to consider yourself tied."

"My Doms usually cuff me, Sir."

"At what point did you confuse me with anyone else?" He grabbed her ass cheeks and squeezed hard, lifting her off her heels.

She gasped, more from shock than pain, he supposed, since his touch hadn't been heavy-handed.

"Oh, God! I'm sorry, Sir."

"Better." He slowly released his grip, and her exhalation was so ragged even her shoulders shook.

It was good to know he affected her in the same way she was getting to him.

He rubbed her body with long, slow, forceful strokes, getting her blood flowing, letting her know he was in charge. "You asked for this." With her words, her body, her actions, she'd been clear about it. "Stay in place. Make me proud of you."

"That's a difficult task, Sir."

"I think you want me to demand a lot from you." She didn't immediately respond. "That's why you approached me. Be truthful." *About this, if nothing else.*

"Yes," she whispered, her words husky with confession.

Fuck. It was a start. Yet it made him want more. "You can count, if you want. I'll stop when I'm ready or when you use a safe word."

Her muscles tensed. Was it from anticipation or the slight fear he was trying to cultivate? "Surrender to me. To yourself." He touched her, soothed her until she exhaled. "Good." He gave her a few gentle strikes on her perfect buttocks. He was not concerned that he might lose his erection. The sight of her skin turning color beneath the supple strands of his flogger would be enough to keep him aroused.

Cole continued to work her with light strokes until her muscles relaxed, draining the tension from her.

Only then did he start the flogging in earnest.

As they connected, breathed in sync, he realized how

much he'd missed this. The last year he'd spent with Gia had consisted of half a dozen emotional meltdowns. She'd believed that once they moved in together, he would be home more, even though he'd said he wouldn't be. She resorted to bratty behavior to get his attention. Twice, he returned from overseas trips to discover she'd moved back in with her parents. She wanted him to chase her. Far too often, he did. She treated him and their relationship as some sort of game.

He'd worked with her, asking her to talk with him. Instead, she'd left him guessing. Toward the end, he stopped responding to her dramatics. The next time she stormed out, he didn't pursue her. Three days later, angry, accusing him of not loving her enough, she returned. For a while, things had gotten better, but then she started avoiding sex.

He'd been wrong to think he could stop her manipulations.

The fourth time she moved out, he changed the locks.

Cole finished his case, then volunteered for extra assignments. He'd avoided relationships since.

While he was abstinent, he'd spent a lot of time in reflection and decided he only wanted to be with women who were self-aware and willing to ask for what they needed. The time he'd already spent with Avery meant a great deal to him, made him think about the future and maybe the sound of laughter in his ridiculously big house.

Appearing relaxed, she rested her head on the armoire. For a moment he stopped, and she shifted her weight from foot to foot. He traced a faint mark on her creamy skin. "How are you doing?"

She attempted to lift her head, only to drop it again. "Wonderful."

He trailed his touch lower to check her arousal level.

"If this is supposed to teach me to ask before touching you, Sir, I'm not sure it's working."

Cole grinned. "If it had been a real punishment, you'd know the difference."

"I'm sure you're right, Sir."

He fucking loved the sound of his title on her tongue. There were a dozen different inflections he wanted to hear. Pleading. Surrendering. Screaming. "Would you like to continue?"

"Please."

Cole crisscrossed her body, using complete strokes, wrapping the strands around her, from her thighs to her buttocks to her waist.

Following his commands, Avery didn't release the piece of furniture, but she readjusted her grip for more support. Despite that, her breaths were rhythmic and deep. Her skin was a tantalizing pink, and her knees wobbled a little. "Talk to me."

"I want to get lost."

"Be specific, please."

"I want it harder."

It wouldn't have mattered to him if she wanted to stop. But her request for more pleased him. His cock was still hard, reminding him how long he'd been without sex.

Cole gave her another twenty strokes. When she sighed with pleasure, he unleashed a little more strength to finish her with a deeper impact.

She swayed, her body relaxed.

Avery had been worth every minute of the wait.

He paused for a moment, flogger at his side, while he fingered her.

Cole threaded both hands into her hair to turn her head to one side. Wanting her, he kissed her, cradling her head in his palm. He was tender, more than he'd ever been with a sub. Her submission cracked the ice around his heart—as a man, not just a Dom.

She tasted of honesty, of the finest champagne, of compliance. Her mouth was soft, her tongue yielding.

And because he was feasting on her response, Cole pulled away from her. He shook his head to clear it. A kiss was incredibly intimate. And with her, one would not be enough. So what the hell was he doing? They'd agreed to a single night and nothing more. Tied in knots, annoyed with himself, he said, "Now…now you can suck my cock."

Cole helped her turn; then he put his hand on top of her head to force her down onto her knees.

She appeared to be in a stupor, from endorphins, from confusion, and he savored it. "Since you used your hands earlier without permission, put them behind your neck and open your mouth." He stroked himself a couple of times while she did as she was told. "Now satisfy me."

She swirled her tongue across his cockhead, then began to lick, pressing her tongue against the underside.

He curled a fist around his dick to control how much she took. "Open wider, sub." Beneath her mask, he saw her green eyes water as he went deeper. If her mascara ran, so much the better. He held the back of her head to prevent her from escaping.

Properly responsive, she choked on him but didn't pull away, taking everything he offered and continuing to move her tongue and suck.

"Enough." He captured her chin with his hand.

When he pulled away, she didn't even try to wipe her mouth. Instead, she looked up with eyelashes fringed with tears. Damn, he wanted more than the measly hours she was offering. "Sexy. Fucking sexy." He helped her to stand. Then before she could walk past him, he put a hand on her shoulder to stop her.

"Sir?"

Cole grabbed his shirt, and he used the bottom of it to clean her mouth.

"I actually liked it, Sir," she said.

His cock pulsed in demand, and she stared at it. Harsher than he needed to be, he clipped out, "On the bed."

She sat on the edge of the mattress while he collected the bowtie from his suit coat.

"Give me your wrists," he instructed. "This will help you to remember to pay attention to your hands." He secured her with his bowtie. The material was slick, and it would open with the slightest effort, but his intent wasn't to prevent movement. It was to make her conscious of his will. He tipped her back as he said, "Spread your legs."

Though she was already aroused, Cole played with her pussy, fingering her again, even as he pumped his still-sheathed cock in his left hand. "Are you ready for me?"

"I am. Yes, Sir."

He said nothing.

She lifted her head off the mattress as best she could, seeking his gaze. "I'm asking. Please put your dick in me, Sir."

Grateful there had already been turndown service, he moved her to the middle of the mattress with her arms over her head.

He took a minute to lave her nipples with attention, tormenting them, causing her to lift her hips from the bed.

"I'm so ready to come, Sir."

"Are you?" He hoped he sounded nonchalant, because in truth he was anything but.

With his knee, he forced her legs farther apart. Then because her pussy was so red and swollen, he slapped it hard.

She screamed, and he leaned over her, placing his cock at her opening and capturing her cry with his mouth.

He devoured her, and she thrashed about. Sexily, her pussy drenched his dick as he slid in.

Cole tried to soften the kiss, but she met his tongue thrust for thrilling thrust. He'd encouraged her to ask for what she wanted. She responded with a demand.

He pulled back, and she moaned. As he fucked her with short, fast strokes designed to drive her mad, her sound became a whimper.

She moved with him and closed her eyes.

His sub struggled against the makeshift bondage and turned her head to the side, breaking their kiss.

"Master Cole, I want to come."

"You don't need permission." He reached between them to press her engorged clit. *"Now."*

She cried out his name as she climaxed, clenching his cock with her internal muscles.

Cole ground his back teeth together to fight off his orgasm. He'd never been with a woman as exquisite as Avery, and the struggle was more than he'd anticipated. He had to dig deep into his military training to find a thought that would distract him.

He pulled out from her a little, needing time to regroup.

When she stared up at him, he stroked into her again.

"I didn't know it could be so good."

Big, strong, tough, hardened Dom that he was, he had no fucking idea how to admit that he hadn't known either. "The night is ours."

Her eyes were wide.

"Stop hiding from me?" He touched the top of her mask and traced one of the delicate lines.

She turned her head to escape.

Cole sighed. Even though it went against his better instincts, he'd promised anonymity.

This time as he fucked her, he set a more leisurely pace so he could prolong her pleasure.

"I need to touch you," she said.

"You can get out of that tie anytime."

"We both know that I wouldn't do that, Sir."

"What a good little sub."

Her green eyes were like sun-drenched gems. And her delicate mouth was parted. She wanted to be obedient. He'd been wrong in his casual assumption that she might be a brat. She was simply a woman who yearned for a man strong enough to accept her gifts.

He clamped a hand on her delicate wrists.

"I learned my lesson earlier, Sir. They'll stay where they are until you say otherwise."

He could fuck her all night long. But it wouldn't be enough.

With long, penetrating strokes, he slid in and out of her, ignoring the demanding fullness in his balls. "Look at me." There was something incredibly powerful about compelling a submissive to meet his gaze. But when his little sub did, he wondered who was truly enslaved by whom. He wanted her as much as she obviously wanted him.

He fucked her tight channel, and she sighed.

For minutes, he continued to watch her reactions. As she became more aroused, she blinked less often, and she opened her mouth a little. Her lipstick had already been worn off by their passion. Her compliance was so damn beautiful.

Primal urges obliterated his restraint, and he began to fuck her in earnest.

Whatever he gave, she responded, hard and fast, short and sweet, leisurely and prolonged.

It unraveled his self-control.

He moved them both so she was half on her side, a leg on top of his, giving him leverage to penetrate deeper.

Then, because he wanted to, he plucked the knot from the bowtie.

"May I?"

"Yes. Touch me."

Instantly she grabbed him, holding his shoulders, wrapping herself around him.

Though he liked having his lover restrained to remind them both of the overarching nature of their relationship, he liked the feel of her hands exploring him.

She curved her body, inviting him in deeper. Obligingly, he filled her heated pussy.

"I love this," she said. "Fuck me hard, Sir."

He gave her what she asked for, one hand tangled in her hair, the other pressed flat against her buttocks to prevent her from moving far.

Her pussy muscles squeezed him tight. He fisted his hands to hold off longer, wanting her to climax first.

"Sir!"

"Come."

She screamed, clenching, coming, grabbing him.

He savored each second that he satisfied his sub.

Only when she was whimpering his name did he allow himself to ejaculate in long, satisfying spurts.

He was a sexual man, masturbating at least once a day, and most times, more. But there was no feeling that matched coming inside a responsive woman.

Inside her.

When he was finished, he framed her face between his palms. "You're stunning..." He barely stopped himself from using her name.

"That was hot, Sir. Can we do it again?"

"You'll be the death of me." Suddenly he wasn't afraid of dying.

Avery had never been much of a snuggler, but she didn't object when he returned to the bed after throwing away the condom and pulled her against his naked body. He didn't ask —he just wrapped her up in the strength and comfort of his arms. She lay next to him, listening to the reassuring beat of his heart.

She smiled, glad she'd found the guts to approach him earlier in the evening. Their time together had been everything she could have imagined.

The only problem was much the same as the one she had with staying at the Royal Sterling. It was difficult to go back to the regular world.

Unlike other Doms she'd scened with, Cole seemed to understand the emotional component she needed. To her, it was about more than just kinky sex or having her ass warmed at the club or occasional parties. She wanted the mindfuck and escape. She wanted someone who understood her—or, better, the sub she yearned to be. The person Dirk had told her was wrong.

Cole trailed his fingers down her arm. "How does your body feel?"

He was big, and his thrusts were powerful. "My pussy aches," she admitted with a blush.

A chuckle rumbled through his chest. "Good. And the rest of your body from the flogging?"

"Warm." He'd wielded the leather strands with confidence and the power she needed. "Relaxed."

"Oh?"

"Fishing for compliments?" She turned to face him with a teasing grin. "You know you're good."

His face was shadowed with midnight-dark stubble that appealed to her. Though his jaw was strong, his smile was transformative. Unable to resist—helpless to keep her hands to herself—she traced the scar on his face. Surprisingly, he didn't stop her.

The raised white line ran deeper than she'd imagined. It was an outward manifestation of the risk he'd taken in his life, so different from her sheltered upbringing.

How many layers are there to this Dom?

"Just making sure I take care of my woman."

The words poured heat through her. *His woman.* She liked that, wished it were true. "I enjoyed it more than any other flogging I've received. You're a master."

"Go on."

She sighed, thinking through what she wanted to say. "The way you started told me I could trust you. By the time you hit me harder and faster, I was ready. I think on some level I was aware that it hurt, but I didn't really feel it." Even to her, that statement made no sense, but he nodded in apparent understanding. "You could have continued a lot longer, and it would have been fine with me."

"You've still got a caning to go."

She froze. "Master Cole."

"If you want it," he added.

"I…" Avery recalled the way he'd been with Gia—tenderness, combined with the indomitable force of his Dominance.

"Bring it to me when you're ready."

"I'm nervous," she admitted.

"And?" He arched his eyebrows.

She blew out a breath. "You seem supremely unconcerned."

"I am. I'm looking forward to seeing marks on your thighs and buttocks. If you're fortunate, you'll feel them for some time."

Leaving the comfort of his arms was one of the more

difficult things she'd ever done. But the temptation was irresistible.

Without being instructed, she crawled to the armoire to collect the cane.

"Your vibrator also." He climbed from the bed.

She rummaged through her purse until she found the small egg and its remote control, then returned to him.

Cole pulled his trousers on, and there was something illicit about her Dom being dressed while she was nude.

From her knees a few feet in front of him, she turned her palms up and offered both toys to him.

"I want you bent over the bed. Do you need to be restrained?"

That offer was a small mercy, and she appreciated it. She was honest when she said, "Whatever you prefer, Sir."

"In that case, no. I want your ass in the correct position because you want this as badly as I do."

Her mouth dried.

"Spread your legs as far apart as possible."

Fighting her nerves, she went to the bed, then draped herself across the mattress and turned her head to watch him.

He put the bullet in his mouth to lubricate it, then pressed it against her swollen pussy. She moaned and swayed, allowing it to slip inside her.

Using the remote control, he turned it on to a slow, frustrating pulse. She generally went straight to the highest setting.

"How's that?"

She wrinkled her nose. "Irritating more than anything."

"Distracting?"

"Yes, Sir."

"Good. I'll give you more when I'm ready."

It pulsed again, and she felt it in her belly. "Now's a good time."

Her evil Dom laughed. "I'm sure it is. Close your legs please."

When the vibe pulsed again, she moved her hips, trying to stimulate her clitoris. Having her thighs together increased the sensations and prevented her from getting any friction. "This is borderline mean."

"Nothing borderline about it, sub." He rubbed her skin.

She squeezed her muscles, dreading the horrid stripes that would follow.

Undaunted, he covered her ass cheeks and thighs with a dozen blazing slaps.

By the time he caught her with the first light smack from the cane, she was ready to climb out of her mind.

He gave her numerous taps that she figured were designed to increase her resistance and pain threshold. She wasn't stupid enough to think he was going to continue to be so gentle.

Suddenly the vibration inside her increased. She murmured in protest.

"Ready?"

Before she responded, he cut into her upper thigh with a brutal strike that only the cane could deliver.

She hissed.

"I take it you felt that one?" He turned the dial.

A long pulse went through her only to gently fade to nothing. "I hate that setting."

"Because?"

Avery struggled for words. Was it possible for him to understand something she'd never tried to articulate? "It feels as if I'm being wound up. When I reach the pinnacle, ready for more, it's gone."

"Ah."

He made no move to change it, even though she expected that he would. "Sir?"

"I told you to ask."

She nodded.

"I never promised to give in to you. I said you will receive everything you need."

"That's fucked-up." *And not for the first time.*

"Dominance and submission." He marked her again.

Avery buried her head into the mattress to ensure she didn't scream.

"Take it." Cole laid another nasty stripe above the first.

She exhaled.

The third felt vicious. Combined with the whirling inside her pussy, she couldn't relax.

"Settle in."

Easy for him to say when it wasn't his ass in the air waiting for the evil rattan to be delivered.

An intimidating whistle sliced the air before the implement connected with her right buttock. She pitched forward, and he increased the torment inside her, making her forget the pain.

He moved on to her left cheek, searing it.

In her experience, there was nothing like the cane. It humbled. Its radiating bite went deep, and it didn't dissipate as fast as a flogger's.

But the vibrator changed her relationship with the pain, helping her to disassociate.

"Three more," he stated.

She'd be lucky to take two.

"Unclench your fingers, sub. Just relax."

Avery hadn't realized she was desperately wadding the sheet in her fists. It took all of her concentration to release her grasp.

"Don't fight. Breathe. It is what it is. In and out."

She nodded.

This time, he placed one beneath her butt cheeks in that tender, perfect strike zone.

"Damn."

He massaged the skin he'd tormented, and her muscles softened, allowing her to accept more.

"Where would you like the next?"

"I wouldn't."

"Slow? Red?"

She exhaled. "No." She'd be proud of herself for getting through this. "On my ass cheeks, Sir?"

"That's what I was hoping you'd say."

He laid one on her, and she gulped back a cry.

Her legs wobbled. She was grateful to be over the bed. If he'd asked her to hold the armoire, she would have fallen over.

He gave her some time to process the pain, file it away.

Then he turned up the vibrator.

He continued to interact with her, touching, massaging, kissing, and she began to slip away. She was aware of him talking to her, but at some point, pleasure vanquished every other feeling. The high from the endorphins wrapped around her. Each stripe from the cane only gave her a new feeling of bliss.

Then she was aware of nothing, just a soothing, enveloping sensation, much like being in a warm bath.

"Well done."

She heard the words but didn't comprehend them, didn't respond to them.

Cole moved back her hair and kissed the side of her neck. "You are an exquisite play partner."

When she opened her eyes, she was sitting up in bed, the comforter wrapped around her bare shoulders, nestled in the crook of Cole's arm. He'd even managed to extract the bullet.

"You're back?"

"Yeah." Her own whisper was too loud. For some reason, all her senses seemed heightened.

"How are you feeling?"

"Incredible." It had to have been her state of otherworldliness that drove her confession. Everything she'd fantasized about had come true. She'd slipped free from the constraints of her body and moved someplace inviting. *Subspace.* Words didn't exist to explain it—the thrill, the way reality fragmented, and the brightness of colors, sensation of soaring through time and space.

The journey had been more exhilarating than she'd dared hope. His exquisite care and tender, infinite patience completed the experience.

He reached toward the nightstand to pick up the bottle of mineral water. "You'll need this."

She accepted it, and he kept his hand cupped beneath it, just in case her grip was still unsteady.

After swallowing a couple of sips, she gave the drink back. Her hand *was* shaking.

"Did you enjoy being someone different for the evening?"

Avery put her hand flat on his chest and pushed herself away from him as much as possible. "Sir?" She frowned.

"Someone you're not usually. Bolder? Braver?"

Her pulse sped, then slowed. "Yes."

His gaze was steely, uncompromising. "How difficult was it?"

"I'm not sure I understand the question, Sir."

"Admitting what you wanted. Asking for it. Did you like it?"

She scowled, confused, his clipped tone making her wary. "Yes."

"Then it's time for you to be completely honest. Take off the mask."

"Don't." Avery reached up to hold it in place. "That's not part of our agreement."

"We fit together well. I'd like to see you again, but in order for that to happen, there can be no secrets between us."

Her world became quicksand.

"I had a sub who resorted to manipulation to get her needs met. Games. Brattiness. Anything to catch my attention and keep it focused on her."

Pain cut through his words, but Avery had her own demons. "I didn't ask for more than one night," she reminded him, even while she fantasized about a thousand more.

"You're a beautiful sub…*Layla.*"

There it was again, that pause.

"And you can have what you want. It takes daring, a big risk. But what are the alternatives? A lifetime of hiding who you really are? Being frustrated? There are costs to your choices."

"There are costs to everything. Asking for too much. *Being* too much." Holding a sheet to her breasts, she bolted from the mattress and snatched up her gown.

He climbed from the bed, spectacular and overwhelming. "The next time I see you, it will be without pretense. No mask. No hiding. Every secret laid bare before me."

What the hell have I gotten myself into? "There won't be a next time." She struggled to get into her dress.

"Let me."

"You've done enough."

"I said *let me.*" His eyes were chilly, like a winter's day.

Damn him and his domineering ways.

Without waiting for another argument, he took the dress from her and raised it over her head.

Once it was in place, she exhaled and reached back to fasten it.

He brushed aside her shaky hands and raised the zipper.

"Thank you." This wasn't ending the way she'd envisioned, with her mysteriously slipping from his bed in the middle of the night. She hated the way they were parting.

Cole picked up her vibrator and remote and offered them to her. "You can reach me through Diana or Alcott. Or call the hotel and ask to be put through." He shrugged. "And you know which room I'm staying in, if you wish to present your ass for a spanking."

That won't be happening. "Thanks for the fuck, Mr. Stewart."

He grabbed her by the shoulders, his jaw tight. His fingers bit into her skin. "It was more than a fuck for me. And it was to you as well, and that's why you're running scared. I'll tell you this—you'll remember tonight. You'll think about it. You may be with someone else, but you'll want this. And you won't be able to have it unless, and until, you stop running."

Pain seared her lungs, but she refused to let him see her distress.

She pulled away, crossed the room to grab her clutch, then stuffed her sex toy inside. Without a look back, she left, pulling the door closed with a decisive click.

Only then did she collapse against the wall.

She put a hand to her throat and drew a couple of breaths to tamp down the adrenaline. How the hell had the evening gone from something so perfect to a stunning disaster so quickly?

Once her legs were steady, Avery pushed off the wall. Squaring her chin, she headed toward the elevator. Inside the compartment, she smiled at the older couple already in there. The pair had their hands clasped, and Avery looked away. Because of the way she protected herself, she might never experience that kind of easy intimacy with a partner.

She exited when the car swished to a stop. Through

willpower, she held her emotions in check while she walked to her room.

Inside, she dropped her clutch on the table, then made her way into the bathroom to take off her mask.

The reflection in the mirror stunned her.

Mascara stained beneath her eyes. Her hair was a wild mess. Worse, her lower lip trembled.

Cole and his opinions didn't matter. They'd shared an evening together, and it meant nothing.

The lie rocked her, making her grip the vanity.

Those hours had been spectacular. She'd achieved the floating sensation that she'd sought for so many years. She'd taken more than she'd imagined she could. He'd given her orgasm after orgasm that left her shattered, not broken, and somehow more complete.

But at what cost?

CHAPTER FIVE

Goddamn it.

He had a reputation as a ladies' man. As such, Cole wasn't known to be a fuckup with the fairer sex. Then again, he'd never been with a woman like Avery Fisher.

When the door had closed behind her, he'd been tempted to ride the elevator to the casino level and drink a few beers at one of the six bars.

Instead, he changed into workout gear. Whether he wanted to or not, he would deal with his emotions head-on, like he demanded from Avery. It was easy to live in denial. But experience had taught him that reality was worth the fight.

He entered the gym, or the Royal Sterling's mind-blowing definition of a gym. Designed by Sean Finnegan, Next Level occupied most of the tenth floor.

Though the aesthetics were stunning, Cole was a simple man. All he needed was a place to run and some significant weights. When he had no other options, his own body could be used for resistance, push-ups, sit-ups, planks.

He bypassed the cardio equipment and went for the free-weight area. Despite it being the middle of the night, the place was busy. Not that it should be a surprise, he supposed. Las Vegas was the planet's playground, and who knew what time zone people were on?

He did squats until his legs burned, curls until his biceps bulged. After a drink of water, he headed for the running track. Maybe the mindless repetition would help him forget the image of Avery's skin turning pink, then red, and her quiet moans of appreciation.

A couple of miles later, a sledgehammer plowed into him. The problem was not her. It was him.

Scening with someone who wanted to keep her identity a secret was fucked-up. And he'd done it anyway. It didn't matter what rationale he used. It had been a bad decision.

But the truth was, he'd have done anything for a night with her.

It had been one hell of an evening. He'd been hot for her curvy, submissive body, and he'd enjoyed every moment they spent together.

If he'd forced her to take off the mask, she might not have had the nerve to scene with him.

The disguise had been the confidence booster she needed and the thing that left him hanging now. He was beyond disappointed that she'd fled instead of trusting him.

He continued to push himself on the track until his lungs begged for a reprieve. And when he began his cooldown, his thoughts were still fragmented.

Honesty was nonnegotiable. And when she was ready, there were a thousand things he intended to do to her, from fucking her ass, to putting her on an iron cross, to scening with her in public, to licking her pussy for so long that the only thing she screamed was his name.

Damn it.

Damn *her.*

On his wrist, his Bonds watch vibrated.

Maybe it was Avery, admitting she'd made a horrible mistake and saying she wanted to be real with him.

Dreamer.

He checked the screen. *Interesting.* A text message from Hawkeye himself.

Go to secure line.

Nothing like work to distract Cole's snarling Dominant beast. *Thank fuck.*

He glanced around to be certain no one was close before selecting the icon for an encrypted line. Then he tapped his earbuds to connect the call.

"Got something interesting."

As usual, Hawkeye didn't indulge in time-wasting pleasantries.

"You interested in taking a trip?"

He slowed to a walk to concentrate on the conversation. "I'm listening."

"We have an appointment in Houston tomorrow. Cristian LaRosa would like to meet you."

What the actual hell?

"He's intrigued by what you've got to offer."

Which was an AI—artificial intelligence—platform unlike anything else on the market. Because Hawkeye protected the world's most valuable people and assets, including secrets, the firm was now Cole's biggest client. But LaRosa? "You busting my balls?" Even as he asked the question, he knew the answer. Hawkeye didn't joke, especially about something like this.

"He's legit."

"Bullshit." Though nothing had ever been proven, the LaRosas were honored as royalty among Mafia families.

"They're planning to open a resort casino here in Vegas, and they have other…business interests stateside and around the world."

Casinos and their resorts were high-profile hacking targets. Which was why he was currently working with Hawkeye on upgrading the Royal Sterling. But working with the mob? That was a line Cole hesitated to cross, despite the fact that Cristian was also a member of the Zeta Society. "Not interested in anything that will raise my profile with the Feds."

"Do your research. Their corporation is completely aboveboard."

Yeah. "Not convinced."

"He's looking at other companies."

"Let him. There's nothing this sophisticated on the market."

"Everyone fucking knows that." Hawkeye's words were clipped with impatience.

Cole wanted to refuse. But a stray image slipped through his brain. One of Avery on her knees looking up at him as she prepared to suck him off. Being in one place for several months was an unheard-of luxury. If he wanted Avery, it gave him some time to plan and execute a strategy.

"I need your answer now, and it needs to be yes," Hawkeye finished.

"Earth to Avery."

She shook her head to clear it then accepted a glass of ginger ale from her friend Makenna. "Thank you."

"Where are you?"

"I'm sorry."

Zara took a sip of her own soft drink, then glanced at Avery. "She's thinking about Cole."

Her friend was right. It had been a week since Avery spent the night with Cole at the Royal Sterling, and she still wanted him. Not just his touch, but his possession.

"There's only one way to get that man out of your head." Makenna scanned the great room of Diana and Alcott Hewitt's astounding home in the John S. Park neighborhood.

For a month, Avery had planned to attend the party, but it had taken every ounce of her energy to change out of the yoga pants she'd worn the entire day. Staying home to watch television was more appealing than interacting with people.

But her friends had texted that they were wondering where she was. Without her customary enthusiasm, she'd wriggled into a tight skirt and bustier. Finally, she donned a bolero jacket so she looked somewhat appropriate for leaving her apartment. With her nose wrinkled, she studied herself in the mirror. The truth was, only one man's opinion of the outfit mattered to her.

Now, she wished she hadn't attended.

"Oh my God. That's Master Zachary…" Makenna fanned herself.

Possessing the fearlessness that came from holding her own against four protective older brothers, Zara grinned. "You should go talk to him."

Makenna shook her head. Though she attended a lot of scene parties, she professed to being far too self-conscious to actually join in. Her favorite spot was in front of the viewing room. "I'll just enjoy watching the demonstrations." She took another sip. Maybe trying to hide her emotions?

"So how about it?" Zara asked Avery "Should we find you a Top to play with?"

Allowing her mind to be consumed with thoughts of a one-night Dominant was ridiculous, but Avery couldn't help herself. "Maybe another time."

For the next hour, they wandered the grounds and observed a few scenes. When a man joined them, with eyes only for Avery, her friends promised to watch out for her, then wandered away together.

He wore leather pants and an unfastened vest that was at least one size too small. Since he'd been invited by the Hewitts, he'd been vetted, which meant he could be trusted. Unfortunately she had zero attraction to him.

"Are you a submissive?"

Unable to find her voice, she settled for nodding.

He swept a glance over her. "Looking for a scene?"

Rather than her heart leaping, disappointment that he wasn't Cole snaked through her. Mentally, she was comparing this man to him. She shook herself. *How screwed up is that?*

Too late, she realized scening with Cole had been a mistake. Everything about him had gotten to her, and she wished it hadn't. He'd ruined her for other men. She was his.

"So, are you?"

Avery blinked herself back to the present. "No. I'm not." Then she smiled to take the sting from the rejection. "Thank you, though."

She wandered into the great room where a woman was dressed in office attire—a tight white shirt, a short skirt, black pumps, and stockings. A man wearing a business suit instructed her to bend over the desk.

Restlessness momentarily abated, Avery watched.

The Dom worked the woman's skirt up, exposing her scantily clad bottom, with the straps on her garter belt bisecting her butt cheeks. Then he shrugged out of his jacket. "What have I told you about surfing social media during work hours?" He picked up a cane.

The sub looked over her shoulder, her mouth open wide with pretend fear. Or maybe the reaction was real. Avery would never be able to face the cane with anything less than complete respect.

"Oh, Mr. Holmes! I promise I won't ever do that again. Please spare me!"

"How many times have you been warned? Hmm? Two? Three? You knew there would be consequences."

Those words echoed in Avery's head. She should have thought through the consequences of scening with Master Cole.

He'd told her he would spoil her for any other man. And he had. But she hadn't been prepared for being adrift without him.

The Dom gathered the material of his sub's panties and moved it all to her crotch, then yanked, lifting her from the floor.

Avery winced in mute sympathy as the Dominant smacked the woman's bare buttocks before letting loose with the cane.

The sound, the way the woman flinched, then the terrible thin line on her skin, brought it all back for Avery.

She yearned for Cole, wanted to be naked, sobbing beneath his dominance. She craved the orgasm he would give her.

The Dom delivered another stroke.

The truth crept up on Avery and hit her as powerfully as a stripe from rattan. It was the connection—emotional as well as physical—that she thirsted for. Cole had held her, caressed her. He'd cared for her, making her feel special. His loving attention had boosted her confidence.

With a hole in her heart, she wandered outside where a couple was demonstrating rope bondage. Watching the slow beauty and intricacies of Shibari often relaxed her. Tonight it made her lonely.

She should have trusted her earlier instincts. Coming here had been a mistake.

Once she accepted that, she found her friends and said her goodbyes.

Avery took her time driving home, avoiding the congestion of the Strip. But it wasn't just the overwhelming traffic that kept her away. It was the realization she would end up at the Royal Sterling, looking for Cole.

And she didn't have it in her to agree to his ultimatum.

She stopped at a traffic light and dropped her head onto the steering wheel.

Why the hell am I making this so complicated?

No doubt, what he had demanded of her would be difficult. She was accustomed to letting her man—her Dom—be in charge. And Dirk's scoldings had been a constant narrative during a scene.

Beneath the mask, she'd become someone different, but what if she could learn to be that person all the time?

The car behind her honked impatiently, alerting her to the fact that the light had turned green. She accelerated, and so did her thoughts and heart rate.

She'd gained confidence from her time with Master Cole. What if he encouraged and supported her growth?

He'd been right when he'd told her she needed to be honest with herself. So she allowed herself to admit she wanted, needed him.

Now what?

It would take a ton of resolve to act on her newfound admission, to either show up at his hotel room or ask Diana for his number.

Unfortunately, Avery wasn't that brave, no matter how much she wanted to be.

Avery spent Sunday doing chores and working out. When she returned home, she tried a couple of different books. When neither held her, she settled in front of the television and binged her way through an entire season of a home improvement show. To prove to herself that she wasn't hopeless, she opened a bottle of expensive special-occasion wine, then poured herself a glass.

It didn't help.

No matter what she did, she couldn't escape the fact that her cowardice was the major contributor to her unhappiness.

Once she was in her bedroom, she slipped the bullet vibrator inside her pussy and masturbated to memories of Cole. They were a thousand times more potent than her imagination ever had been.

Even more frustrating, she was unable to climax.

Annoyed, she removed the toy, cleaned it, then dropped it back into her drawer.

At work on Monday morning, two of Avery's coworkers followed her into the break room to chat about their weekend outings, the movies they'd seen, the parties they'd attended. When asked about her time off, she replied noncommittally, then went into her office and got busy on her spreadsheets behind a closed door.

She stayed later than most people, and at six o'clock, Aunt Scarlet dropped by her office.

"Darling girl." Her great-aunt took plopped into a seat without waiting for an invitation. "You didn't return my call."

Since her aunt was too perceptive at times, Avery had dodged the two Sunday calls. She should have expected Scarlet to show up in person.

"It's a man, isn't it?"

"I'm sorry?"

"When you hide from me, it's because of a man."

"I wasn't hiding."

Aunt Scarlet's eyes went wide, sending her lashes soaring. "You were hiding."

"Okay." Avery sank a little lower in her chair. "Maybe I was."

"Tell me about him."

"You seem to have done quite well without a man."

"That's because I had dozens. Still do. I like"—she waved a ring-covered hand—"variety, shall we say. I like rich ones and creatives ones. Skilled lovers. Men who will jet me to their island. Mostly, I like my independence. It's cost me some relationships." She took a breath, and she blinked rapidly. It couldn't be tears, could it? "Some I regret."

The moisture in her aunt's eyes vanished so fast that Avery was sure she'd imagined it. "Do you?"

"Yes. Not many. But I do wonder about Billy."

The mobster? "What would you do differently?"

"Nothing. I have to live with some scars, but to me, it's worth it. You, however, are different. Such a tender heart."

"So what do you recommend I do?"

"Oh, heavens! I would never give you advice!"

"But if you did?"

"Live with no regrets. Do what makes you happy. Anything can be undone. Except, perhaps, chances you didn't take."

Avery exhaled.

"It's the delicious secret agent man, isn't it?" Aunt Scarlet leaned forward, as if soliciting a secret. "Cole."

"Yes."

"Oh, honey. The way he looked at you." She shimmied, and in the process moved forward a couple of inches in her chair. "He wants you."

"He gave me an ultimatum."

"Ah," she replied, as if she understood. "A man who knows what he wants. He's good to you?"

He was.

"And you wouldn't be suffering if you didn't care for him."

Avery exhaled.

"So, if I were to give advice, which I don't, I'd say give it a try. Well, unless the terms of his ultimatum are dreadful. Are they?"

"Emotionally, maybe."

"It's up to you, then. If the risk isn't worth the reward, spend the next six months moping."

Offended, she responded. "I'm not moping."

"You are. And that's not living. So, forget him and go have some fun tonight. See a movie. Try a new restaurant. Or be brave and see where it goes. If it doesn't work out, at least you'll know. You might get hurt, but you won't have the scars of never knowing and always wondering what might have been."

"When did you get to be so wise?"

"I was born this way. And so were you." She winked. "Chin up, darling girl." Aunt Scarlet grabbed the handle of her oversize purse. Rising, she said, "If you'll excuse me, Gerard is in town. And this is an evening I fully intend to embrace. No show tonight. Well…except for his command performance."

"Wait." Avery blinked. "Gerard who?"

"He was in a few movies or…something on television. He looks good in a kilt. Very nice legs."

"You've got to tell me," Avery demanded.

Scarlet rounded the desk to drop a kiss on Avery's forehead. "Remember to choose the path that will help you live with no regrets." Without another word, Aunt Scarlet breezed out, letting her wisdom linger on a cloud of perfume.

Avery collapsed against the back of her seat. For several minutes, the conversation replayed in her mind.

Walking away from Cole had left a hole deep inside. She could go on with her life, but one point that Scarlet made continued to resonate. If she agreed to Cole's terms, Avery might very well get hurt, but she wouldn't have to live with not knowing how it might have turned out.

Contemplatively, she tapped a finger on the arm of her chair.

Could she do it? Take the chance?

It would mean being honest. Not just with him, but with herself.

She blew out a breath to steady her nerves. The truth was, if she didn't at least try, she would be disappointed in herself. She needed to be as brave without a mask as she had been wearing one.

Before her newfound resolve fled, she picked up her phone to text Diana for Cole's number.

It didn't mean Avery had to contact him. It just meant she could, if she decided to.

Instead of staring at the phone, waiting for a response that might not come, she dropped the device into her purse, then straightened her desk before leaving for the night.

Her phone chimed while she was navigating traffic, so she waited until she was at a stoplight to check her messages.

Diana had replied in her customary precise way. She'd

attached Cole's contact card, with all his information—email address, social media accounts, and his cell phone. His number showed up in blue, which meant all Avery just had to do was touch the screen to be connected.

She moved her finger toward the number and hovered over it.

But she couldn't make herself tap the number. Thank God, the light turned green, allowing her to put off the action a little longer.

By the time she arrived home, nerves were pouring through her. She was going to call him. But then what would she do if he didn't answer? Leave a message? What would she say? What if he didn't call back? Her mind skipped through a dozen different scenarios before she harnessed her thoughts and took a breath, drawing on the coaching he'd given her when they scened.

She made herself face the fact that he might reject her. If so, at least she would know. She'd be no more hurt than she was right now.

But if he wanted to see her...

That possibility made her tighten her grip.

By the time she arrived home, she'd made her decision.

She walked down the hallway leading to her apartment, and her step faltered. A man stood near her door. Not just any man—one who was tall, broad, unshaven, sexy. He wore a charcoal-gray suit, and his only concession to it being after work hours was the loosened knot in his tie. Stunned, she stopped near him. "Master Cole."

"Avery." He pushed away from the wall.

"You know who I am." *Of course.* He had all of Hawkeye's resources at his fingertips.

"I've known all along."

Nervously she tucked her hair behind her ears. "There's no way."

"I saw you, that night when I was at Alcott and Diana's with Gia. I overheard your friends calling you Avery, and the name was unusual, beautiful, so I remembered it. It could have been a scene name," he allowed. "But I didn't get the sense it was. Then I noticed you at the club about six months ago."

"Those sleuthing skills come in handy."

"I was hoping you'd be brave enough to come to me. Or hell… I was so intrigued by you that I would have made a move if you'd shown enough interest."

She lurched, as if the world had suddenly started to spin backward.

"Your eyes, Avery. They give away the world. The way you walk, your ass swaying? Your body is so damn sexy. Hair length, color? Mask?" He shrugged. "It wouldn't matter how you altered your appearance. I would always know you."

Damn, he'd told her he could be counted on to give her what she needed. He left her speechless.

"Since you contacted Diana, I wanted to meet you halfway. I would never ask you to take all the risk. I do want you to ask for what you want, but I will make it easy for you. You will always know I respect and value you. I brought you a cupcake in case I need to bribe my way inside." From behind his back, he presented a gorgeous pink box wrapped with a white ribbon. "It's triple chocolate."

"You're an evil man." But oh, so wonderfully sweet.

"I'm holding it hostage."

It might have been her imagination, but she swore she could smell the sugar in the frosting.

"I was going to give you another couple of days; then I'd have been all over you. I've been crazy with missing you. If you refused to see me, I planned to hang out near the cupcake machine, figuring you'd show up eventually."

A neighbor and her two boys who were punching each

other entered the hallway.

Avery moved her keys from hand to hand. "I think you should come in."

Seconds later, he locked the door behind them, and she hung her purse from the coatrack.

In the kitchen, he placed her gift on the counter.

"I missed you too." Her words were soft. "Terribly." This was difficult, but the longer she talked, the easier it got. "Being honest with you has to be easier than not being with you."

"That night, before you left, you said there were costs to everything. Asking for too much. *Being* too much. Tell me about it."

Her first test. "Can we, uhm…? How about something to drink?"

"No. I'm fine. But you can, if you wish."

She shook her head. "But I would like us to sit in the living room."

He followed, and she perched on the edge of an armchair, while he lowered himself onto the sofa. He leaned forward and laced his fingers on top of his knees.

"I've been single for over a year." Avery drew a breath. She hadn't shared these details with anyone. Cole remained silent, waiting while she collected her thoughts. "My boyfriend—Dominant—said I wanted to scene too often." She paused. That wasn't quite the truth. His wording had hurt more. "He was supposed to be in charge, so that meant everything in our relationship was up to him." With a little shrug, she went on. "I stopped asking. I accepted what little he offered, and I was grateful for it. I was…but at the same time, I wasn't. I began to think he was right. Maybe my sex drive was too high. I was restless, feeling neglected. We played once a month, if that. I made the mistake of asking if we could go to Diana and Alcott's one night, and Dirk snapped." After a breath, she confessed the shame. "He called me an ungrateful bitch. Then he left. I never heard from him again."

"Jesus, Avery. I had no idea."

"That night, behind the mask, I could be the woman I wanted to be. I needed that crutch to shut out his voice in my head. It was my first scene in a really long time."

He dragged the knot from his tie. "What he told you was bullshit. You're exquisite in every way."

She gave a ghost of a smile as relief poured through her. "It's going to take me some time. But if you have the patience, I want to try."

"Will you come to me?" He extended his hand.

On shaky legs, she stood.

She crossed the room to him; then he eased her into his lap, facing him with her knees on the cushions. His eyes were melted steel, offering promise and reassurance. "You're enough. We will figure this out together."

Drinking in his approval, she nodded.

"Tell me what you want."

"I want you to kiss me, Sir. I want to wrap my arms around your neck. I want you to be hard with me. I like it rough. I want you to put your leg between mine so I can rub my hot pussy on you. I'm desperate to come. I've been masturbating, but I haven't been able to have an orgasm. And if you tell me I can't have all of those things—any of those things—I will say yes, Sir, and be happy. Just be my Dom."

He put his hands on either side of her head and kissed her, long, slow, stoking embers until the flames roared into an inferno. She inhaled his spice and the freshness of honesty. His breath was warm on her face, and he moved his thigh between hers, achingly close to her pussy.

"Are you horny for me?" His eyes narrowed, and she shuddered.

"Yes. As always."

"I want you, Avery. First, you need to be rewarded for your honesty. Lift up your skirt."

Because it was so tight, it took her a few seconds to do as he instructed.

"Ah. Panties. Just like the night at the Royal Sterling. I guessed you were the type of woman who would wear them unless your Dom instructed otherwise."

She met his eyes.

"Consider yourself instructed."

She shivered. "Yes, Sir."

"Get rid of them."

Since that was a difficult task in her position, he helped her.

"Now put your arms around my neck." He dampened his finger, then glided it across her clit.

His touch was exquisite. She wrapped her arms around him and moved in rhythm with his strokes. There was no place she would rather be.

"I want you to be thinking…"

"Sir?"

"About how many stripes you're going to get from my cane."

Fear, excitement, doubt, hope all surged through her. "You don't have it."

"In the car, I do," he countered. "I'm thinking three for each day you've been gone."

"That's too many," she protested, scared, hungry.

"Better idea?"

"No, Sir."

"Let's go get my cane."

In that moment, she knew—*knew*—he would give her what she needed. She sighed, content, maybe for the first time ever.

EPILOGUE

"So..." Avery reached for her Dom's tie and began to loosen the knot at his throat. Four months prior, she'd moved in to Cole's beautiful house. Built on more than half an acre on a cul-de-sac up against a mountain in a gated community, it was as much a fortress as it was a place to retreat. The fenced perimeter was protected by a state-of-the-art security system designed by Cole himself and tweaked by the tech genius, Julien Bonds.

Anyone approaching the fence was greeted by a rather polite British voice advising that they were trespassing and that the police had been notified. In addition, video was livestreamed to the authorities. There were other fences and tripwires, and, of course, the house itself had a secure room with numerous monitors that also could be accessed from Cole's cell phone.

A little at a time, he'd shared some stories from his past, and she understood his need to know what was coming before it arrived. To his credit, though, he'd realized she needed more comfort than he did. They spent most of their weekends working together to transform the six thousand square feet into a home. She'd set up a place to work, and the previous day, he'd surprised her by having several potted palms delivered for their living room.

They'd spent considerable time discussing their relationship and expectations. He had cut back his travel schedule, and when he returned to her, he always pulled her tight and kept her there.

"So…?" he prompted.

She took a breath. Each time she stated her needs, it was easier. But it was still far from natural, even though he was true to his promise and made it as easy as possible for her. "Diana and Alcott are having a play party next weekend."

"Are they?"

Avery tugged the knot open and left the ends of the bloodred tie hanging down his jacket. She couldn't get enough of him. Every day he assured her it was more than mutual. "I'd like to go, Sir."

A slow smile crossed his face. "Would you?"

"I ordered a new outfit. Just in case you said yes."

He lifted one eyebrow in a sexy way that showed his interest and shot heat through her. That was something she adored about him. When they were together, all of his attention was devoted to her. Many nights they took a dip—naked—in the pool. Sometimes they curled up on their new couch and watched her favorite drama. At least twice a week, he spent considerable time planning a scene that shattered her, healed her. "Tell me about the new clothes."

"The top is called a bralette. But it's a little more complicated than that."

"Lace?"

"Leather, and it sort of looks like a harness."

"That may be my new favorite word." He pulled her against him. "I'm thrilled to have people see you wearing it."

He touched her collarbone. "And of course, I will want to attach a leash to it when we attend the party."

His cock was raging hard, and she guessed what was next. Still, she waited on the command she knew was coming.

"Drop your clothes, Avery." His words were forged in steel, instantly dropping her into a submissive state of mind. Cole knew her sensual triggers, and his voice was the most powerful.

He released his grip on her. In a fluid movement, she pulled her sundress up and off, then dropped it to the floor before kicking off her sandals.

He swept his approving gaze over her. "Let me see you."

She drew a steadying breath, no longer from concern. He appreciated *her*, everything about her, even the things she considered flaws.

Avery turned her back to him, spread her legs as wide as possible, then held her ankles.

"So gorgeous." He grabbed her ass cheeks and squeezed. Hard.

His fingers dug deep enough to hurt, but she didn't wince. Instead, she closed her eyes in submission.

"All day, I thought about this," he said, spreading her wide for his inspection. He skimmed his finger across her private parts, being sure she'd complied with this morning's order to be clean-shaven.

Not knowing what to expect was an extra bonus. At times, he wanted her natural. Once he'd directed her to be neatly trimmed. Mostly, he wanted her bare. He didn't allow her to anticipate and in fact had chastised her for doing so. Since it had hurt to sit down after that, she'd learned her lesson.

He was the Dom—in charge—in the best way possible. Over their months together, she'd learned to trust him. He didn't criticize her or have mercurial moods. They'd had a few disagreements, but they'd sat together at the dining table, across from each other, taking turns talking, with no raised voices.

Over time, trust had blossomed into the first tendrils of love. She'd passed infatuation, and the more powerful emotion was new and a little scary, leaving her giddy.

"How long since you've tasted my belt?"

Her world swam.

"Answer me." His words were soft, but his tone was not.

She thought back. His cane, she remembered. And his hand. Even the flogger. "Too long, Sir."

"I agree. Let's rectify that." He released her. "I want you over the back of the couch."

Conscious of him watching her every move, she brought herself upright and walked across the room to get into the position he'd requested.

Cole said nothing, allowing the time to drag and her tension to build.

Something crinkled, and she turned her head to the side to see what he was doing, but he wasn't in her range of sight. She could guess what he was doing—removing his suit coat? And his tie? Rolling up his shirtsleeves?

Her breath whooshed out when he lifted her, tipping her forward. Frantic, she grabbed for a cushion for stability. "Sir!"

"Much better. Don't you agree?"

Her feet no longer touched the stone floor, but she knew better than to argue. "Yes, Cole." Something cold and wet pressed against her rear. She froze.

"Clenching will make it worse, Avery."

Breathing deep in this position was almost impossible—especially with him doing evil things to her.

He pressed forward. Avery's tightest hole stretched to

accommodate him, as it always did. "Urgh." The metal snuggled in.

"Very nice." Cole twisted the plug around and around, driving her out of her mind. "I love having your ass stuffed full."

Because it heightened her arousal and because it pleased him, she liked it too.

To warm her up, he smoothed his hands over her back and shoulders, then her buttocks, even the tops of her thighs. She allowed her body to go limp, going to a place deep inside her mind where she could push away the stresses of the world and connect with her Dom.

The first few strokes of his belt were soft, a hint of what was to come. As the minutes drew on, he deepened the intensity.

"Leather was made for your ass."

"Yes." The word emerged as a mumble, but he understood, as he always did.

The next stripe caught her beneath the buttocks. She yelped from the wave of pain. Within seconds, it eased off, and pleasure surged in.

He slid his finger between her labia. "You like this."

Avery struggled to stay in place, but she was so aroused that she jutted herself backward, seeking more.

He laughed, a diabolical sound, and moved his finger away from her.

Protesting would earn her a longer spanking, so she clamped her lips together.

"You are a quick study." Approval laced his words, making her glad she'd remained quiet.

He gave her ten more stripes, each one making her cry out louder. And when it was over, he helped her up.

Overwhelmed, she slipped to her knees.

Shocking her, he knelt too, facing her. He took her hands

in his, and she met his eyes. For once, they were unreadable, their gray color lighter than normal, like liquid silver.

"Sir?"

"I love you, Avery."

His words and the pure conviction in them made her shake. A lump lodged in her throat, making it impossible to respond.

"I've known it for a long time, but I didn't think you were ready to trust the words, until now." He continued to hold her with one hand, and he used the other to notch her chin up. His smile was tentative, and it was one of the few times she'd caught a glimpse of him without his customary alpha male confidence. It humbled her, revealed the depth of his honesty. "It's okay if you don't return the sentiment—"

"I..." Desperately trying to swallow the wedge of emotion, she nodded. The tears spilled.

With exquisite tenderness, he used his thumb to capture one, but he didn't try to wipe them away. "I'm taking it that means you love me too?"

The words, admission, came from deep inside her. "Oh Cole..."

He kissed her intimately, with domination, but also with affection. She clung to him and his strength as if she never wanted to let go. He tasted of promise. Of a hundred thousand tomorrows.

When neither of them could breathe anymore, he ended the kiss.

"That was..." She managed to dislodge the knot in her throat. "I love you, Cole. There's never been anyone like you in my life."

"Precious, precious sub." He grinned, a cocky tilt to his mouth. The macho Dom was once again in control. "We should order some food. You've got a long night ahead of you, and you're not leaving the house for a very long time.

Now that I have you naked and plugged, I plan to keep you that way."

Oh. "For how long?"

"The rest of your life will do." His eyes gleamed. "For a start."

SLOW BURN

TITANS: SIN CITY, BOOK TWO

SLOW BURN

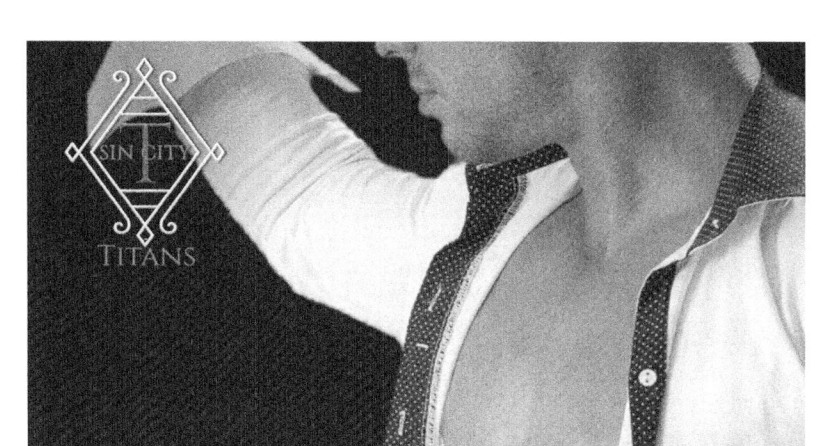

USA TODAY BESTSELLING AUTHOR
SIERRA CARTWRIGHT

CHAPTER ONE

"What do you see?"

Makenna jumped, sending diet soda over the rim of her glass to splash on the polished hardwood floor. The question, unexpectedly sexy and growly against her ear, rocketed sparks of desire down her spine.

Although they'd never been introduced, she'd recognize his commanding baritone anywhere. For at least a year, Zachary Denning had starred in her dreams and strolled through her fantasies.

The renowned Dominant was ridiculously rich, movie-star handsome, a battlefield hero…and a notorious heart-breaker. Master Zachary could have any woman on the planet, and from what she'd witnessed—tonight even—fans clamored for his attention.

So why are you talking to me?

"I didn't mean to frighten you."

She started to turn, but he clamped his strong hands on her shoulders, igniting a firestorm inside her.

"No. Please. Stay where you are."

Her pulse skittered, and her breath caught. Did he have any idea how intoxicating his effect was on her?

"That scene has you fascinated."

Since she was momentarily speechless, she settled for nodding.

Every few months, she and her friends from a businesswomen's group attended a play party here at the home of Las Vegas's hottest legal eagles, Diana and Alcott Hewitt.

Not only were the couple partners at the law firm bearing their name, but they owned one of the city's most unique properties—a house that was over twenty thousand square feet with grounds that sprawled over three large lots. The U-shaped home had an amazing courtyard complete with lush tropical foliage and a swimming pool with attached hot tub. Beyond it was a dramatic and rather noisy waterfall. And for clandestine meetings, a grotto was tucked away in the darkest recesses of the garden.

This evening, Makenna stood in front of her favorite place, an observation room, complete with one-way glass. The hot BDSM scene transpiring between her hosts held her riveted. That was the only explanation possible for not noticing Master Zachary's arrival.

"Tell me what you see." It was his second prompt, and command laced his request, compelling an obedience she'd never before experienced.

Unnerved by the billionaire as much as her own response to him, she cleared her throat. "I was about to move on."

"Were you?" His tone was warm, with an underlying mocking note. He'd caught her in a lie and called it out.

Impossibly he moved in closer. She imagined the abrasive rub of his pants against the bare skin of her legs.

Master Zachary had a reputation as a considerate Dominant, which meant she could excuse herself and make an escape at any time. Maybe that was why she remained rooted in place.

"You want to watch every moment until the very end." He slid the words into her ear, his breath warm on her already heated skin. "That's why you're here, isn't it?"

In a rush, she exhaled the painful admission. "Yes."

On the other side of the glass, Master Alcott held up a palm. Diana, naked and collared, sank to her knees and lowered her head. Then, in a move both beautiful and practiced, she cupped her breasts, offering them—and herself—to her Dominant.

"Is that what you want? To be in that position?"

Frantically Makenna shook her head. "I'm not much of a submissive." But if she were, it would be with Master Zachary. He was blessed by the gods with an exquisite body.

"You're not much of a submissive?" A gentle tease roughened his question. "You haven't moved from this place for at least ten minutes."

Which meant he'd been watching her. Had he noticed the way she squirmed when Master Alcott stripped his wife? "Ah…I find it interesting." Makenna cleared her throat. "A curiosity."

"Are you aroused?"

"What?" Heat rushed through her. She was glad he couldn't see the way excitement vanquished her shock.

"Is your pussy wet?"

Oh my God. Embarrassment clogged her throat.

"Be brave."

She couldn't.

"Take a chance. For me."

Because his order was as compelling as it was nonnegotiable, she nodded.

"I'd like to hear the words."

"Yes." Could she do this? Could she not? "I'm wet."

"That pleases me immensely. Yet you hesitated. What are you afraid of?"

"I'm an event planner. I deal with brides and demanding C-types all day long. Nothing scares me." She tried for an air of lightness she didn't feel.

"There are things in this world that are absolutely terrifying."

Of course he would know. She'd read an article about his exploits in her favorite gossip magazine, *Scandalicious*. Though he was from a wealthy background, all the Denning men were expected to serve their country. He'd graduated from a military academy and served heroically in battle before joining the family business. How they made their money, she had no idea. But she'd heard plenty of whispers.

He eased closer, rocketing a response through her and forcing her to admit she was afraid of something. *Him.*

In front of them, Master Alcott took a bit gag down from the wall. His obedient wife continued to stare at him and, without being told, opened her mouth. He placed the gag between her teeth, checked it for fit, then buckled the strap tightly behind her head.

At the sight of Diana's compliance, a bizarre buzzing scrambled around Makenna's ears.

"Describe the scene to me."

Like a moment ago, his command was absolute. Zachary Denning was a man accustomed to being obeyed. The problem was, until now, even though she had her private daydreams, she wasn't a woman accustomed to being told what to do.

"I'm waiting."

This surreal experience was giving her the opportunity to live out her fantasies, if only for the moment. Despite a rush of nervousness, she spoke. "Master Alcott is helping Diana to stand." Makenna tightened her fingers around her glass.

"Now she's walking to the center of the room where there's a massage type of table."

"Keep going."

Is this really happening? "She's bending at the waist, and he's securing her wrists to the far end of the table."

"So she can't move?"

Makenna squirmed. "Not much."

"So theoretically Master Alcott can do whatever he wants to her?"

A shiver rippled through her. "Yes."

"And since she's gagged, she can't say anything. She can't beg for mercy or protest in any way."

Words failed her.

"Do you wonder what it might be like to be in there? To be completely helpless to your Dominant's whims? To have others watching you?"

Her mouth dried. She took a sip of the soda, trying to ignore the fact that her hand was shaking. "Of course not. I've already told you I'm not submissive."

His soft chuckle was more of a scoff. "And your reactions tell a different story. Your breathing." He stroked a finger down the side of her throat. "The fluttering here." He pressed a thumb against her pulse.

If he hadn't kept one hand clamped on her shoulder, she would have fled.

"You haven't told me to go to hell."

Because foolishly she wanted this.

"Let me take your drink, Makenna."

Her pulse skipped a beat, then slammed the next dozen together. "How do you know who I am?" Maybe she should have selected a scene name to hide her identity, though she suspected he would dig through as many layers as it took to discover the information he wanted.

"I make it my business to know all of Diana and Alcott's guests, particularly the beautiful ones."

Beautiful? Not at all, and especially not when compared to the women he was known to date. Despite eating more lettuce than a rabbit, skipping chocolate for long enough to bankrupt Switzerland, and sweating at the gym three times a week, she had bulges and ripples everywhere. "I'm afraid you have the wrong person."

"Be assured, I don't."

What game are you playing?

With a strength that gave her no chance to run, he turned her to face him. For a moment, he stroked her shoulders, so sensually that her insides began to unravel. Then, when he tightened his fingers again, she tipped back her head to meet his gaze.

This close, he made her tremble.

He wore black trousers rather than leather pants or jeans. Light winked off the masculine gold ring and expensive watch that he wore. A tailored white dress shirt conformed to his body, emphasizing the athletic cut and definition of his well-honed biceps. Expensive shoes added an inch or two to his height, not that he needed it. He was already over six feet tall, towering over her, even in her heels.

His strong jaw was set in a firm line. But his eyes grabbed her attention. They were dark and deep—a blue-gray like the Atlantic during a tumultuous storm. Tiny grooves were carved next to them. Master Zachary had clearly seen more of life than she ever would, and it gave him an air of confidence, of mastery. No matter how hard she tried, she couldn't bear to look away from the intensity that suddenly blazed in his expression.

At that moment, a male server wearing tight black slacks and a red bowtie approached.

Master Zachary finally released her to take her glass.

After placing it on the tray, he snagged a napkin to wipe up her earlier spill.

His thoughtfulness surprised her.

When they were alone once more, he took a slight step back and swept his gaze over her. If what her ex-boyfriend said was true, Master Zachary was cataloging her numerous flaws.

"Gorgeous. Simply gorgeous."

She blinked at his reaction.

"Now, I'd like your legs shoulder width apart."

She had no idea what he had in mind, but if she offered him the control he wanted, she would be changed forever.

"You're hesitating. And again, you haven't told me to go to hell."

Master Zachary's presence was as undeniable as it was compelling.

"Courage, Makenna. Why not seize the moment?"

With a shaky breath, she did as he'd instructed, terribly aware of how short her skirt was.

"You follow directions well. You please me."

His approval weakened her knees. It had been so, so long…

"Now face the scene again."

As before, he placed his hands on her shoulders, but this time, his grip was possessive.

While they watched, Master Alcott slid his hand between Diana's legs. The woman arched her back, as if silently asking for more.

"Please continue your narration."

"Master Alcott seems to be stroking Diana's…" Makenna trailed off. "Her clit."

"And does she seem to be enjoying it?"

"Yes." As much as possible, Diana lifted her body, seemingly begging for her Master's touch. Makenna couldn't help but picture herself in Diana's place, with Zachary's strong fingers parting her labia.

Master Alcott moved away. Diana's hips swayed side to side gently and invitingly.

"What is he doing?" Master Zachary asked.

"Ah…" Her eyes widened. "He's getting… Oh my God." Little points of metal winked in the overhead lights. "Vampire gloves."

"Have you ever used them?"

She shook her head. Then she revealed more than she intended. "I haven't experienced most things related to BDSM." Truth was, while she yearned for more, she lacked the courage.

"And are you curious?"

"About the gloves in particular?" She shivered as Master Alcott checked the fit and flexed his fingers. "No. They terrify me."

"I can understand that. Yet the simultaneous dance of pain and pleasure can be addictive."

The image of Master Zachary exploring her body sashayed through her mind.

Intently focused, Master Alcott traced the little spikes up the outsides of his wife's thighs, then the insides, forcing her to rise onto her toes.

Diana turned her head to the side, so Makenna could read her expression. As the Dominant neared his submissive's pussy, she closed her eyes.

Instead of touching her most intimate place, he grabbed hold of her buttocks and squeezed.

Makenna yelped.

Master Zachary chuckled. "Sympathy reaction?"

"That had to hurt."

"Most likely."

Master Alcott said something inaudible before uncurling

his fingers to spank the tops of Diana's thighs. Though Makenna winced, the submissive wore a soft smile.

"He knows what she likes and ensures she receives it."

When Master Alcott again traced his way up the insides of her thighs, Diana parted her legs as far as her restraints allowed, giving herself over to her Dominant. She didn't pull away when he reached her apex.

"Notice the way he's taking in every one of her responses."

To Makenna this was about far more than BDSM. Submitting would mean she trusted a man to keep her best interests at the forefront, something she'd never experienced.

Diana wiggled her ass in invitation, and her Dominant removed his gloves, then picked up a serious-looking broad leather paddle and used it on the places he'd scratched.

Desire drove Makenna out of her mind, and she whimpered, even though she tried to hold it back.

"Have you ever been spanked like that?"

Tiny shakes overtook her. "I've never been spanked at all."

"Would you like a taste?"

God. Yes. "I…"

"Do you have a safe word?"

Though she'd never needed one, this was something she was familiar with. "Red."

"And green to let me know you're okay?"

Driven by the response unfurling in her, she nodded.

"Yellow to slow down?"

At this moment, she couldn't imagine ever wanting to say that.

"Tell me what you want."

No one was near, and she was fully dressed. "Green."

"Very good." Master Zachary slid his forearm in front of her. "You can brace yourself on me."

Before she could respond, he squeezed her right buttock,

and she sighed. It had been so long, and his touch, even through her clothing, made her delirious.

"I smell your arousal." His statement was a silken scandal, unraveling her resistance.

Firm, but not too hard, he delivered a single swat.

"Ohh."

"Green?"

She nodded.

"Remove your panties for me?"

Shock froze her vocal cords.

A primal part of her brain recognized that he was forcing her to be part of the experience.

He didn't press her again. Instead, he remained silent, allowing her the space to make a decision.

This was mortifying. If she took them off, he'd know what size they were. One time, she'd accidentally left a pair in the dryer, and her ex had picked them out, then brought them to her and mentioned that he'd had no idea she was that big.

She wasn't sure she could endure that kind of embarrassment ever again.

"Makenna?"

"I, uh..." Maybe it was better he know all her flaws from the beginning. Not that it mattered. After tonight, she'd never have the opportunity to be with him again.

With a sigh, she used his arm for balance as she removed the bikini-cut underwear.

"Perfect. Now give them to me."

Unable to help herself, she turned as much as possible, hoping to read his expression. The only thing visible was the cold, hard set of his jaw. "You're serious?"

"I'm not known for my sense of humor when giving my submissive a command."

She shuddered. Though they'd been together less than

five minutes, and he'd barely touched her, her mind already spun out of control.

"Your obedience would give me great pleasure." His growly, gravelly, turned-on voice was persuasive as fuck.

With a sigh of resignation, she crouched to scoop up the lace and satin.

"Thank you." He plucked the material from her nerveless fingers and tucked his prize into his pocket. "I'll reward you with several spanks."

Reward? Before she could form the question, he slipped his arm back into place and kept his promise, four times in quick succession.

Then he went on, delivering dozens more, matching the cadence of the ones that Diana was receiving.

Each stroke was hard but dulled by the material that covered her skin. She loved the way he curved his fingers into her, firmly and possessively.

It was mesmerizing and seductive, leaving her dizzy and hungry.

When he finished, Makenna jerked, but he was there, tightening his hold, offering support.

"How was that?"

Breath constricted in her chest. "I'm not entirely sure."

"Can you try to explain?"

Makenna scowled. How was she supposed to answer him? She dug deep in order to understand her own reaction. "It hurt. But it went away fast. And it was only one…"

"Ass cheek?" The suggested words, fed softly into her ear, were light, despite the fact that he said he wasn't known to joke around. "And you want to have a longer, more authentic experience?"

In front of her, the paddling continued. Diana's eyes were closed, and her breaths were long and relaxed.

"Wondering what it might be like to be as euphoric as Diana?"

Because her back was to him, she found an honesty she hadn't with any other man. "Yes."

"Good. Because I want to give you exactly that. And for what I have in mind, we need a little more privacy."

Run.

"Accompany me to the grotto."

She couldn't go any further with him. If she did, she might fall off an emotional cliff, never to recover. "I'm not your type, Master Zachary."

"On the contrary. You absolutely are." He brushed aside a long lock of her blonde hair. "Stunning." Then he placed a gentle kiss on the side of her neck. "Curvy."

That was a kind word, unlike the one her ex had used to describe her.

"Inexperienced yet interested."

Maybe the fact that she hadn't fawned all over him was the appeal. But to her, this was no game. "And you want to be the one to corrupt me?"

"In every way I can think of. And ruin you for every other man."

As if he hadn't already. "That's quite…egotistical."

"Not in the least."

Even though Master Alcott continued to spank his wife, he moved his free hand between her legs to masturbate her.

The peaceful expression on her face vanished, and she bucked wildly, Diana arched toward her Dominant. He rubbed her even harder. Seconds later, she went still before collapsing with a gentle shudder.

Master Alcott faced the glass and smiled, then pressed a button to close the blinds, effectively ending the scene. There was no longer any reason for Master Zachary to stay with her.

"What will it be, my innocent?"

If Makenna didn't seize this moment, would it ever happen again? Her innate sense of preservation warred with her desire to give herself over to the moment.

When she met his gaze and read promise and urgency, she was lost. Everything he offered, she wanted.

"Are you brave enough to turn yourself over to me for the next hour to see what pleasure awaits you?"

CHAPTER TWO

"Makenna!"

At the exclamation, she looked up to see her friend, Avery, striding toward her, accompanied by her fiancé and Dominant, Master Cole Stewart.

"I won't forget that we have unfinished business." Master Zachary's promise was rich and foreboding.

Fortunately she was saved from replying as Avery swept her into a hug.

The men shook hands, and once again, Master Zachary's ring caught a light beam. This time, two emeralds winked, even more noticeable because a similar flash came from the ring Master Cole wore.

After everyone had exchanged greetings, Masters Zachary and Cole turned slightly for a quiet conversation.

Makenna appreciated seeing her friends as it gave her a hint of normalcy. "I didn't know you were going to be here."

"It was last minute." Avery, with her signature sweep of pink in her blonde hair, glanced toward her future husband before leaning closer to Makenna and lowering her voice. "Master Cole bought this outfit for me." She twirled around.

Avery's short skirt flared out, then settled over her hips with a teasing swish. Her black mesh shirt was formfitting, low-cut, and sexy.

"I love it." And she adored the fact that her friend was radiant.

"He wanted me to save it for our honeymoon, but I was dying to wear it."

"Now he'll have to buy you something else."

"Exactly!" Avery grinned.

"Speaking of your honeymoon...?"

"Finally. Yes. Everything is arranged, thanks to you." Avery exhaled.

"Good." One of her professional acquaintances, Elizabeth Gallagher, had been promoted to a VP position in the Sterling Hotel organization. She was a whiz at securing the high-end accommodations at luxurious resorts.

"We're going to a private island in the Caribbean. We'll have a chef, if we want it, groceries delivered by boat, great sunsets, snorkeling, sunshine. It should be"—Avery glanced at her fiancé, who was still talking to Master Zachary—"memorable."

"Sounds perfect."

"I still have a million details that are keeping me up at night." Avery sighed. "Tell me we're still meeting on Tuesday."

"Wouldn't miss it. We have five o'clock reservations for the martini bar at the Bella Rosa." Though they were friends, Makenna was also Avery's wedding planner, and they liked to combine business with pleasure every chance they had.

"Do you mind if we invite Zara?"

"That would be great." Makenna nodded. "I haven't seen her in a month or so."

"Good. Some girl time will help my stress level. And I want to work my way through the happy hour menu, starting with the Italian Wedding Cake drink." Avery grinned.

"If you love it, we can add it to your cocktail hour menu."

"Something other than wine or beer? I like the idea. Budget? What budget?"

Avery was a numbers whiz, and she watched every penny. But Cole wanted to give her a wedding fit for a princess, and he was willing to foot the bill, much to Avery's consternation. She would have been happy with a small event at one of Las Vegas's wedding chapels or even elopement, but Cole was insistent on everything being first class.

After a resigned shrug, Avery slid a glance toward Master Zachary. "Now tell me about you and Master Dreamboat."

Makenna laughed. Avery was one of the few people who knew about her long-term attraction to the stern Dominant. But Makenna had never expected that he'd actually choose her over the throngs of women who hounded him. "I'm not sure what to say." She sighed. "Or what I'm doing."

"Are you enjoying yourself?"

"More than I thought possible."

"Good." Avery smiled. "And I'm going to want all the details on Tuesday."

"I wouldn't think otherwise." Truthfully Makenna was grateful she knew someone she could share her emotions with. No doubt it was going to take some time to sort through them all.

"If you need me before that, make sure you call. Anytime. Night or day. I mean it."

"Thank you." Makenna gave her friend another quick hug.

The two men—self-assured and gorgeous Dominants—ended their conversation, and Cole lightly touched Avery's shoulder. "If you'll excuse us, I'm anxious to get my future bride to her appointment at the spanking bench."

Avery smiled shyly.

"Shall we?"

"Yes, Sir." Then she gave Makenna a little wave. "Tuesday. *All* the details."

For a moment, Makenna watched the couple walk away. Master Cole placed his palm against the curve of Avery's back in a protective, easy intimacy.

Makenna had never experienced anything similar. Her parents had been cool toward their only child, somewhere between indifferent and aloof. As a result, she'd wrapped her emotions in armor so she didn't get hurt.

"You two are close friends, I assume?"

She shook her head to clear it. Until this moment, she hadn't realized how much she'd missed, and how badly she wanted something like Avery had found.

"Makenna?" he prompted when she didn't answer.

"We met at a women-in-business breakfast group, and a few of us have developed our own circle of friends. I'm her wedding planner."

"Excellent job on the invitations."

She faced him, her lips slightly parted. "You're on the guest list?" What a ridiculous question. The city's elite would be in attendance, including everyone whose address was on Sin City's Billionaire's Row.

"I'll get to see you in action."

Which meant that—no matter what—she would have to see him again. She wasn't sure whether the idea thrilled her or terrified her.

And then it occurred to her. Of course he'd bring a date.

That she wasn't sure she could survive.

"Now that we're alone again, I'd like to revisit our earlier conversation. Are you brave enough to accompany me to the grotto?"

She frowned, considering the question.

It was one thing to have secret fantasies about the Dominant. But the reality was, they were from two different worlds. She'd earned college scholarships. Even at that, she'd worked at a catering company—nights, weekends, and holidays—while attending classes. She'd spent a lot of her life waiting on people like him.

Even though she ran her own company, her clients moved in his social circles—evidenced by the fact that he'd be at Cole and Avery's wedding.

It would be foolish to allow herself to believe she was anything more than a diversion to him. And yet, she didn't indulge in random experiences. She needed to care about someone to sleep with them.

Instead of pressing her for an answer, Master Zachary stood there with his hands clasped behind his back, allowing the silence to expand while he took in her reactions. Surprising her, he never looked away, giving her the gift of his complete attention.

"Just a scene?"

"Everything you want, and nothing more." His voice was as gruff as it was sexy, turning her on.

So why am I hesitating? He wasn't asking her about their future. In fact, he wasn't even suggesting they go out on a date. He was offering to fulfil her fantasies. And if she turned him down, he might never approach her again.

The grotto was a safe place to hide her self-doubts. Since it was remote, it was safe from onlookers. From what she'd heard, the interior was dimly lit, which meant she'd be able to hide her embarrassment as well as her body. "I um…" After clearing the sudden knot of fear from her throat, she nodded. "Yes. I'll go with you."

"I'm honored." His smile was slow and wicked.

No doubt he intended to appear gentlemanly, yet it was

anything but, and the predatory gleam in his eye sent a shiver through her.

"I promise you, it will be an evening you won't forget."

Earlier she'd suggested he was egotistical, and this comment was in the same vein. Yet even after the small taste of a BDSM experience, she was afraid he meant every word.

"My play bag is in the foyer."

Which meant he'd fully intended to scene this evening.

"Walk with me? I'm afraid you'll succumb to your doubts and vanish on me if I leave you alone."

How well he already knew her.

Oftentimes, Tops had their partner walk a little behind them, and she'd noted some wearing leashes. Yet he was behaving as they might at a vanilla event.

"Is the grotto available?" he asked the attendant when they reached the home's foyer.

She glanced at the sign-in log. "Yes, Master Zachary."

"I'd like to book it for an hour."

"Of course, Sir. Will you need your bag?"

"Please."

Less than two minutes later, she returned. The owl embossed on the side caught Makenna's attention.

After thanking the attendant, he extended his hand in front of him, indicating that she should lead the way toward the rear exit. Once there, he leaned over her to open the door and held it for her. Such elegant manners in real life would sweep her off her feet.

The Nevada evening with its hot breeze wrapped around her, sultry and inviting. Her heart quickened as they passed other guests. Within thirty seconds, the music from unseen speakers high in the palm trees became fainter, and the boisterous shouts from attendees splashing in the pool receded.

As they neared the grotto, solar lights dotting the garden provided the only illumination.

"Nervous?"

She glanced over her shoulder.

"Your breaths... I can hear them."

Was there no way to keep secrets from this man?

"You're perfectly safe with me."

Safe? No doubt that meant something different to him than it did to her.

The cavelike grotto structure was sealed shut by two heavy arched wood doors. A metal bolt was in place across both. After sliding it open, he tugged on the handle to allow them entrance.

The cavernous space shocked her.

Despite the outside heat, the grotto was cool. Flickering lanterns hung from the ceiling. Though there was enough light to see by, it wasn't bright, and the dimness created an intimate ambience.

The floor was made from uneven slate-gray flagstone. Numerous pillows, in various sizes, shapes, and colors, were scattered about.

Long lengths of gauzy material were draped along the walls, and for a moment, she was swept away into an Arabian-nights fantasy.

She startled when he sealed them inside and secured a lock for privacy.

"What do you think?"

Against one wall was a low purple bench, and also a shelving unit where Master Zachary stowed his toy bag.

"It's a lot to take in." A Saint Andrew's cross stood near the back of the area, and now that her vision had adjusted to the light, she noticed the gleam of rings—shackles—attached to the walls.

"And it's soundproof."

She turned to stare at him. His arms were folded, and his jaw was set. Never had she seen a man look so Dominant.

"Are you serious?"

"You can cry and scream all you want. No one will save you."

Makenna shivered.

"Would you like to test my words?"

Quickly she shook her head. He'd made it clear he didn't joke.

"Now come to me, my innocent one." He paused. "If you dare." With great deliberation, he unfolded his arms and crooked a finger, beckoning her forward.

On wooden legs, she did as he commanded.

He turned away long enough to grab his bag and place it on the bench. Then he looked at her. "Go ahead and open it. If you're interested in trying out any of my toys, we can. Or we can continue what we started in the house, using my bare hand."

The sound of the zipper was unnaturally loud, bouncing off the stone enclosure.

He had a dizzying array of implements. She'd been around the scene long enough to recognize them. Large and small floggers, paddles, several slappers, an evil-looking tawse, even a single tail. "The whip is a definite no."

"Understood. Off-limits. As for the rest of them?"

The courage she wanted was nowhere around. After sighing, she turned her head to look at him. "I'd like to start with your hand again." Even though it was more personal, which meant her choice was a greater threat to her emotions.

"My preference as well." His smile was the reassurance she needed. "For what happens next, I want to see your body."

Mortification swamped her. *"What?"* The only time she'd been nude with her ex was when the lights were completely off. And this man wanted her to expose her flaws to him.

"Can you do that for me? It's part of the mental preparation for your submission." He plucked at a wayward strand of hair, then curled it around his finger. "You're beautiful, Makenna. You may not see it, but I promise you, I do."

"I—" She'd been about to protest, but instead, stopped herself. He was a charmer, no doubt. Disagreeing with him would beget more arguments.

Nerves swarming through her, she closed her eyes.

"No. Watch me watch you."

She exhaled.

"Look at me." He gave her a moment before adding, "That's your first order." His voice was different, sharper. Uncompromising.

"You don't ask for much, do you?"

"Is that what you want? A man, a Dominant, who will expect nothing from you? Who will allow you to be passive?"

"No." Her whispered admission was painful. That wasn't what she wanted at all. This was the man of her fantasies, of her dreams. No matter what, she would always have this evening to remember. And the more memories, the better.

"Start with your shoes."

Once they were off, she became even more aware of their height difference, how big and powerful he was.

"Keep going."

She drew her shirt up and over her head. But before she could let it fall to the ground, he snagged it in midair and reached over to place it on the bench.

He sucked in a sharp breath. "You're even more gorgeous than I imagined."

This evening, she dressed in a lacy, delicate demi bra that barely contained her voluptuous breasts.

He traced a fingertip from the hollow of her throat downward a couple of inches before pausing. "May I?"

As she nodded, she lowered her head.

"No. Please remember my command. I want your gaze to be locked on me."

"I'm not sure I can do that." She wanted to hide from this, from him. And yet his demand encouraged her to enjoy every moment.

"I'll remind you as often as it takes. But I won't be denied."

Fighting her demons, her slamming heart, she summoned the courage to meet his gaze.

"Good. Your eyes are so expressive, revealing your reactions. And that pleases me." Gently he slid his palms beneath the fabric covering her breasts. Then, his touch warm and firm, he gently squeezed. At the same time, he scraped his thumbnails across her nipples, abrading them. Instantly the tips rose, and she involuntarily groaned.

"Responsive." Master Zachary smiled. "And sensitive." Sincerity flared in his shocking blue eyes.

Her body might be bigger than she wanted, but he made it clear that to him it was perfect. Maybe she could do this after all.

"May I?"

As she nodded, he reached around to unhook her bra. Slowly, as if savoring the moment as much as she was, he eased the straps down her arms.

With perfect precision, taking care of her belongings, he placed the lingerie on top of her shirt.

"How much nipple play do you like? A little? A lot?"

As if he had all the time in the world, he caressed her. He squeezed her nipples, tugging on them until they thickened and elongated; then he lowered his head to suck one into his mouth. He laved it with his tongue, drawing the tight flesh deeper inside his mouth. The swirling, teasing pressure drove her mad. Unsure how to ask for what she wanted, she leaned forward, giving herself, offering herself to him.

"Yeah. That's exactly right. I like my submissives to willingly give me everything I want."

The jarring words crashed her back into reality. That was what she was to him. Another woman in a long line of submissives who lined up to be the object of his desire.

Before she could react, giving voice to her doubts, he sucked her other nipple into his mouth, this time with more pressure, making her cry out. When she might have pulled away, he placed his hand on the middle of her back, holding her steady and preventing escape.

Finally he was done. He sighed deeply and passionately, making her wet, making her moan, making her forget her traitorous thoughts to the point that she wasn't sure she could even remember her own name.

"You're doing great. Surrender to the experience, to the moment, and just let it happen. No past, no future." He smiled, but it didn't make him any less dangerous. "And yes, I do know what I'm asking for and how difficult it is for you. So we'll start with an over-the-knee spanking and go from there?"

That seemed overwhelmingly personal. If she were attached to Saint Andrew's cross, he'd likely be using an implement, which meant there'd be distance between them, and he wouldn't be physically touching her.

With a gentleness that surprised her, he captured her wrist and drew her to the bench where he took a seat. "Ready?"

He offered his support as she lowered herself into place. The position, with her ass in the air, pulled the skirt tight and made it ride up. He placed one arm across her to hold her in place and then angled his thighs to move her closer to him. Since he'd thrown her off-balance, she pressed her fingertips to the floor for stability.

"That's better." He captured the hem of her skirt and drew it up over her buttocks. "So very spankable."

She wished she could accept his compliment without embarrassment.

"Surrender to the experience. The more you relax, the easier this will be, and the more you'll enjoy it."

"That's totally impossible."

"It's not. Take a breath." With small, gentle motions, he massaged her upper thighs.

For a moment she tensed, but he continued to soothe her.

"I recognize that trust is difficult. But I promise you that I will do everything it takes to earn it. I see you, Makenna, and I appreciate every single thing about you."

"All my flaws, you mean?" Maybe it was a good thing she was facedown; at least this way she could hide her humiliation.

"I see a woman who has the type of curves that men fantasize about. That I fantasize about. You're womanly."

Maybe it was from the lack of oxygen going to her brain, or from his featherlight caresses and reassuring words, but she began to relax.

"Keep breathing and let go."

She exhaled with a shudder.

"That's perfect. May I have your permission to touch your pussy?"

He was stroking everywhere, and arousal made her resistance collapse. "Yes." It was more a plea than permission.

With maddening lightness, he brushed across her clitoris, igniting raw feminine hunger.

Before bringing her to completion, he resumed spanking her, first with love taps and then increasing the intensity.

"Remember to breathe." He covered her exposed skin from the tops and insides of her thighs to her lower buttocks. And then the fleshier parts.

If he inflicted any pain, she didn't register it. Her entire body was heated, feverish. Then when she wasn't sure she could take any more, he pressed his thumb against her clit and slid two fingers inside her.

"So wet. So damp. Are you going to come for me, Makenna?"

The truth was, in this moment she was his, incapable of resisting. She was so far gone, she would do anything he asked.

"Is this what you want? An orgasm at my hand?"

"Yes."

As he moved inside her faster and faster, she dug her toes into the stone floor, lifting herself higher, begging for him to take even more.

"This is the reaction I hoped for. *This* is what I wanted."

Her breaths were too shallow and too fast for her to respond. Masterfully he slid a third finger inside her, then changed the angle of penetration to find her G-spot.

She went rigid as a breath strangled her and she came, whimpering through her screams. Even though she was in the throes of an ecstasy she'd never experienced before, he continued to finger-fuck her. *"Oh my God."*

"Ride it.*"*

Beneath his skillful ministrations, she shattered, losing track of time and space.

When she returned to full consciousness, she was in his lap, cradled in his arms, comforted by his strength and the reassuring thud of his heartbeat. His scent, that of the desert after a stunning electrical storm, filled her senses.

Blinking, she placed a hand on his chest and pushed away from him. "I apologize." Her memory had a gap in it. One moment she was writhing, the next, it was over, and now she was in his arms. "I'm not sure what happened there."

"You gave yourself to me completely." He captured her

chin so that she had to look at him, see the sincerity in his eyes. "And that makes it as spectacular for me as it was for you." His lips twitched in a half smile. "At least I hope you enjoyed it?"

"It was..." Where was her ability to put words to emotion? "Everything I could have hoped for, maybe more. Better than my fantasies." *Did I really admit that?*

"It's completely about you. You came to this with honesty and curiosity, and I merely facilitated the experience."

"I think perhaps you are underestimating your contribution, Sir."

"And you're having a difficult time accepting my compliment," he countered.

Shocking her, he brushed a gentle kiss across her lips. The world around her tilted. What was happening here?

Makenna warned herself not to read anything into his action. His actions—and every word he uttered—had been constructed to make her feel like one in a million. No wonder he had an entire line of women at the ready. She, however, was too smart to become one of them.

"Have you had enough? Or would you potentially like to try out a flogger and the Saint Andrew's cross?"

Again, her survival instinct screamed at her to run while she had the opportunity. Yet the spell he wrapped around her made her want this evening to last forever. And this was her one and only opportunity to scene with him. "I'm curious." Who was this wild, new person inside her?

His smile was the greatest reward.

"Your choice—I can secure you in place, or you can simply hold on."

Being with him had taught her the power of letting go. Interestingly, being in bondage would also allow her that freedom.

"What will it be? Would you like to wear my cuffs?"

His cuffs.

"Makenna?"

"Yes, Sir. I'd like to wear your cuffs."

He helped her to stand, then caught her around the waist when she wobbled.

A moment later, the world righted itself. "Thank you."

"If you're unsteady, then I'm doing my job well." Even in the dim light, his eyes twinkled with masculine deviltry.

"Your ego again, Sir?"

In pure alpha style, he countered her. "Is it ego if it's true?"

With a shake of her head, she grinned.

"When you're ready, walk to the cross and face it."

A moment later, he released his hold on her.

As she drew closer, the structure loomed a little larger than it had from a distance, a little more intimidating. Then, remembering his coaching, she took a couple of deep breaths to settle herself.

Each of his movements echoed off the stone surroundings, and she glanced over her shoulder to see what he was doing. Confoundingly his back was to her, blocking his movements.

When he turned, he held two pieces of leather. Unable to look away, she followed each of his steps as he closed the distance, then walked to the other side of the cross.

She had to tip back her chin to see his face. While he was still the implacable Dominant, the tenderness in his eyes stole her breath.

"Now raise your arms, please."

Within seconds, she was cuffed and secured in place.

"Not that I think you'd ever flee, but I enjoy having you in bondage—your body available to me." He severed their gazes. "And you can't escape as I do this." He captured her breasts, pressing their heavy weight together.

Her breaths were coming in frantic little bursts.

"Do you like this, being at my mercy?"

This was different than the spanking he had just given her. He was more ruthless now, and this new side of him was scarier, but just as compelling—or maybe even more so.

"Do you?

Instinctively she pulled back, only to discover that she couldn't move more than a couple of inches.

"I noticed the way you whimpered when Alcott squeezed his wife's breasts while he was wearing the vampire gloves."

"That was terrifying."

"But tantalizing, yes?"

She pressed her lips together, unable to give him the confession he wanted.

Relentlessly he pressed his fingernails into her flesh, then captured her nipples, pinching them between his thumbs and forefingers.

She sighed as a fresh wave of need made her weak.

"You like it. Is your pussy getting wet again?"

Impossibly it was. She'd never had multiple orgasms. And the fact that she was already turned on again stunned her.

"I'm going to remove your skirt so that it doesn't impede my swing." He walked around her to tug the material over her hips, then down her legs, leaving her completely exposed and vulnerable to him.

He placed a gentle kiss to her shoulder before leaving her once more.

When he returned, he stood in front of her and held up a short emerald-green suede flogger. "This one is more thuddy than stingy. A perfect choice for your first experience…or as a warm-up."

She gulped.

"Feel free to use your safe word, and I'll slow down at any point. Understand?"

"Yes, Sir." At least she thought so. How could she truly know what to expect?

"We will start slow, and I'll check in with you."

Master Zachary walked behind her and allowed the strands to fall on her buttocks in such a gentle manner that she barely registered the impact.

For minutes, he explored her entire body in that same way, dancing the leather across her skin. Because he was such an expert, she relaxed. Only then did he increase his tempo.

"Are you doing okay?"

"More green than I could have imagined." The leather licked her in bites and whispers, and it was the most exotic, erotic thing she had ever experienced.

Her temporary Dominant flogged her in earnest, and each crisscrossed strike made her wetter and wetter.

Then he stopped and slid a finger between her legs, rubbing so vigorously that her breath caught. *Fuck.* I think I'm going to come."

"You absolutely will. But not quite yet." He moved his hand away.

In frustration, she stamped her foot.

Instead of showing sympathy, he chuckled. "I would have never guessed you were a brat."

"You, Sir, are a tease."

"There's plenty more where that came from." He fisted a hand in her hair and pulled back her head as he pressed his body against hers, trapping her between his strength—and his dizzying erection—and the unyielding wooden structure. Then he ferociously plundered her mouth, seeking and demanding her surrender.

Helplessly she gave him everything he asked for. He'd made her pussy wet and her nipples hard. She was on fire from his mouth.

Eventually he ended the kiss, leaving her changed. Because of his physical reaction to her, she now had a confidence she'd never before experienced.

After taking a step back, he resumed the flogging, this time harder than before.

Jesus. How was it possible that this was no longer enough? "I…I need more."

"That's my perfect innocent." He flogged her in earnest before dropping the implement to the floor with a loud clatter.

Master Zachary masturbated her, filling her channel with his fingers, going knuckles- deep with long, demanding strokes. "Now, *now* you've earned the orgasm. Give it to me."

She whimpered, arching her back to thrust herself toward him.

He dug his fingers from his free hand into her ass cheek, creating a starburst of pain that rocketed her over the edge. She screamed out his name and climaxed hard, not just once, but twice. And still he wouldn't give up.

"Keep going."

"I can't!" There was nothing left in her, and she wouldn't have remained upright if he hadn't affixed her to the cross.

"You can. I'm hand-fucking you, and I want your orgasm. And you're going to be a good submissive and give it to me. Aren't you?"

He gave her no choice. He took what he demanded, wringing it from her body.

Makenna had no idea how long it went on, but all of a sudden, even in the warm Nevada desert, she was completely chilled.

"Let's get you out of those bonds." He reached around her and pressed his wet fingers to her mouth. "Now lick."

Unable to find her voice, she complied. The eroticism of the act shocked and thrilled her.

Efficiently he detached her from the cross, then rubbed her arms as she slowly lowered them.

Hands on her shoulders, he turned her to face him. "You're shivering." He removed his shirt and draped it over her shoulders, then swept her up and carried her to the bench so swiftly she didn't have time to protest that she was too heavy for him.

And the truth was, he held her as gently as if she were made from spun glass.

She settled against his already familiar body.

What an odd dynamic BDSM was. Some of his spanks had been hard enough to make her yelp. Yet she drew comfort from the same hands that had tortured her. It was a euphoric marriage of pain and pleasure. No wonder so many people were completely addicted to it.

Even though they hadn't had sex, she'd never been closer to anyone—or more vulnerable to emotional hurt.

"How are you doing?"

To mask her real answer, she reached for something that would unravel her tension. "I take back what I said earlier."

"Oh?"

"You're not egotistical."

He responded in kind. "I've ruined you for other men, then?" With the pad of his thumb that still smelled of sex, he traced her lower lip. "It's been a memorable evening for me as well. I'm honored to be the first man you've played with in this way."

First man—which meant he fully expected her to move on to another. Which she'd known all along. So why did his statement sting? "Thanks for a great introduction." She slid from his lap. "And for taking such good care of my things." She'd expected to find her skirt on the ground. But it was neatly stacked along with everything else.

"Let me take off your cuffs."

Grateful for the shirt that gave her some cover, she extended her wrists toward him.

While she dressed, he sanitized the Saint Andrew's cross and repacked his bag. Then she offered him his shirt back.

While he slipped it on, she feasted her gaze on his breathtaking body—the flat, honed planes of his abdomen, the raw strength of his broad shoulders, and the ripple of his bulging biceps.

Though she'd fantasized about him plenty, he blew away every single expectation. More than ever, he'd be the star of her dreams.

He tucked his shirt into his trousers; then, instead of refastening his cuffs, he rolled them up, leaving his forearms exposed. Simply, he was the picture of male perfection.

"Shall we?"

The return to reality was as inevitable as it was unwelcome, leaving her mentally and physically exhausted. "I'm ready to go home."

"I'll see you out."

"That's nice but not necessary. Thank you, though."

"I'm not flexible on this." His jaw was set, and his tone was harsher than anything she'd heard from him. The accommodating Dominant who'd taken her to the dizzying depths of sexual hedonism was gone. In his place was an alpha who would not be dissuaded. "After you, Ms. Helton."

She squared her shoulders in an attempt to gather her composure.

Rather than leading her back through the house, they followed a path that led to the driveway. Once they reached the valet station, she described her car, and the young man nodded and then headed off at a sprint.

"All set. There's no need for you to stay any longer."

"I can only guess what kind of man you're used to being with, but do not confuse me with him."

An eternity later, the valet pulled to a stop in front of them.

Master Zachary handed the man a nice tip. "I've got it from here."

"Yes, sir." With a nod, he moved away to help another guest.

Master Zachary walked Makenna around the car and handed her into the driver's seat. Taking a moment to regain her equilibrium, she fiddled with the air conditioner's controls, even though the setting was fine.

"I'd like to see you again."

Before she could respond, he went on. "May I have your phone number?"

Makenna shook her head. "This was…" She paused. *Magical. Amazing.* "I know you're a busy man, Mr. Denning." She used his surname as a way to distance herself from the temptation. "I had a nice evening."

"Nice?" For a second, he frowned, and his eyes seemed to darken as something flitted through the blue depths. Surely her rejection couldn't have caused him pain.

She reached for the door handle. "I need to be going."

With a tight nod, he stepped back, and she seized the opportunity to seal herself off from him.

As Makenna accelerated, she looked in the rearview mirror and saw him standing where she'd left him, arms folded, legs planted shoulder width apart, looking absolutely fucking furious.

It was then that she realized he'd never returned her panties.

CHAPTER THREE

The driver pulled up behind a long line of limousines and gleaming black vehicles, waiting for his turn to pull under the spectacularly lit pink brick porte cochere.

Because of her job as an event planner, she'd already visited Las Vegas's newest resort and casino several times—once for a soft opening meant to wow—and it still impressed her.

WELCOME TO THE BELLA ROSA was written in massive letters. This afternoon, the gold leaf shimmered in the afternoon sun, offering a mirage-like greeting.

"I'll walk the rest of the way." She paid her bill on the app.

"Fair warning. Give yourself plenty of time when you're ready to leave. It can take forever to get a car out here."

Not a surprise. The billionaire owner, Lorenzo Carrington, had decided not to give the property a theme. Instead, he wanted to offer a high-end luxury experience. From the buzz in the press, it was a good call. Despite its location at the end of the Strip, the property was reported to be packed with customers and thrill seekers who craved elegance. She'd expected that for a period of time after the grand opening, but the number of nights they sold out was on the way to be record-setting. "Thanks for the advice." She handed him a nice cash tip.

"So, give me a call anytime. If I'm available, I'll meet you over there." He pointed to a place separate from the line for taxis and rideshares.

"Thank you." She accepted the business card he offered.

Glad she hadn't opted to wait for a doorman, Makenna walked toward the entrance. The line had barely moved, and guests of all nationalities were buzzing around, laden with designer luggage.

Crisp, cold air engulfed her when she walked through the wide-open entrance. Instantly she was lured by enticing electronic chimes from high-stakes slot machines anxious to separate her from her money.

Numerous nearby tables offered card games and more. Ladies sipped champagne, and men dressed in suits and tuxedos drank whiskey.

A hand-lettered sign indicated the way to the Rose Martini Bar. Every time she visited, she noticed some nuance she'd missed before, from the stunning chandeliers to walls covered with murals that could have been painted by Renaissance masters. The meeting space was stunning as well, and so far away that trams—of course outfitted with opportunities for gaming—shuttled attendees back and forth.

She checked in at the podium and was grateful she had made reservations. Although it was only five o'clock, the place was already standing room only. Makenna wore her work outfit— a royal-blue dress and shoes that matched her purse—and was slightly underdressed for the exclusive lounge. Many places in town were filled with casino-hopping tourists in shorts and flip-flops, but not at the Rose —as the Bella Rosa was already being nicknamed.

"Right this way, Ms. Helton."

She followed the hostess through the space with its signature glass bar pulsing with neon lights. Behind it, three bartenders were pouring and shaking with entertaining flair.

Avery was already seated at a table, studying a leather-bound menu. She slipped from the bar-height stool to give Makenna a hug. "Isn't this place magnificent?"

"Sensational." Makenna had been looking forward to this evening, hoping to get some answers. Since Saturday night, thoughts of Master Zachary had consumed her, and she'd spent far too much time on the internet reading stories about him—including the fact that he was reputed to belong to the Zetas. Known as Titans, the secret society was comprised of the world's richest and most powerful people. World leaders, actors, scientists, writers, and billionaires belonged, along with philanthropists and politicians. Even though no one had confirmed the organization actually existed, plenty speculated that it did.

They both took their seats, and Makenna picked up her menu. A quick glance confirmed that prices started at twenty dollars, even during happy hour. There were at least thirty martini choices—from classic to unique creations.

"I'm sticking with my original idea. I want to try the Italian Wedding Cake. What are you starting with?"

Makenna put down her menu. "Death by Chocolatini."

"I should have guessed!"

The server arrived, and they placed their orders. "May I bring an appetizer?"

They both agreed to wait to order food until Zara arrived.

"All right." Avery leaned forward. "I've been dying of curiosity. How did you end up scening with Master Zachary?"

"It wasn't on purpose." She exhaled. "I was watching the Hewitts in the observation room. And I was so entranced that I didn't notice Master Zachary behind me until he put his hands on my shoulders."

"Dang." Avery shivered deliciously.

"He asked me to describe what was happening." Makenna left out other scandalous details like the fact that he'd asked her to remove her panties. And that he'd spanked her right there in the open. "And then he invited me to the grotto."

"So how was that?"

Complicated. "Everything I could have hoped."

"Are you going to play with him again?"

"No." Makenna knew better than to allow herself to be consumed with a billionaire. But she'd spent the weekend thinking about Master Zachary, even succumbing to temptation and spending Sunday afternoon reading articles about his life.

One socialite had been particularly scathing, saying he wasn't a playboy—he was a manwhore. "You know he never sees the same woman twice." Makenna had scrolled through the pictures that proved it. "Even if he did, I wouldn't be a consideration. I don't have the required social pedigree."

"He's not that shallow."

She wasn't as sure. Men like him wanted a wife who would be an asset, a woman who'd gone to the right schools, had successful parents. With her working-family background, Makenna had nothing in common with him. "I'm not his type, and I don't belong in his world."

"That's what I thought when I met Cole. Being his wife will have some demands, but it's also exhilarating. And I wouldn't have missed this opportunity for the world."

"Despite the stress of the wedding, you seem really happy."

"Honestly? It's beyond my greatest expectations. It meant taking a risk, but it's been worth it."

Her thoughts twirled, and she considered them before speaking. "You're stronger than I am."

"No." Avery placed her hand on Makenna's. "Your asshole ex did a lot of damage, and I hate that he's allowed to impact your future."

She winced. Though Avery was her usual gentle self, her words were barbed, and they stung when they found their target.

"Zachary would be a fool if he didn't want you, and he's a smart man."

"What do you know about him?"

"Not much, except from what I've seen in his interactions with Cole. Zachary is honest, maybe brutally so."

"Maybe. I guess I don't want to be someone he fucks and forgets."

"As if that would happen." She rolled her eyes. "Look, Kenna. Think about giving him a chance. He'll be straight with you about what he wants. At least hear him out?"

And risk my heart?

"You can't stay single your entire life."

"Well…"

They both laughed.

"What if you thought of him as a bridge back into the dating world? He would treat you like a princess."

No doubt that was true.

"You deserve to be wined and dined." Avery's eyes twinkled. "And spanked."

Makenna gasped.

"Go have fun. Don't expect it to be forever. Enjoy his company and a few orgasms."

The drinks arrived in glasses with Z-shaped stems, interrupting conversation.

Avery took a sip of hers. She closed her eyes in bliss. "Oh

my God. It's decadent." She put down her glass. "Now try yours."

Makenna licked some of the sugar and cocoa from the rim, then took a tiny sip. Her taste buds exploded, dancing from the combination of sweet and bitter chocolate, complemented by top-shelf vodka. "Amazing. It's as rich as the man I hope to marry one day."

Giggling at the absurdity since they had both achieved business success and were more than capable of taking care of themselves, they clinked their glasses together.

"And now..." Makenna put down her beverage. "We absolutely have to talk about your wedding plans before we finish this; otherwise I'll never remember anything." She pulled her tablet from her purse and called up Avery's file. "We need to finalize the cocktail hour menu. Are we adding your martini to the list?"

"Absolutely."

Makenna made some changes to the menu, then showed the future bride the new estimated bar tab.

"That'll work."

"How are the RSVPs coming?"

"We already have thirty more people attending than we had planned on."

Makenna nodded. "Would you like to increase the budget, or would you like to make changes to the menu for a less expensive entrée?"

"As I'm sure you've already guessed, Cole is completely against changing the menu."

"Okay then. An increase in budget it is. I'll send you an updated amount tomorrow."

Avery nodded. "And one other thing. Cole would like to have an ice sculpture."

For a wedding, it wasn't a common request, but it was certainly doable. "What did you have in mind?"

"An owl." Avery picked up her cell phone, tapped it a few times. "Let me send you a picture."

When it appeared on Makenna's tablet, she cocked her head to the side. "Athena's owl."

Without answering, Avery took another sip.

"I did a little research." *Hours of it. Days of it.*

"And?"

"Admit it. He's a Titan?"

"I can neither confirm nor deny the allegation."

It wasn't like Avery to hedge. "Saturday when they shook hands, he and Cole were both wearing rings with owls on them. The same one you just sent me."

"I can neither—"

"Confirm nor deny the allegation." Makenna sighed. "You're not going to tell me anything more?"

Zara arrived, forcing them to abandon the conversation. Several men had turned their heads to track her movements. A short formfitting dress hugged her curves. She wore sky-high strappy sandals and had accessorized like crazy with jewelry and a tiny silver clutch. Her hair, brunette burnished with blonde and copper highlights and lowlights, swung at her waist. She owned a marketing company, and she was recognized as a social media influencer, which meant she was her greatest asset.

Makenna admired her friend. She was the youngest of five children. And whereas she could have been the spoiled child of a multimillionaire, she'd stayed away from the family business and instead worked her ass off to make it on her own.

Zara gave each of them a quick hug and kiss on the cheek before sliding into her own chair, adjusting her hem so it didn't reveal more than she wanted to.

The server joined them. "Nice to see you again, Ms. Davis."

"Thanks, Julio." Her smile was as genuine as her delight. "Good to see you."

"The usual?"

She nodded. "Thank you."

"Another round for you ladies?"

"You're a regular," Makenna surmised when they were alone again.

"It's a great place to be seen." She grinned.

"So what's your usual?"

"Rose martini, of course."

Avery scowled. "I read the menu twice. How did I miss it?"

"I'll let you have a taste. Are we ordering food?"

"Any recommendations?"

"Everything is to die for. I think we should get them all and share them."

Avery and Makenna looked at each other and shrugged. "Since Avery and I discussed the wedding, this is a business expense for me."

"And this is one of my last nights out before I'm a married woman. That means I'm in."

Makenna finished her drink, only to find a partially melted piece of Godiva chocolate stuck to the bottom.

Zara provided the first suggestion. "Use your tongue."

Makenna laughed.

"How about a knife or fork?" Avery handed her a wrapped set of silverware.

The confection was gooey and alcohol-soaked, and she held it on her tongue while it dissolved. "I could die happy."

Two stunningly gorgeous men were walking through the bar area. Each stood well over six feet tall, and they were as broad as they were fit. Their dark hair was cut in military precision. Even in a room full of expensive suits, theirs were a notch above. And they were wearing sunglasses.

"Security." Avery lifted her eyebrows.

Since Cole was in that line of business, no doubt she knew what she was talking about.

Zara grinned. "Makes me want to do something naughty."

"And get spanked for it?" Avery laughed.

Shocking Makenna, the men paused at their table. "Ladies."

Zara crossed her legs and sat up a little taller. Did she know them?

This close, the pair bore a striking resemblance. Twins? Brothers? Cousins? And each wore a black tie with a pink rose embroidered on it.

"Ms. Davis." After nodding in Zara's direction, they continued on.

"Something you want to tell us?" Avery demanded.

"No." Her smile was saintly.

The server returned with Zara's drink. The martini was a pale pink, and a rose petal floated on top.

Avery looked at the server. "I'll have one of those.

"For you, ma'am?" He addressed Makenna.

"Lemon drop." Something not quite as sweet as what she'd just finished.

"Any appetizers?"

Zara nodded. "All of them."

"Of course." He closed his order pad and slid it into his apron.

Before her brain became any cloudier, Makenna looked at Avery. "I've been meaning to ask, are we having a bachelorette party?"

Avery nodded. "But not like everyone else does. I was thinking we could do a spa day at the Royal Sterling. I was planning to invite a couple of other friends and maybe some people from the businesswomen's group."

"That would be a strategic move." Makenna nodded. "We can make an afternoon of it and rent out the whole place."

After they all checked their calendars and agreed on suggestions, Makenna made a note to call the spa.

"I'll provide champagne and snacks." Zara shrugged when Avery started to object. "Part of your wedding present."

"That's far too generous."

"Not at all. It's my way of ensuring you'll throw a bachelorette party for me if I ever find a man."

Their drinks and food arrived, and Avery entertained them with gossip about who her eighty-year-old great-aunt Scarlet was dating this week. The Brit was an actor less than half her age and, in her words, a bit too old for her tastes. The burlesque phenomenon was considering dumping him for a recently divorced prince who was still in his thirties.

Avery swirled her drink. "She thinks maybe he can keep up with her. She's tired of waiting for the Brit's little blue pill to make his dick hard."

Makenna laughed so hard that people at the next table turned to face them.

The server paused to ask if they wanted another round.

"I wish I could." Avery sighed. "But I have an early morning."

"I'm attending an open house for a real estate agent. So I have to get going." Zara reached for her purse. "Can we get the check, please?"

"Separate checks?"

"Just one," Makenna replied before anyone else could. "And bring it to me, please."

"I'll get it right out." The server headed back toward the computer.

"Kenna, you don't need to do that." Avery was always the first to protest.

"As I said, it's a business expense."

"In that case, I'll treat next time. We need to do it soon so we're not too far out of balance."

"It's a deal." In that moment, awareness, hot and irresistible, tingled at the base of her spine. Sensing she was being watched, Makenna turned, and her heart slammed into her throat.

Master Zachary stood with a small group of men around a table, and he was looking at her.

Breathless, she returned her attention back to her friends, pretending an earthquake hadn't rocked her world.

"Ah..." Avery glanced over at the other table. "He's headed this way."

Makenna traced the stem of her glass. "I'm sure he's not."

Zara glanced too. "Are you talking about Zachary Denning? Oh! You saw him at the party on Saturday night?"

"Yes." Her thoughts were in pieces.

"Did you play?"

Makenna cleared her throat. "We did."

"And he wants you."

"Definitely not." Makenna dug her credit card from her wallet. Anything to distract herself.

"I can tell you this—he's a man on a mission. But he has to work hard to deserve you. Don't forget that."

Though Makenna tried to steel herself, the effort failed. She was too besotted with the billionaire to pretend otherwise.

"Five seconds," Avery warned. Then she smiled. "Zachary!"

He hugged Avery, then lasered his focus on Makenna. "Ms. Helton." He captured her hand and raised it to his lips, crashing memories through her, reigniting awareness.

"Mr. Denning."

With a knowing, terrifying smile, he released her.

"I know one of your brothers, but we've never been introduced." He turned to Zara. "Zachary Denning."

As was custom, he didn't let on that he recognized her from the scene.

"Zara Davis." The pair shook hands.

"Nice to meet you." But rather than continue the conversation, he returned his attention to Makenna, with the same intensity as he'd shown on Saturday night. "I was hoping to see you again."

Never had she'd been more grateful to be leaving.

The server approached with the check, and Zachary extended his hand. "I'll take that."

"It's mine."

Without argument, Zachary plucked the folio from the server and inserted his black credit card inside without even glancing at the tab.

"You don't need to do that."

"I already did." He returned it to the server.

In true traitorous form, her friends abandoned her.

"Look, Mr. Denning…" She sighed when he slipped into Zara's empty chair. "I don't want to be beholden to you."

"As I said the last time we were together, I don't know what kind of men you've been with, but don't confuse me with them."

"Why are you doing this?"

"I should think it's obvious. Or am I losing my touch?"

"We had a scene. It's over."

"Do you know you look away and blush when you lie?"

She brought her head up sharply. "I'm not—"

"You haven't thought about me? Not even once?"

Did he know the truth? That he'd seeped into her dreams, as well as every waking moment? He was a constant distraction, and she had no idea how to get him out of her mind.

The server dropped off the folio and thanked them.

She couldn't resist a glance as Zachary totaled the bill. The tip he added was exorbitant. Despite herself, she was impressed. As her past taught her, waiting tables was a grueling, difficult job. Customers like him were as rare as they were welcome.

"Have dinner with me."

Makenna blinked. "What?"

"We're already here, and I have reservations at the steak house. My colleague canceled, leaving me at loose ends."

"Thank you, but I have an early morning."

"Another lie."

Her mouth had watered at his suggestion. But the only thing stronger than temptation was the sense of self-preservation. Despite what Avery had suggested, Makenna knew this man would never be a bridge back to the dating world. She was convinced that what he'd said the first night was pure truth. He would ruin her for any other man. And that was a risk she couldn't take.

"I might think you're a little bit of a coward, Ms. Helton."

"Okay, Mr. Denning. You want the truth?" With bravery she didn't really feel, she met his gaze. "You're right, about many things, but not all. I don't have an early morning, and yes, I have been thinking of you. It was a hot scene, so that's natural. Am I a coward? I guess that's for you to decide. I think it's smart, more than anything." She took a breath before she continued. "Will I have dinner with you? Also no. I know your reputation. You want me because you can't have me." Paradoxically, if she gave in to him, he would no longer want her. The trouble was, she'd be left broken. "My answer is no. It will always be no. Keep it up, and I'll tell you to fuck off."

"Fair enough."

She narrowed her eyes. Relenting didn't seem to be something he was familiar with.

"At least let me drive you home."

"I was planning to catch a ride share."

"In that case, I'll walk you out."

Knowing she couldn't win every argument, she gathered her belongings. He stood instantly and offered a hand when she slid off the chair.

As she now expected, he showed a possessive streak by placing his fingertips in the small of her back as they walked to the exit.

She sighed when she saw the line for rides, remembering too late that she should have called her driver. Though they stood under a small shelter, the sun was still brutal, shimmering off the pavement. A tiny drop of perspiration traced down her spine.

"Any other objections to me taking you home?"

She sighed.

"You can say thank you at any time." He strode to the valet stand and handed off his ticket. Before the line had moved at all, his car was brought around.

He dismissed the valet and opened her door, handing her into the luxurious passenger compartment of his low-slung and ultra-expensive sports car.

"Thank you."

"That's better."

Within moments, they were on the road. Following her directions, he threaded his way through the city to her townhome in Henderson.

"Nice place." He slid the gear shifter into Park.

She looked at the stucco structure that shared walls with three other units. At least hers had some flowers on the tiny front porch. "It's not what you're used to."

"You make a lot of assumptions."

"Do I?" She faced him. "You're not a billionaire? A Titan?"

"You've been busy."

"A manwhore?"

"A—" He blinked, and then he laughed. "That's a new one."

She hadn't expected that reaction.

"To respond the same way you did... Do I date? Yes. A lot?" He shrugged. "I guess that depends on your definition. Do I use women?" Something dangerous pulsed in his temple. "Hell no." He bumped down the temperature in the car. "I don't care what opinions of me are out there. The only thing I care about is what you think."

"You're good." She scoffed. "I'll grant you that. Almost good enough to make me believe you mean it."

"Good night, Makenna." That ticking became more pronounced. The way he said it was his version of *fuck you*.

He pressed the button to kill the engine. "I'll walk you to the door." Motions deliberate, he exited the vehicle and waited for her to do the same. Then he followed her up the path.

Once she inserted the key in the lock, he turned and strode back to the car.

Her hand shook. What had she done?

You saved yourself.

So why didn't she believe that?

The engine kicked back on, and she went inside, closing the door and collapsing against it.

Tires squealed, and then she was left with nothing but the loud and horrible deafening sound of silence.

Zachary strode across the red carpet to reach the back of Bella Rosa's whiskey and cigar bar where Cole was already seated.

This was one space where the owner had exercised his

personal preferences and designed it based on his interpretation of an old-world gentlemen's club with oversize leather chairs arranged around small tables. Walls and partitions were decorated with black-and-white pictures of old Las Vegas, including signed pictures of the era's best-known entertainers. The lounge boasted Sin City's best bartenders, a walk-in humidor, and a dizzying number of whiskeys.

Seating was limited, and admission was for members only, making it a perfect place for deal-making and clandestine meetings.

Cole stood, and the two shook hands.

After Zachary took his chair, he leaned forward. "Do you have the file?" On Sunday morning, after his team hadn't turned up the information he hoped to find on Makenna Helton, he'd contacted Cole. If she was hiding any secrets, he would find them.

"I do." He extracted a thumb drive from a pocket inside his sports coat. Instead of turning the device over, he placed it on the table directly in front of him.

"Problem?"

"You tell me."

Zachary sat back. "I wouldn't have hired you if it wasn't important."

"Why the interest in Makenna?"

"It's personal."

Cole, too, sat back, and he steepled his hands.

Before Zachary could guess what fucking game Cole was playing, the server arrived bearing a tray that contained a sealed bottle of whiskey and two glasses.

"I'll take it from here." Cole gave the woman a quick smile of dismissal. "Thank you."

Zachary had readily agreed to meet Cole here. The ambience of the whiskey and cigar bar was second to none, and it had quickly become one of the best places to meet up with other Titans. He'd been one of the first people to buy a condominium in the residence tower, and the fact that he had access to several private elevators allowed him to move around the resort without being seen. "Nice bottle."

"Ridiculously expensive. Julien Bonds sent me a bottle recently."

"Nice."

Bonds was a quirky fellow, tech billionaire and dreamer, with his fingers in every pie.

"I liked that shit so much that I ordered a case. The bar manager ordered a few bottles for my private reserve."

Not only did Lorenzo have a whiskey sommelier on duty, but he'd also installed private liquor cabinets. For a ludicrous annual fee, members could rent one of the glass lockers. The member's name was inscribed on a brass plaque and affixed to the wood beneath.

Of course, no one could bring in a bottle. It had to be ordered through the hotel's preferred distributor, and the price was marked up considerably.

Cole broke the seal. "Bastard knows what he's doing. Gives away one bottle and gets an order for twelve more."

Zachary nodded. "Brilliant."

"Fucking genius," Cole corrected, pouring a couple fingers' worth of the premium whiskey in the cut crystal glasses.

By unspoken assent neither of them returned to business until after they had completed their first whiskey.

Then, after Cole had refreshed their drinks, he leaned back. "Makenna is one of my future wife's best friends."

Zachary nodded.

"Avery will kill me if I have any part in hurting her."

"I assure you that is not my intent."

In silence, Cole regarded his friend. "Then what is?"

"Being sure."

Cole scowled. "Of what?"

How the hell did he explain something even he didn't understand? The untamed passionate response he'd had for a woman he barely knew.

He was willing to admit he loved scening with newbies. Coaxing their reactions, teaching them about their own bodies' pleasure receptors was intoxicating.

And yet... Makenna was different. She was more real than any other submissive he'd been with. They'd had a connection he hadn't known possible.

He'd envied Cole when he found Avery, but Zachary hadn't understood how any man would willingly throw away the perks of bachelorhood and get involved in wedding preparations.

Now? *Yeah.* He got it. He more than wanted Makenna—he burned for her, and it was fucking consuming him. Sleep was impossible, and far too many business details had slipped.

And yet... Was he blinded by his own lust? Making a second mistake? "There was a woman."

While Zachary struggled, Cole waited.

"During my stint in the military, I avoided relationships. That changed when I came home. My mother set me up with a woman of impeccable background. I was prepared to refuse to take her on a date, but Blythe was beautiful, and I was smitten. She played hard to get. The more she turned me down, the more I chased her. I was in love. Or I thought I was." He picked up his glass and rolled it between his palms. No one had ever heard this story. "It took forever to get her in my bed, and even longer to get her to accept my marriage proposal."

"I'm listening."

The memory still burned. A few months before their wedding, he'd arrived home from work to find her in the bathtub. He was surprised to hear a man's voice. Quietly Zachary opened the door to discover she was videoing herself while she masturbated. And the words he heard seared into his memory.

"What do you want?" the male on the screen had demanded.

"Your big dick. I need you to fuck me so I can forget my miserable life. The asshole made me sign a prenup. If we get divorced in the first five years, I don't get anything for putting up with his shit."

Fury seared Zachary.

"How long until you can see me? I gotta fill that hot cunt of yours."

"Next week. I'm on one of his credit cards, and I told him I have a girls' weekend."

He'd heard enough.

With icy calm, he crossed the room and plucked the phone from her hand.

"Zach! I can explain. It's not what you think."

He turned and slammed the screen on the sharp edge of the quartz counter; then he tossed the device into the bathtub with her.

By then, she was standing, and bubbles clung to her body in invitation. With a smile, he took her hand.

"Zach?" Her eyes were wide, and her breaths were short, frightened.

As she watched, he slid his grandmother's ring off Blythe's finger. He turned, walked away, and never spoke another word to her.

He shook his head, realizing Cole was still waiting. "I got played. It could have cost me big—nearly did. She was in love with someone else, and they intended to be together, using my money. I was a fool, and I'm fucking embarrassed to admit it. To say I don't trust people easily is accurate."

Cole nodded, and he leaned forward to slide the thumb drive in front of Zachary. Continuing to roll his glass, he stared at the small USB that would expose every one of Makenna's shortcomings. Once he opened the dossier, she'd have no secrets from him.

After a moment's hesitation, he picked up the drive and dropped it into his pocket.

Because part of him hated what he'd done, he finished the rest of the whiskey in a single swallow.

For the next few minutes, they continued to talk, and his tension eased; then he followed Cole's gaze toward the other side of the room and saw the casino owner walking toward them.

Zachary and Cole stood to shake Lorenzo Carrington's hand. As always, he was impeccably dressed in only the finest bespoke garments from Italy. Though his mother had tried to distance herself from her family, blood ran deep, and Lorenzo had fully embraced her side of the family. Don Marco La Rosa himself was reputed to be an investor in the property.

Cole would know for sure, and Zachary wouldn't be surprised to learn that the rumor was true. After all, not a lot of people had the resources to invest billions of dollars in a brand-new resort.

"Join us?" Cole invited. "It's the Bonds whiskey."

Lorenzo raised an eyebrow. "I believe I will." He signaled to the two men who were with him. One took his place several feet behind Lorenzo, while the other positioned himself at the back of the room, where he could watch all the comings and goings.

Instantly, the server appeared with another glass. This one contained a hand-carved ice ball.

Cole poured while speaking. "Avery tells me we haven't gotten your RSVP for the wedding."

"I'll be there." He inclined his head toward his bodyguards. "Plus two. They will not require meals."

The billionaire no doubt garnered significant interest from the female population, but he never dated as far as Zachary knew.

Lorenzo took a sip of the whiskey. "Excellent. Perhaps we'll consider stocking it."

"If you do, tell Bonds I want a commission."

He placed his almost untouched glass back on the table. "I'll allow you to handle those details."

Lorenzo's man moved closer to him. With a brief nod, Lorenzo stood. "If you'll excuse me, duty calls."

With that, he exited through an unseen door next to a perhaps unironic picture of Bugsy Siegel, a legendary Las Vegas mobster.

"Speaking of RSVPs…" Cole finished his drink. "I guess you can't invite Makenna as your guest because she's the wedding planner."

"Asshole."

"Between you and Lorenzo, I'll tell Avery we need a table for the Lonely Hearts Club."

"Don't rub it in, man."

Cole grinned.

"Thanks for the report."

They both stood and shook hands. "Don't make me regret it."

Cole's words stayed with him long into the night. Around midnight, he inserted the USB into his computer.

But instead of opening the file, he typed in a command to reformat the drive, erasing all the data.

CHAPTER FOUR

"You are absolutely radiant!" Makenna exclaimed. She'd been with her friend when she found her gown, but now—waiting to walk down the aisle—Avery looked like a fairy princess.

They exchanged air hugs so that the makeup artist's work wasn't ruined. "Are you ready?"

"Emotionally?" Avery exhaled. "Yes. But nervous about all the details."

"That's why I'm here. Most of the guests have arrived." Including more VIPs than she'd ever dealt with, from Lorenzo Carrington to a reclusive associate of Cole's known only as Hawkeye—Makenna had no idea if that was a first or last name. "The minister is on-site. And I have to say, the ballroom is even more beautiful than our renderings. I'm sure you'll be pleased."

The event space had been transformed with pipe and draping, balloon arches, several beautiful spots for pictures, massive flower arrangements on pedestals, and multiple bars had been set up strategically to minimize waiting.

The ballroom opened onto a patio. Tables were arranged

in conversational style, and bright-purple umbrellas added a festive flair. And of course, a bar had been set up outside as well.

"Has Cole arrived yet?"

Makenna grinned. "He's been at the hotel since noon."

Avery opened her eyes wide. "Are you serious?"

"He's been greeting people and pestering me. He wants to see you."

"*What*? No." She shook her head vehemently. "I haven't kept this gown secret for months for him to ruin the surprise."

"That's what I thought, but I promised I'd relay the message."

After glancing around to be sure no one was in earshot, Avery leaned close to Makenna. "You can only guess what his favorite form of stress release is."

Makenna pressed her lips together so she didn't laugh out loud. "I'm not sure that would be good for your dress or your hair."

"Not to mention my rear end. And it's been tormented enough."

"Okay, okay." Makenna laughed. "I'll make sure he doesn't get within ten feet of you. He's afraid you'll change your mind."

"The man is impossible when he wants something."

"He's in love."

"Yeah." Avery's expression softened. "So am I."

Makenna checked her watch. "Less than half an hour. I want to do a final check. I'll be back in about fifteen minutes."

There was a knock on the suite's door.

"Want me to get it?" Zara was serving as one of Avery's bridesmaids, and she was the only one who'd finished getting ready.

"Thanks." Avery nodded. "But if it's Cole, don't let him in."

Moments later, Avery's great-aunt Scarlet swept in wearing a long sequined gown and an ornate fascinator hat. No doubt her picture would be on social media before the ceremony began.

Scarlet smiled at everyone before homing in on Avery. "Darling girl! You are positively sensational!"

Makenna left, not that anyone noticed.

Once she was in the service elevator, she glanced at her tablet and was relieved not to see any messages. Things seemed to be under control.

Downstairs, she surveyed the anteroom where the cocktail hour would be hosted. Bar-height tables were scattered around and festively decorated with the wedding colors. Servers were prepping trays for champagne and hors d'oeuvres.

Then, for one last time, she walked through the ballroom where the reception would be held. Everything was complete, and the band was setting up.

Satisfied, she continued through to the patio. Zachary was there, elbow propped on top of a metal fence. He was devastating in a charcoal-colored suit. His tie was perfectly in place. Despite the heat, he was cool and composed.

Even though it had been over a month since she had seen him, he took her breath away. Time and distance had done nothing to quell her desire for him. In fact, it had made it worse.

At night when she was lonely, she wondered what her life might have been like if she had agreed to dinner or another scene.

He looked her up and down, slowly, measuredly taking in every detail.

Though she should make polite conversation and then

leave, she remained where she was, not wanting the moment to end.

"How am I doing?"

In confusion, she blinked, not following his question. "I'm sorry?"

"At fucking off?"

Makenna winced. Then, to hide her reaction, she clutched her tablet closer to her chest.

"Since you're such a detective, how many dates have I been on in the past month?"

"I have no idea." She refused to admit that she searched his name nearly every morning when she arrived at her office.

"Either you're catching a sunburn, or you're lying again."

Damn you.

"None. And you know it." He pushed away from the fence and devoured the distance between them. "I was in love once."

With his fiancée, Blythe, no doubt. Makenna had read a couple of articles about the short-lived engagement. Shortly thereafter, his office had issued a short statement, saying he wished her well while asking that their privacy be respected.

Unsure where his comment was headed, Makenna waited. She had a lot to do, but she didn't want to dismiss him right away.

"Blythe was in love too. With another man." His words were flat, but no doubt pain lingered behind them.

"I'm sorry."

"Don't be. I'm glad I found out when I did. She and her lover concocted a scheme to make me fall for her. Scary thing was how close it came to working."

"Meaning you sleep with a different woman every week because you have trust issues?" This close, he overwhelmed her. He smelled of spice, and his body language spoke of determination.

Instead of responding to her barb, he took a half step toward her. "She knew how long we had to stay married to get the amount of money she wanted." A combination of anger and pain was mixed in his voice.

"Why are you telling me this?"

"You don't have a monopoly on pain, Makenna, or on the need to protect yourself."

The idea of self-assured billionaire Dominant Zachary Denning having an emotional weakness was so stunning she couldn't respond.

"Or the fact that our behavior doesn't always make sense. After Blythe, I wondered why I'd ever want to get married. I have nieces and nephews, charitable organizations I support. There was no reason for me to have my own children. And then I met you."

"I…" Aware of the time ticking, she frowned. "I don't understand."

"You're different." He propped a finger beneath her chin. *"I'm* different with you. And you know it. There comes a time when we have to stop letting our pain define who we are. When you're ready, I'll be here."

With that, he strode off, leaving her standing there staring after him. She wasn't sure how long she looked at the closed door, but she missed a call from her assistant, Riley.

Her heart still thundering, mind spinning with the implications of everything he'd said, Makenna forced herself to refocus as she hit redial on her assistant's number.

Despite a few momentary lapses, she managed to get back to Avery's suite within the promised fifteen minutes. After advising the bride that it was time to go, she took a staff elevator so that she'd be available at the wedding if anything went wrong.

Makenna blinked back her emotion when Cole saw Avery for the first time. The big, tough secret agent man wiped a tear from his cheek.

Despite herself, Makenna sought out Zachary, but he never glanced back at her.

Avery and Cole exchanged vows they'd written themselves, and then the minister pronounced them husband and wife, partners for life. "You may now kiss your bride."

Cole capitalized on the opportunity, to the cheers and applause of their guests.

Zachary's words still heavy on her heart, Makenna dived back into action, helping organize wedding photos while Riley oversaw the cocktail hour, complete with Avery's favorite martini.

Before the ballroom doors were opened, Makenna double-checked to be sure the ice sculpture had been placed.

Then the reception began in earnest.

A few times during the evening, she was aware of Zachary's gaze on her, and she wondered what she was going to do about him.

Follow Avery's advice and take a chance? Or hide and let her past dictate her future?

Near midnight, the band struck up a ballad, and he strolled over to her. "Dance with me?"

"I'm the hired help."

"You're also one of her best friends."

Was there anything she wanted more than to be in his arms?

"You have an assistant who is keeping watch."

His earlier words returned to her. *"I'm different with you. And you know it. When you're ready, I'll be here."* She sighed, foolishly giving in to temptation. "Just one."

"I'll settle for that...but I'll ask for more."

"You're impossible."

A devilish grin transformed his features, making him even more dangerous, and when he extended his hand, she accepted it.

With effortless ease, his steps graceful, he led her around the floor. "Where did you learn to dance?"

"Something all Titans are required to do."

"That's ridiculous." She laughed and relaxed, surrendering to the pleasure of the moment. Being this close with him was natural, and every one of her feminine instincts responded to him.

The song ended, and he released her. "I enjoyed that. Thank you."

"The pleasure was mine." With a small bow, he walked away, and she had to fight off the temptation to call him back and tell him she was ready for the dinner he'd once suggested.

Her phone chimed. Of course she still had details to attend to, including getting Cole to take care of the bill.

Generally at this part of the evening, the person responsible for the final payment made a crack about the cost of everything, but Cole merely scrawled his signature on the bottom line. "A bargain at ten times the cost." He handed her the pen. "Thank you for being such a good friend. I hope I can attend your wedding soon."

"I'm in no hurry. It's enough to see you happy."

"We'll get together for dinner after we return from our honeymoon."

"Let me know if you need help with anything while you travel."

A few minutes later, Avery sought out Makenna. "I'm sorry you didn't get to enjoy yourself."

"Don't worry about me. I had a good time." The dance with Zachary had been the only thing she needed.

"This has been everything I could have hoped for." She

squeezed Makenna's hands in gratitude. "You're the best wedding planner ever. I couldn't have done it without you." Then she caught sight of her husband. "I'm going to treat you to a spa day when I'm back."

Arm in arm, Avery and Cole headed for the elevator, her veil billowing beautifully behind her.

"Another successful evening, boss." Bearing a glass of champagne, Riley joined her.

Makenna accepted the gift. As a rule, she never drank at an event until it was almost over. "Thank you." Tonight, she really appreciated the expensive glass of bubbly. "You can go ahead and leave anytime."

"It's my turn to stay."

"I don't mind." Especially since Zachary was still here. "But I'm going to sleep for two weeks."

"Meaning you'll be at the office at seven on Monday morning?"

She blew out a breath. "About right." Work was the story of her life. But at least she could take off most of tomorrow. And maybe before bed she'd soak in a hot bath to ease some of the stress of being on her feet—and in heels—since noon.

Over the next hour, other guests left, some saying they were heading to other bars, a few to the casino floor. The cleaning crew got to work—sweeping up glitter, boxing the cake, scooping up balloons.

And then she saw him. Zachary. All thought of resistance fled.

He stood near the exit, his tie loose, and his suit coat slung casually over his shoulder. "You look exhausted."

"Such a charmer."

"I was going to offer to buy you a drink, but I see you already have one."

"Unfortunately I can't finish it since I need to go home."

Makenna half expected him to offer to take her, but he surprised her instead.

"We could go to my condo."

"Which is where?"

"The Bella Rosa."

"Are you serious?" She gaped. "You drove me all the way to Henderson last month, even though you live at the Bella Rosa?"

"Spending time with you is no hardship. Well, until you tell me to fuck off."

"I didn't." She recalled the way his tires had burned on the pavement. "Well, not exactly."

"What do you say? A nightcap at the martini bar? Or I can have catering send up a bottle of champagne."

She couldn't believe she was considering his idea.

"I have a soaker tub."

Tempted, she wrinkled her nose. "You were right about me being tired, and I need my Epsom salts."

"Got you covered. Pulled my hamstring a few months ago. My massage therapist recommended I buy a bag. I still have most of it left—eucalyptus and spearmint scented."

"Mr. Denning…"

"Everything is on your terms. If you want to kick off your shoes and have a glass of champagne before you go to sleep, that's all that will happen."

She shouldn't.

"What do you say?"

"You had me at eucalyptus and spearmint."

"Your home for as long as you desire, my innocent." He pressed his thumb pad on a touchscreen on the wall, right below a plaque that read PENTHOUSE TWO, and the door snicked open.

"Welcome home, Mr. Denning."

The greeting was disembodied, female, and Australian, if Makenna's guess was right.

"Temperature is sixty-eight degrees. A shipment of whiskey arrived this afternoon, compliments of Julien Bonds, and you have an 8:15 a.m. appointment with the London office. There have been no updates of note to the world money markets. Though your cryptocurrency has made moves in the past hour. You're on track for your new car." Silence hung for a moment as Zachary closed the door behind them. *"Do you have a guest with you?"*

He looked at Makenna. "Cole installed this. It's a version of Bonds's *Hello, Molly*. Everything electronic in the house talks to her—refrigerator, freezer, wine chiller, air conditioner, water heater, all the security devices. She's one hell of a computer."

"Hmph. I beg your pardon?"

"I mean her AI is state of the art. She's not just a computer."

"That's better."

Makenna laughed. "And she has personality."

"You clearly have a guest, Mr. Denning."

"I do."

"May I say it's about time? You've been a member of the Lonely Hearts Club for too long."

He groaned. "Uhm, system glitch. She's not perfect yet."

"Care to tell me more?"

He rolled his eyes. "Cole. The VIP table?"

"With Hawkeye and Lorenzo Carrington and others?"

"He said it was for us loser bachelors. Even wrote that on the invitation. He filled in the RSVP card himself—*plus zero.*"

"Ouch." She flashed him a mock wince.

"Yeah. Asshole makes his happiness known every chance he gets."

"Mr. Denning, would you like to introduce me to your company?"

"I would." To Makenna he explained, "She will learn your voice. If you are introduced, it means that she will respond to your commands."

"What happens if you don't do that?"

"Then she won't follow orders. It's a security precaution." He crossed to a thick glass control panel that was at least eight feet tall. It resembled something out of a science fiction movie. After touching it with his thumb, he gave an instruction. "Miss Ellie, I'd like to you to meet Makenna."

"Hello, Makenna."

Zachary nodded to Makenna. "Say anything in response."

This was so tech-forward her mind whirled. "It's nice to meet you, Miss Ellie."

"I await your commands."

"Wow. That's impressive."

"She is when she wants to be, and when my friends aren't messing with her programming." His grimace was more of a snarl. "Miss Ellie, open the blinds."

Makenna expected to be wowed, but nothing happened.

"Fuck me running." He sighed. "Miss Ellie, *please* open the blinds."

Silently they rose.

As he no doubt intended, Makenna was instantly drawn toward the floor-to-ceiling windows. "It's like being on top of the world." Whenever she was on the Strip, she expected to look out and see neon everywhere, but since they were so high up, she looked down on nearby buildings. "It must be spectacular during the day."

"Mountain view. I'm sure it'll take your breath away, if Miss Ellie decides to cooperate."

She grinned. "Do you always have to say please?"

"Only when she's annoyed at me. Bonds said I can be too impatient, so he programmed an etiquette module into this particular system. At times, I consider disabling her."

"I heard that."

"Let me show you around."

Penthouse Two was spectacular. In addition to a kitchen with high-end appliances and finishes, he had a formal dining room and a separate bar area, perfect for entertaining.

He showed her two of the three bedrooms, and one served as his office. Instead of facing a wall, his desk was situated so he could stare out the window.

She wandered over to his credenza, the only spot in the condominium that was in the least bit messy. Here, file folders and papers were stacked haphazardly.

"I wasn't expecting company."

Makenna couldn't resist teasing him. "As a card-carrying member of the Lonely Hearts Club, of course you weren't." That inadvertent piece of information from the posh Miss Ellie soothed Makenna. She picked up a framed picture of him, taken from behind. He stood with his hands propped on his waist, looking outside. The caption read, "Sky's the limit."

She put it down and turned to him.

"One of the reasons I wanted to live in the clouds." He shrugged. "It's a visual reminder every day to keep working my ass off."

"I like it."

"Let me show you to my bedroom."

His suite was enormous, with an informal seating area at the far end, with two barrel chairs—each with a matching ottoman. A small metal table stood between them. He'd angled them so they faced the window. True to his word, an ice bucket stood there, champagne chilling in it. "May I pour you a glass?"

"Thank you."

He uncorked the expensive bottle and filled two flutes. Before their first sip, his phone rang. "I apologize."

"It's late."

"Overseas, it's tomorrow." He checked his watch. "Or, actually, later today since it's almost one o'clock. Make yourself comfortable. I have an extra robe in my closet, and you'll find the jar of Epsom salts on the teak bench near the tub. Good place for your bubbly as well."

While he answered the summons, she found the promised robe. Holding it close, she crossed into the bathroom. The tile and marble exuded the same elegance as a world-class spa.

Within minutes, she sank chin-deep into the hot, fragrant water.

More tired and relaxed than she'd been in a long time, Makenna lifted her hair so it didn't get wet, then rested the back of her head on the attached pillow. With a sigh, she closed her eyes.

The soft rumble of Zachary's baritone reached her, soothing her. She must have drifted off for a moment, because when she opened her eyes, she was chilled.

Sitting up, she drained the tub and stepped onto the bath mat to reach for her robe. The fluffy material swaddled her in luxury. After picking up the still-full flute of bubbles, she returned to the bedroom to find him seated in one of the chairs with his feet propped on an ottoman. He wore a soft black T-shirt and black pants and was peering out the window over his steepled hands.

As she approached, he turned and smiled. "A fantasy come true."

"You flatter me too much."

"Join me?"

She curled up in the chair. "Maybe I should book a night

at a hotel after every event. Relaxing and not driving... I could get used to this."

"Certainly factored in my decision to buy here. I travel frequently, and I keep similar though much-smaller homes in London, New York, Los Angeles. You'd enjoy them."

"My life is here."

"And you do a hell of a job. No wonder you're in high demand."

"You had a good time?"

"I shared a dance with a very special lady." He refreshed his champagne. "Then she accompanied me home. Yeah. I had a good time. And it's just beginning." In silent invitation, he extended his hand toward her.

This—he—was something she wanted more than her next breath.

They both placed their drinks on the small table.

With a confidence unlike her, she went to him. Then, facing him, she lowered herself into his lap, her knees on either side of his legs.

His eyes darkened and then narrowed. "I've thought of this for weeks, months."

"Months?"

"I had my eye on you at the Hewitts' parties, waiting for my opportunity."

How could she be less vulnerable than he was? "I've wanted this also."

"Have you?" He parted the lapels of her robe, then slid the material over her shoulders. "Your breasts are gorgeous. A gift from the gods." He cupped them in his palms, then tightened slightly. "Since we've had a drink, we can't enjoy a formal scene."

"I promise you I'm not tipsy." Maybe a little bit in an altered state from being near him.

"Earlier I said nothing would happen here unless you wanted it. And I meant it."

"You can believe me when I say that I want you to fuck me."

"Hell no. I want to make love to you. I won't allow you to use words that put emotional distance between us."

"Zachary…I just want to enjoy the moment."

"I'll see to it that you do."

She dropped her hands onto his shoulders as he tightened his grip on her breasts. "Ruin me for any other man?"

"I was honest about my intentions from the start." He placed one hand behind her head and drew her to him so that he could kiss her passionately, asking, seeking, demanding, taking.

When he released her, she moaned and leaned heavily against him.

"Fuck, Makenna. You're everything I want. Everything I need." He tormented her nipples until they were hard and throbbing. Then he sucked on one, laving it with his tongue, swirling and twirling, driving her mad.

She ground herself against his already-hard cock.

"Do you have any idea how much I want you?"

"Maybe as much as I want *you?*"

"I have condoms. But they're across the room."

"I'm not on birth control." She bunched his T-shirt in her hands. "What are we going to do?"

"Solve the problem."

Impossibly, with her laughing and protesting, he managed to stand. "Wrap your legs around me."

"I am way too big for you to do this."

He began to walk, and she yelped. "You'll drop me!" Quickly she grabbed hold of his shoulders.

"At some point, we're going to have sex in this position."

"You'll definitely need the Epsom salts after that."

"One more self-deprecating comment out of you, and I promise I'll turn you over my knee tomorrow and paddle you so hard you won't sit for a week."

Not doubting his sincerity, she clamped her mouth closed.

"That's better." They reached the nightstand. "This is going to take some teamwork."

"You could put me down."

"Not happening."

"Do you know how ridiculous this is?"

Immediately he countered her objection. "Do you know how much I fantasized about having you ride my dick while I watch our reflection in the window?"

Her mouth dried.

"You're not the only voyeur, Makenna."

"Uhh…"

"I'm going to keep hold of you. And you're going to open the drawer and pull out a condom."

On the second attempt, she managed to do as he asked. But trying to close the drawer again was futile.

"Leave it. We have other things we need to focus on." He strode back to the living room and managed to sit without either of them losing their balance.

"If you'd have asked me, I would have said that was impossible."

He cracked a grin. "Sky's the limit."

"I'm starting to believe you."

"Where were we?"

"You were sucking my nipple, and I was trying to get myself off on your dick. I want you inside me."

"And it will absolutely happen." As he swept his gaze over her, he sucked in a breath. Very deliberately, he pushed her breasts together and traced gentle circles on her nipples.

"This is overwhelming."

"Good. Now open your mouth for me."

When she did, he stuck a finger inside. "Wet it."

Despite the fact they weren't scening, the man was still every inch a Dominant. When he was satisfied, he pulled it out. "Now, kneel up for me." He slid the damp finger between her feminine folds, tantalizing and arousing her. I want you wet for me."

The mere thought of him was enough to make her needy.

"I want to have sex with you a dozen times and in a dozen different ways. So I need to make sure you don't get too sore."

She clamped her mouth shut; arguing with him would get her nowhere. He played with her pussy and her breasts until she tipped her head back, sending her hair cascading over her shoulders.

His touch left her breathless and desperate. "If you keep this up, I'm going to come. But I want to orgasm with you inside me."

"There's no doubt that will happen as well." He inserted a finger inside her, then slipped in a second.

Trying to rub herself on him, Makenna jerked her hips. *"Please."*

"I need you up on your knees again."

Makenna wiggled around, and somehow he managed to lower his pants and kick them aside. Beneath them—thank God—he was commando. Her first sight of his cock made her gasp. "It's enormous." And a drop of precum leaked from the tip.

"Look what you do to me, my innocent. Can you give me a little room?"

She did as he asked, holding on to the curve of the chair for balance while he rolled the condom down his shaft.

"I'm thinking that your dick is the Eighth Wonder of the World."

"Okay, now it's certain. I will never let you go." With primal intent, he caught her mouth once more, plunging in deeply, simulating sex, claiming her in ways no one else ever had.

With a groan, he captured her hips and drew her toward him once again. His constant approval gave her newfound confidence, and she reached between them to hold his cock while she lowered herself onto his shaft.

She took only a small amount of him inside her before she lifted herself away from him. "It's been a really long time for me."

"We can go as slow as you need."

God. Could she even do this? "That was only your cockhead."

"We're going to be the perfect fit."

He squeezed her ass so hard that she pitched forward. Master Zachary definitely knew what he was doing.

"Now ride me." He kneaded her flesh and gave her multiple swats that made her writhe, and each motion took her lower on his dick until he was seated balls-deep.

With a sigh, she rested her forehead on his shoulder.

"What did I tell you? Perfect fit."

"Is that what you call it?" He filled her completely, owned her. Like the scene they'd shared at the grotto, he was focused solely on her pleasure.

The moment seared into her memory. Zachary Denning, with his approval and the way he continually saw to her well-being, had gotten past her well-constructed defenses. Not only did she care for him—he'd earned her trust.

Slowly she began to move, and she grabbed hold of his shirt and tugged it from his waistband.

He took over from there, pulling it up and off, then tossing it aside.

"Damn." His chest was magnificent, and his abs were honed. "You're absolutely beautiful."

He swiveled the chair slightly. "Look at your reflection. Watch yourself. Watch us." With great deliberation, he gently spanked her, reddening her buttocks.

The image of them moving together, the way his jaw was set, the way his muscles flexed from exertion, drove her to the edge.

"Are you getting ready to come, little innocent?"

"Yes. Y*es*."

He stopped moving his hips, and she changed their angle, taking what she needed. "That's it." He fisted a hand into her hair to pull back her head, then kissed the hollow of her throat.

She had never been so lost before.

Zachary squeezed one of her nipples. Then he gently bit. The pinprick of pain rocketed her over the edge. Whimpering, crying his name, she took her orgasm, riding it for everything she could. And then her body went limp. He was there, cradling her. When she caught her breath, he brushed a lock of hair back over her shoulder.

"Now I have an idea for your second orgasm."

CHAPTER FIVE

Zachary rearranged the furniture and beckoned to his beautiful, hesitant lover. "I want you to grab the far end of the table, facing the window."

She scowled. "This will never work."

He was taller than she was, but not so much that the position was unachievable. "I assure you, it will."

"Maybe the back of the chair would be better?"

Was she stalling, or doing geometry? "Humor me."

With a skeptical sigh, she did as he said. Zachary moved behind her, placed his hands on her hip bones, then brought her back toward him, holding her steady, effectively imprisoning her.

His cock throbbed with demand. And he held himself in check. This had to be wonderful for her. He'd been waiting for weeks. What were a few more minutes? "Spread your legs as far as you can."

Makenna glanced back, and her eyebrows were knitted together over her expressive cornflower-blue eyes.

"There's no doubt I'm going to fill your tight little cunt." She was still wet, and he inserted the tip of his cock into her.

She did a little dance but then faced forward.

In the window's reflection, he watched her long blonde hair fall forward to frame her face.

Her upturned ass was a dream, reminding him of the night she'd lain across his lap at the Hewitts' party. She'd been shivering from anticipation and maybe a touch of fear, but still she'd trusted him.

He admired her. No doubt it had been difficult for her to keep her insecurities in check while he skimmed his fingers across her skin, exploring her innermost secrets, then spanking her until she wore one of his handprints like a badge of glory.

He eased into her, looking at their bodies in the window. Soft and hard, feminine and masculine. "Your breasts are magnificent." They swayed and bounced, making him even harder.

Zachary shook his head to clear it. If he wanted to last more than thirty seconds, he needed to change things up.

He pulled out slightly, then took a breath. Control regained, he slid his forearm in front of her, so she couldn't escape. Then he reached to play with her clit. The little bundle of nerves was already swollen, and when he pressed his finger against it, she sucked in a sharp breath.

"Zachary!"

Hell and back. He loved the sound of his name in her mouth. And no matter how many times she screamed it, he'd never tire of hearing it.

He fucked her, tormented her, then moved faster and faster until her tiny whimpers became a solid never-ending cry for release.

"This is too much."

Her feminine heat squeezed him, demanding his orgasm in a mating ritual as old as time.

"I'm going to..." Gasping, she cried out, her wet pussy convulsing.

Though Zachary moved his hand away, he continued to hold her. While she shook her head, he traced his damp finger down the cleft of her ass.

"That was..." She fell silent, and he wondered if she was searching for the right word, or whether she wasn't thinking at all. "Indescribable."

"We're not done yet."

She exhaled a shuddering breath.

After untangling their heated bodies, he helped her to stand.

"You've almost worn me out."

"Almost? Then I need to work harder." Too impatient to wait, he swept her from her feet and carried her to the bed. Smartly she didn't protest, even when he joined her. "And now you're going to come on my face."

"But..." Frantically she shook her head.

"It's what I want." He plumped a pillow, then laid his head on it. "Get your sweet little ass over here and straddle my face." His eyes narrowed in warning. "Before you say anything, remember what I said about you making any negative comments about yourself."

"That's not—"

"Brace yourself on the headboard. I'm going to eat your pussy. We can argue all night, but I will prevail. You might as well get on with it."

Rather awkwardly, she placed her thighs on either side of his head. Her musky, sexually satisfied scent drove him wild. "Lower yourself onto me."

When she didn't react quickly enough, he pulled her down.

"Master Zachary!" She lifted herself up.

Holding her firmly, he licked her, back to front.

"Oh my *God.*" She gasped and jerked away.

"Last warning," he growled.

Her body shaking like it had the first night they played together, she whimpered.

Patience gone, he took control, moving her where he wanted so that he could insert two fingers into her pussy while pressing his thumb against her anus.

"This is…" Her knees trembled. "I've never experienced anything like this."

He tasted her, tongued her, savored her, and the more she relaxed, the more responsive she became. "Play with your breasts."

"Then I'll have to let go of the headboard."

"You don't want me to repeat myself."

"*No.* No, I don't, Sir."

Zachary moved his tongue faster, and she groaned. "Squeeze your nipples, tug on them, pinch them the way I would." He knew the moment she followed his order because she spread her thighs farther apart, resting her pussy on his face. *Perfect.*

Like a starving man, he ate her out until she came, drenching his face with her juices. Eventually he slowed his strokes and eased his fingers from inside her. "And now, *now* you're ready."

Driven by a primal alpha need to mark his woman, he tossed her beneath him without the consideration he usually granted.

Her eyes were wide, but no fear lurked in their depths.

"You're mine, Makenna. I'm going to make sure you accept it."

He grabbed her hands and yanked them over her head, pinning them against the mattress. Then he plowed into her pussy with one long, satisfying stroke.

In recognition of his power, her body yielded to his. Satisfied, he sucked in a breath. *"Fuck."* His entire life, he'd waited for this—for her. "Spread your legs." Though he was deep inside her channel, it wasn't nearly enough. He needed her complete capitulation. For a moment, he pulled out. "Lift your legs."

When she complied, he braced his shoulders on the backs of her knees and bore forward.

She gasped at the force of his penetration.

"Take all of me, Makenna." An image of her belly swollen with his child urged him on, both real and inevitable.

She called out his name, part plea, part desperation.

Finally his balls drew up. He groaned, unleashing the force of the orgasm he'd held back for weeks. "Jesus."

Moments later, spent, he rolled to the side, then pulled her toward him. With a heavy exhalation, she rested in his arms. Maybe she was recognizing the same thing that he was. This was forever.

"What is this?" Tightening the belt around her robe, Makenna walked into the living room.

Zachary—her lover—stood there, shirtless, wearing only a pair of casual pants, grinning as he poured a cup of coffee.

There were several silver carts lined up, all stacked with food.

"I figured you'd be hungry after last night, and I wasn't sure you'd even had time to eat dinner." He shrugged. "I had no idea what you'd like."

"So what did you do? Order the entire room service menu?"

"Pretty well. Crepes, waffles, bacon, eggs, toast, oatmeal, granola."

"And coffee?" She needed it.

When he suggested they have sex in front of the window, she'd been apprehensive. There were no other tall buildings nearby, so they couldn't be seen. But knowing he was watching made her tummy tumble. And then, when he'd made her look too... It had been beyond sexy. Their bodies moved together perfectly, and there had been unadulterated pleasure in his eyes, proving his attraction to her was real and honest. As they'd continued, her self-consciousness faded, and their lewd acts appealed to her own voyeuristic fantasies.

Afterward, they had dozed in each other's arms until he had gotten up out of bed to discard the condom, and he returned with a warm, damp cloth to soothe her tender nether region. A couple of times during the night, they made love before drifting gently back to sleep.

But now, in the light of day, anxiety gnawed at her happiness. Last night was over. And they both had to go back to their real lives. She might be emotionally changed, but he was still a billionaire playboy. Despite her resolve, she had become another notch on his bedpost.

"Makenna?" His head was tipped to the side quizzically, as if he'd been trying to get her attention.

"Sorry." She offered a quick smile. "I must be still half-asleep."

"Cream and sugar?"

"Just cream. Thanks." She walked across the room to accept the cup. "Manna from heaven."

He held it back until she kissed him.

Danger zone. From the moment they met, he'd encouraged her to remain in the moment. And as long as she did, things were fine, but when she looked to tomorrow or the next day, the future was bleak.

"What would you like to eat?" He removed the lids from the assorted plates.

"Maybe a little of everything." After all, he'd ordered a private buffet.

But instead of choosing anything healthy, she went straight for the crepes and covered them with strawberries and whipped cream. Then she snatched up a piece of bacon. "For protein."

He laughed. "Protein is good."

Once his plate was mounded with food, they moved to the dining room.

The blinds were lowered, but the sun still filtered through. "What time is it?"

"A little after ten. I needed to get up for a conference call with London."

"Sorry I slept so long."

"I wouldn't have blamed you if you'd stayed in bed until noon. In fact, we could both probably use the rest."

It had been a physically demanding night for him too.

"What would you like to do today?"

She put down her bacon without taking a bite. "I was planning to go home. Did you have a different idea?"

"I'm leaving town in the morning on business, but if you have no plans, we could be tourists in our own city."

The invitation caught her off guard. With his reputation, she'd expected he would take her home.

"Alternatively we could spend the day at the pool, have dinner after you get a massage." He grinned devilishly. "Or I could fuck you so hard you can't walk."

"Uh... The last part is already dangerously close to happening."

Greedily he perused her, taking in her mussed hair and the robe's gaping lapels that revealed her cleavage.

Since yesterday, her survival instincts had gone into hiding, and she ended up agreeing to spend the day together. "We can't stay out too late."

"I can take you home in the morning."

"You have a flight, and I am expected at the office by seven."

"I'll drop you off before I go to the airport."

More than anything, she wanted what he offered, even if it was dangerous. She had makeup in her bag, but she couldn't rewear yesterday's clothes. "I'd need a few personal items and maybe a sundress. And definitely a pair of shoes." Since she'd been meaning to buy some walking sandals, this was the perfect excuse.

"As you know, there's a shopping mecca attached to the resort."

Most with brands she'd never be able to afford.

"I'll go with you."

Her protests were ignored, not that she expected anything different.

Even though she took over an hour finalizing her purchases, he didn't check his watch or look at his phone, and he pulled out his credit card at every vendor.

"You don't need to do this."

"If I had let you go home, you wouldn't have needed all these things. Besides, Miss Ellie told me my crypto is still on the rise."

"Who am I to argue with that logic?" And honestly, it was nice to be spoiled. "You've been totally patient. I think your male complaint mode is defective."

He grinned. "I'll see if we can get Julien Bonds to install an upgrade."

As they took the private elevator back to PH2, as he called Penthouse Two, she couldn't resist her question. "You're friends with him?"

"With Bonds? Close enough."

Which meant… "He's a Titan."

"Are you referring to the organization that may or may not exist?"

The compartment arrived at the fifty-third floor so fast that her vertigo was triggered.

"The Bella Rosa believes in expediency. The quicker you get people to the casino floor, the better."

"I'll say."

Once they were back in his condo, she took a quick shower and got ready to go. He was dressed and doing some work in his office when she went looking for him.

"That dress is fabulous."

"Why, thank you." She twirled, and the hem flared a little.

"I'm going to wreck your hair before we leave."

Makenna gasped. "Are you serious?"

He pushed away from his desk and advanced toward her, eyes narrowed with purposeful intent. "As you know, there are certain things I don't joke about."

She stood her ground. "But I just—" Her breath whooshed out as he swept her off her feet and carried her to the bedroom.

"Since I'm a generous man, I'll allow you to keep your shoes on." He lowered her so she could put her feet on the floor.

With swift motions, he stripped her, then once again picked her up and placed her on the mattress, this time on all fours.

He rolled a condom down his thick shaft, then ensured she was ready for him before taking her from the rear.

When they were finished, she was overheated and dotted with perspiration. A quick glance in the bathroom mirror proved he had totally destroyed the bun she'd swept her hair into.

"Fair warning." Wearing only his trousers and a triumphant smile, his body gleaming from exertion, he stood behind her. "Seeing you all made-up ignites my inner beast." He pressed his cock against her.

In the mirror, she locked her gaze on him. "You're hard *again?*"

"You put your hair up." He shrugged fatalistically. "Of course, if you left it loose…" He swept the blonde locks aside to kiss the side of her neck. "Then I'll need to close my fist in it."

She shouldn't poke him. But she was caught up in her own tide of lust. "And do what?"

"This…" He caught a handful of hair at the root, firmly—just short of painfully—and pulled her head back. Then he kissed her…hard.

To remain upright she had to wrap her arms around his neck.

With his mouth, he claimed her completely, communicating something she was afraid to acknowledge.

When he finally released her, she grabbed hold of the vanity for support. "Thank you for the warning."

"Unless you want to spend the afternoon in my bed, I recommend you be at the front door in under two minutes." With that, he left.

She didn't point out that they would have already been at their first stop if he hadn't ripped off her clothes.

With a half shake of her head, she repaired the damage to her mascara and lipstick and did the best she could with her hair.

Once they were outside the casino, the Las Vegas heat blasted her.

Hand in hand, they wandered down the Strip, and she took in the sights that she normally missed because she was so busy working. When she visited a property, she paid cursory attention to the tigers or flamingos and instead spent her time evaluating the logistics of the meeting space. Some might enjoy dancing fountains as an amenity, but she wanted to know how responsive the catering staff was and if the manager was someone she could work with easily.

Because the day was growing hotter, they purchased bottles of water and continued their stroll, ending up at a resort that was featuring a showing of impressionist art.

"I'm so glad we came." On a normal Sunday, she'd be getting organized for the next week. If time permitted, she'd take a yoga class.

They stopped in front of the final painting. "This is absolutely amazing."

He nodded.

"There's all these wonderful things to do in Las Vegas. People come here from all over the world, and I've never been in this gallery before."

"We need to take the time to appreciate what we have."

She looked over at him, but he was still studying the work hanging on the wall.

"Next stop?" he asked eventually.

After buying ice cream sandwiches—a full scoop of butter pecan wedged between two chocolate chip cookies—they sat at a small metal table.

"How about a comedy club?"

"I've actually never been."

"Another thing I can corrupt you with." He opened an app and purchased tickets before booking early dinner reservations.

"I'd feel bad about the crepes and ice cream, but I think we've walked it off."

"There's no doubt."

At the restaurant, still quiet because it was relatively early, she opted for a Caesar salad with grilled chicken. He went straight for a steak and vegetables.

The stand-up comedians were superb.

Then, evening falling, they walked back on the other side of the street for a change of view. As he had all day, Zachary took her hand.

"I haven't done anything like this in forever." She savored the moment. "Thank you."

"We should plan another one soon."

By the time they reached his condo, her feet were throbbing, and she looked forward to soaking in the tub.

But he turned and narrowed his eyes. Her insides liquefied.

"I can pour you a glass of champagne. Or I can give you the spanking that you're craving."

All of a sudden, he was the masterful Dominant, rather than the solicitous man who'd spent the day catering to her every whim.

"Be mindful of your decision." His voice was roughened with command. "Because I'm inclined to give you forced orgasms if we play together."

"Fuck the champagne, Sir. I'll take a bottled water."

"Good morning, Mr. Denning and Makenna."

Miss Ellie's cheerful voice cut through Makenna's dreams, and she groaned. "Ten more minutes."

Zachary soothed her hair and kissed the top of her head.

"Please?" Last night, after he'd thoroughly spanked and fucked her, they'd agreed on a five a.m. wake-up call. It had seemed like a good idea. But that was before he'd made love to her two more times.

"I'll be back with coffee."

"With cream." She buried her head beneath the pillow, but without him in the bed, she couldn't go back to sleep.

With a resigned sigh, she tossed the blankets aside and padded into the bathroom. He was already in the walk-in shower, steam billowing around him, droplets of water sluicing down his sexy chest, and his cock magnificently hard.

Maybe sensing her presence, or hearing her gasp, he glanced over. "Join me?"

She knew better than to protest that it couldn't be done.

"Grab a condom?"

By the time she was back, he'd stepped out and toweled his lower body dry. Zachary rolled the condom down his shaft; then she followed him into the shower.

After kissing her, he turned her to face the wall, then reached around to play with her breasts and clit, ensuring she was turned on.

Once he was fully inside, he moved slowly, creating a sexy rhythm that made her wet. He kissed her neck and squeezed the ass he'd spent so much time tormenting last night.

When Makenna came, it wasn't with a huge shudder, but a soft, satisfied sigh.

"Lovemaking," he murmured.

She tipped back her head, and warm water trickled over her as he increased the force behind his thrusts until he came, gritting out her name in three distinct syllables.

Once they were done, he released her wrists. Still lethargic, she turned around. He tucked damp strands of hair behind her ears, then kissed her. "Now are you glad you didn't stay in bed?"

"Having sex with you is worth the lost sleep."

"Good." He lathered a bar of soap to wash her, and she luxuriated in every caress.

"I'm still going to need coffee."

"Miss Ellie has already brewed it."

"I think I love her."

"That's the nicest thing anyone has ever said to me. You could learn something, Mr. Denning."

Makenna laughed. "Can I take her home with me?"

"I shall make the inquiry of Mr. Bonds."

"Hell no." With his palm, Zachary wiped the water from his face. "I'll tell him to send you one."

By the time Makenna had finished her second cup, she was mostly awake, and running late.

Near the elevator, he stood waiting for her, freshly shaven, wearing a tailored suit, his addictive scent of power and spice branding the air.

Would he always have the ability to make her senses swim?

"Ready?"

"Don't you have a trip?" She looked around. "Where's your luggage?"

"I keep a full wardrobe and a complement of electronics on the jet."

Of course he had a private plane. *Who doesn't?*

"And my home in New York has everything I need."

In the same dizzying way that she'd never get used to, the elevator whisked them to the lobby. Outside, his snazzy yellow car was waiting, already purring. "You never have to wait." She, on the other hand, a mere mortal, spent half her life in frustrating lines.

"Miss Ellie notified the valet when she started the coffee."

"Wow. Again, I'm impressed."

Because traffic was light, he parked in front of her house five minutes ahead of his projected schedule.

"Thanks for the ride." She reached for the door handle but didn't pull it. "Have a successful trip."

One hand on the steering wheel, he angled his body toward her. "This is awkward."

A flutter of nerves teasing her, she asked, "What is?"

"I don't have your phone number."

She grinned. "That's ridiculous, isn't it?" Given the fact that she'd slept in his bed, and they'd had wet, steamy shower sex only an hour ago.

"I could track you down, but I don't want to call in any favors or put our friends in an awkward situation."

"Agreed."

He pulled out his Bonds device to program in her information. "You'll be hearing from me."

"I know you're busy." She hoped he meant it, but his dating history said otherwise. "Thanks for the weekend. It was nice." This time, she opened the door.

By the time she gathered her purse and the gym bag he'd loaned her for her purchases, he was standing beside her.

He walked her up the path. Once they were on the porch, he gathered her into his arms and kissed her in a way that curled her toes.

"That's a promise of things to come."

Her heart was thundering when she let herself inside, and she stood in the foyer until the purr of his car engine vanished into the predawn silence.

Then she straightened her shoulders. She had to put the fairytale fantasy of the weekend behind her.

Less than an hour later, Makenna was on the road. Because the caffeine she'd consumed wasn't nearly enough to power through this Monday morning, she drove through her favorite coffee place. She ordered their largest American for herself and a frozen chocolaty thing for Riley. And because she'd skipped breakfast, Makenna added pastries to the order.

As soon as she reached the first traffic light, she broke off a piece of maple nut scone and popped it in her mouth. Going to the gym after work was a small price to pay to indulge in such deliciousness.

About half an hour after she arrived at the office, her assistant swept in. Over coffee and their breakfast treats, they briefly chatted about their day off. Riley had gone to dinner with a friend. Makenna was vague about how she'd spent her time.

"But you had fun?"

"Yes. I did." Other than with Avery or Zara, Makenna wasn't willing to share any information about Master Zachary. "Ready to get to work?" She pulled up their joint calendar. "Can you meet Joelle and Nick at the cake-tasting appointment?" Attending food samplings was something she rarely did. But Joelle's mother was overly involved in the wedding preparation, so she wanted support with her at all times.

"No problem."

She assigned the appointment to Riley. "Good. I have a video pitch with a couple from Colorado today at two. This morning, I want to attend the preview of the new wedding chapel. Forget Elvis. You can choose about anything from a king to Merlin the magician." She laughed. "Only in Vegas."

"Can I go with you?"

"Why not? We can take a car together, but I'm heading from there to lunch with an event planner who's a bit miffed that we didn't consider them for the last tradeshow."

"Sounds like a plan." Riley brushed her hands together to wipe away the crumbs. "That was decadent." After a cheery wave, she vanished into her own office.

An hour before they were scheduled to leave, Riley knocked on the open door.

Makenna removed her reading glasses and looked up

from the spreadsheet she'd been studying. Riley's phone was clutched in her hand, and her cheeks were pale. "Is everything okay?"

"Can I come in?"

"Of course." Makenna frowned as Riley walked across the office.

"Have you…umm…" She extended her phone as she sank into a chair. "I think you need to see this."

"Okay." She accepted the device.

A picture of her and Zachary at the Rose Martini Bar leaped out. It had been snapped while he was kissing her hand. The headline was in all caps and bolded. FULL-FIGURED FABULOUSNESS. NEW ROMANCE FOR SIN CITY BILLIONAIRE?

A horrible roar echoed in her ears, and a headache slammed into her.

"God, Makenna. I'm so sorry."

With nerveless fingers, she scrolled down. The salacious words blurred together, and there were other pictures. Of course there was one of her taking a big bite from her ice cream sandwich. As if that wasn't bad enough, an arrow invited readers to discover the entire photo gallery.

Riley reached for the phone before Makenna dropped it.

"Are there more?"

"Yeah."

"Worse than that?"

"Makenna, look—"

"So, yes?" Her silence told Makenna all she needed to know. Her phone buzzed with an unknown number.

"Don't answer it."

She shouldn't have been surprised. After all, she'd seen pictures of his other conquests online. But now she understood the sickening invasion of privacy, knowing they'd been watched. And the comments on her weight...? The coffee she'd been drinking turned to acid.

The office phone rang, and automatically Riley answered with her customary cheerful greeting.

Makenna overheard enough to know it was a columnist seeking a comment. She shook her head and motioned for Riley to hang up.

"If you'd like to leave a message, I'll have Ms. Helton return your call when she's available."

On Makenna's desktop, her email chimed.

Trying to think, she squeezed her eyes shut. She'd never dealt with anything like this before and was at a loss.

Her cell phone rang again. "We'll let calls go to voicemail for the rest of the day. I'm sorry, but you'll need to listen to the messages so that we don't miss anything urgent. But we're not going to talk to the paparazzi." Another call shattered the silence. "This day is going to be awful."

When she'd first scened with Zachary, she'd known he was a player. But she'd had no idea that their relationship and her *full-figured fabulousness* were going to be laid bare for the entire world to muck around in.

Her phone lit up again, this time displaying Zachary's name. Her humiliation was complete. He'd obviously seen the same things she had—*Lots to Love. Thick is the New Thin.*

From the beginning, her intuition had warned her to stay away from him. But because of the fatal sexual attraction, she'd allowed herself to be seduced, and worse, to fall in love.

God. How could I have been so stupid?

She blinked back angry tears as she turned her phone facedown.

He called back two more times before sending a text.

DO NOT read the articles. They're trash.

. . .

Less than a minute later another message arrived.

I'm so fucking sorry, Makenna. This is on me. I should have thought to warn you that this might happen. You had a right to know what you were getting into.

The moment she finished reading, another appeared.

Call me.

Then a final one.

Please.

Aware of Riley watching her, Makenna shook her head. More than anything, this horrible experience had taught her one thing. She wasn't from his world, and she didn't belong in it. More than that, she wanted nothing to do with it.

"Do you want me to cancel your appointments?"

"No." She needed something to occupy her mind. Besides, some creeper had gotten a picture of her on the porch this morning. Which meant they knew where she lived. "I mean it's not like the whole world has seen the articles. Right?"

"Right."

Neither of them were convincing.

When she was alone again, she picked up her phone and

reread Zachary's messages. Then, her jaw set, her finger trembling, she typed in her response.

Don't ever contact me again.

And then, because she didn't trust herself not to weaken, she blocked his number.

CHAPTER SIX

God fucking damn it to hell. Zachary slammed his phone down. "Penny!"

With a polite smile, his flight attendant hurried over. "Yes, sir?"

"Let the pilot know I need to return home." No doubt there'd be a dozen details to attend to, but she was ultra-capable.

"Of course, Mr. Denning."

He picked up his phone to try Makenna's number again. Immediately it went to voicemail.

What the hell is she going through?

The constant speculation and harassment were the things he despised most about his life. The women he'd dated in the past had expected it; some had even thrived on having their names associated with his. But Makenna was different. *Innocent.* And this time the paparazzi had gone too far.

Since she was refusing his calls, he had no option but to do an internet search for her work number. And when he called that, he received an electronic greeting stating all lines were busy.

Shit.

In frustration, he sent several text messages. Thank God, he got a read receipt.

His next call was to the person who would help him coordinate the responses to the horrible articles—Celeste Fallon, a fellow Titan. Fallon and Associates had been in the PR and fixing business for well over a hundred years.

Despite the fact that he hadn't needed her services since his engagement ended, she picked up her private number on the first ring.

"Zachary. To what do I owe this pleasure?"

"It's not a fucking pleasure call."

"In that case, how can I help?"

"There's a young woman. And it's not what you're thinking." Her firm had dealt with some of the biggest scandals in history, events that had rocked the world and kept people glued to their televisions and computer screens. It was her job to change the conversation, and she was very good at it. "Nothing needs to be spun."

"I'm listening."

"Makenna Helton."

In the background, keys—presumably to Celeste's computer keyboard—clacked. "She's beautiful."

"She's mine."

"Generally you'd respond by saying no comment and letting it go."

"She's not from our world." She'd never been exposed to the nasty, relentless viciousness of the paparazzi, and they'd attacked her where she was most vulnerable. Zachary hated himself for bringing it down on her. "She's not going to know how to deal with this. I'm in the air right now, and…" He took a breath. "She won't take my calls."

"I'll reach out."

Maybe hearing from a woman would help. "I want the

vultures kept away from her."

"Of course."

"I want the uncomplimentary goddamn disgusting articles removed. Not apologized for. Not retracted. Gone."

"That may take some time."

"Frankly, I don't care if you blow up the entire fucking internet." Because his world had been destroyed. He'd been attracted to her for months, and he'd cared about her since they'd first played. But over the weekend? He'd fallen in love. Completely, totally, making rational thought impossible.

"Zachary?"

He plowed his hand into his hair.

"I was asking for Ms. Helton's contact information."

He sent across her information. "As for her business number—"

"Already got it."

She was good. "Call *Scandalicious.*" They were a gossip site, but bigger and more reputable than most. "I'll give them an exclusive if they keep this shit off their front page."

"Consider it done."

He had no doubt she'd been deploying resources the entire time they'd been on the phone. She was as competent as she was efficient, and her network of people spanned the globe.

"I'm turning around and heading back home."

"I'll provide hourly updates, more often if warranted."

"Thanks, Celeste." Anger and agitation warred inside him, fighting for supremacy.

He'd done all he could for the moment, and he had to figure out how to harness his cold fury before he destroyed everything in his path.

A few minutes later, his phone pinged, and he grabbed it from his pocket and glanced at the screen.

Seeing Makenna's name, he sighed and opened the

message.

Do not ever contact me again.

This time, her fuck-off was pointed. But it was going to take a hell of a lot more than that to make him stay away.

Late in the day, the office door opened, and Makenna looked up, expecting to see Riley. Instead, two people—a man and a woman—entered the anteroom, and her heart thundered. *Press?* Wary, she stood and went to greet them. "Can I help you?"

"Ms. Helton?"

"Who's asking?"

The woman spoke first. "I'm Mira Araceli, and this is Torin Carter."

The tall, brooding man with electric eyes nodded.

"We're Hawkeye agents."

"Okay." She'd met Hawkeye at Cole and Avery's wedding, and she knew that Cole was associated with the security organization.

"We were told you were expecting us."

"No."

The pair exchanged glances.

"I'm confused. What can I do for you?" Surely they weren't here about an event.

"We were hired on behalf of Zachary Denning."

She pressed a finger to the bridge of her nose. "Look, I think there's a mistake." She shook her head. "I don't need... whatever it is that you do."

Mira smiled warmly, easing Makenna's tension. "I'm sorry we caught you off guard. But our orders are clear. We'll be staying with you for an indefinite amount of time."

"I beg your pardon?" Mutinously, she folded her arms across her chest.

"The paparazzi can be aggressive."

"They're assholes, ma'am." Torin spoke for the first time. "That's a technical term."

Even though tension was swarming through her, she gave him a half smile. "At least we agree on one thing."

"Anyway, we're here to be sure no one takes pictures of you. And we also want to do a sweep of your neighborhood, including the sky. Some of them are using drone technology."

Makenna shivered.

It was almost quitting time, and it had crossed her mind that she might be followed. Looking over her shoulder all day while she'd been out on business had been nerve-racking.

In her skilled, reassuring way, Mira went on. "We know this isn't comfortable for you. We'll be with you during your workday and if you go out in the evenings. We'll pick you up and take you home. A surveillance team will work overnight at your house. We'll do our best to be as unobtrusive as possible."

As if Torin Carter could be unobtrusive. He was massive, and drop-dead gorgeous. If her guess was right, he was a Dominant—he had the air and bearing about him. "How long will this go on?"

"Until Mr. Denning gives us the all clear."

"And you have no idea when that might be?"

Torin spoke up again. "No, ma'am."

Even though she hated the intrusion in her life, she appreciated Zachary's gesture, especially since she'd told him she never wanted to hear from him again.

"Do you have a garage door opener in your car?" Mira asked.

"I do."

"Good." Torin nodded. "Can we have the keys?"

As she handed them over, she gave them the make and model, along with the license plate number and location of the parking garage.

"No hurry, but let us know when you're ready."

She gathered her belongings, then answered a call from Zara.

"You okay?"

"It's, uhm... Stressful."

"You know they're haters, right? They intentionally use shitty angles to make their targets look bad. It's more sensational that way." She exhaled. "Everyone can see Zachary is besotted with you, and that makes the story clickbait. Don't let the trolls get to you. Pull your shoulders back and be a badass."

"Good advice." She just wished she could take it.

"Would you like me to come and stay with you?"

"That's really sweet." She hesitated to mention the security detail. "But I'm okay."

"You're absolutely beautiful, Kenna. And don't let anyone tell you otherwise. Promise you'll call if you need anything?"

"I swear."

"Let's go out for drinks after this blows over. You'll need a martini or two."

"Maybe three." After exchanging goodbyes, Makenna checked her office one last time before slinging her purse over her shoulder.

Torin outlined their strategy for moving her as quickly as possible and instructed them to give him a thirty-second head start.

"You're doing great," Mira said. Then she opened an

umbrella. "Stay under it and keep it low. It will make getting a decent snapshot impossible."

Outside, the rear car door stood open. Within seconds, she was in the passenger compartment, and Mira slid in after her. Simultaneously, Torin climbed into the driver's seat and pulled into traffic.

"This is surreal."

"Hopefully it's only for a day or so."

"How does this work with dinner and such?"

"If you want to order food, you can." As always, Mira was as soothing as she was practical. "But we'd like to ask for contactless delivery if you do."

Torin added his own opinion. "Assholes have been known to pretend to be florists, plumbers, delivery drivers."

She nodded. "Understood."

Mira shook her head. "While we'll have surveillance on you, we don't want to take unnecessary chances."

"Of course."

Later that evening, she grabbed a glass of wine and carried her tablet to the couch. Even though it was probably a very bad idea, she opened her web browser.

And now, even her favorite site, *Scandalicious*, had an article about her and Zachary. The headline sucked the breath from her lungs. SIN CITY'S FAVORITE BILLIONAIRE IS OFF THE MARKET!

Her hand shaking, she continued reading. *Billionaire banker Zachary Denning hasn't been seen much in recent months, and now we know why. He's been wining and dining a new love whose name is secret. And he sure looks happy.*

There were pictures, of course, but these were different. Though they hadn't been retouched, the angles and lighting were better, and she didn't hate them.

Zara was right about the haters. And no doubt her words had come from experience.

Makenna took a drink before continuing, surprised to see Zachary quoted. In other articles, except business exposés, he always responded with, "No comment."

"She's beautiful on the inside and out, and I'm a lucky man. I don't deserve her. But I'm not going to stop trying."

She choked on a sob.

Though they were heartfelt, his words changed nothing. She refused to spend her life wondering who was lurking in the shadows, hoping to catch her looking awful.

After powering off the device, she went to take a bath. And then, sinking into the bubbles, she gave in to her tears.

The next day she was shocked to realize that all the articles—except the one in *Scandalicious*—had been removed from the internet. How was that even possible?

At the end of the week, Mira let Makenna know that their assignment was over, but they'd be back immediately if needed.

Which it won't be. Makenna was no longer in the spotlight. And though that was a welcome relief, being away from Zachary burned more than she could have imagined.

She went to the Hewitts' next party but left early when Zachary didn't attend.

A couple of weeks later, she returned to the office after lunch to find a massive bouquet on her desk.

She picked up the small, attached envelope to read the greeting.

Happy two-month anniversary.

I miss you.

Love, Zachary.

The constant ache in her heart accelerated into a throb. The scent of the roses spiraled her back to Avery and Cole's wedding, and Zachary's words returned to haunt her, this time with more meaning. *"There comes a time when we have to stop letting our pain define who we are."*

For years, she'd done that—allowed her ex to ruin the way she saw herself.

She eased one of the flowers from the bunch. Unbidden, a memory returned to her—of Zachary and her having sex in his living room, and her being captivated by their reflection in the window.

To him, she was beautiful. His reaction was authentic. With both his words and actions, he'd repeatedly shown her how much he cared.

For too long, she'd allowed her ex's nasty words and unflattering paparazzi pictures to ruin her happiness.

Then she remembered the rest of what he'd said. *"When you're ready, I'll be here."*

Now, like before, he'd respected her need to be alone. And that made her fall even harder for him. Every day she'd looked but hadn't seen a single mention of him dating anyone else.

Their time apart hadn't damaged her affection for him. It had only increased it. She put down the rose and reread the card.

He'd signed it *Love*.

Did he mean it?

Life with Zachary, even with challenges, was better than life without him.

Her hand was shaking so hard that it took her two attempts to open the tab where she could unblock his number.

Because she wasn't brave enough to call him, she sent him a text message.

The flowers are beautiful.

. . .

The response took so long she wasn't sure that he would actually reply.

Dinner?

Her knees weakened. God, she'd missed him and ached to be with him.

I can send a car and bring you in via the private entrance. We can have dinner sent up to my place.

She considered that. But she refused to hide, even if photographers were lurking around. This was the new Makenna.

Actually I'd like to try out the steak house.

Eight o'clock? I'll make reservations.

The time dragged, and she was a nervous wreck by the time he met her at the hotel's private entrance and keyed her in.

Her breath caught. He was even more stunning than she remembered. His blue-gray eyes were dark, haunted, and his expression was stark. Though he was broad and strong, he looked as if he'd lost a few pounds that he didn't need to.

"*Jesus*, Makenna. I've fucking missed you." He pulled her into a small space just past the elevator and kissed her deeply, making her head spin and the ground ripple beneath her. "I was afraid this day would never come."

"I took your words to heart. I'm tired of letting my past define me."

"I'm so proud of you. But that was a fucking mess, and I'm sorry it happened."

She shook her head, and a tendril of hair curled alongside her face. "It's not your fault."

"I should have protected you better. Prepared you. Been more on guard." He raised his hands helplessly. "Something. I've kicked myself a million times, and I've slept with regret every night."

"I survived it. And learned to appreciate what I have. You said that to me at the art gallery."

"Makenna, my little innocent, I vow to always appreciate you."

They kissed again, only stepping apart when someone approached. "More later."

"Is that a promise?"

"It is."

Over a scrumptious meal, they caught up on the events of the past few weeks, and then the waiter rolled the dessert tray over. The sight of a slice of cheesecake topped with bittersweet chocolate made her mouth water.

"Have it," Zachary encouraged.

"I think I will." She nodded to the server. "With a cup of coffee."

"Very well. And for you, sir?"

"The same."

Once they'd finished dessert and were relaxing with their second cup of coffee, Zachary regarded her. "If you're amenable, I'd like you to stay the night."

She exhaled a great burst of relief. "I didn't bring a bag."

"We'll work something out. For what I have in mind, you

won't need a lot of clothes. Can you take tomorrow off work?"

"Uhm..." She bit her lower lip. "Maybe I can talk my boss into it."

Since she was her own boss, he grinned. "Good. Because you're not going to get much sleep tonight. And I want to spend time getting reacquainted."

After he'd taken care of the bill, they headed for the elevator.

Her stomach lurched as the car whisked them upward. "I'd forgotten how fast this thing is."

"And I was hoping to be the one to sweep you off your feet."

In his living room, champagne was chilling in a tall silver ice bucket.

"Miss Ellie, close the blinds."

Nothing happened.

Makenna grinned. "Please, Miss Ellie."

"Why certainly, Makenna. My pleasure."

Zachary groaned. "I'm being ganged up on."

"If you remembered your manners, you'd be fine."

His eyes darkened, and he tipped back Makenna's chin. "I have other things on my mind."

"Oh?" Desire unfurled in her stomach.

He released her. "Champagne?"

"So... That means you are not planning to scene?"

"We have our whole lives in front of us, and I assure you, my little innocent, I certainly do intend to tie you up and paddle your delectable ass tomorrow. Tonight, however, is our anniversary. I want to make it memorable."

Her heart skipped a beat. "Every moment with you is unforgettable." She yearned to be in his arms, sleeping next him, making love.

After tossing his suit coat on the back of the couch, he

walked to the ice bucket to pour them both a glass.

"My beautiful Makenna." He offered her a flute, then raised his in a toast. "To the future. To you."

"To us." She'd only taken one sip when he took the drink from her and set it down alongside his on a nearby table.

"It's been… Unendurable. Worse than any battle I ever faced." His voice was raw, rubbed with emotion. "I miss you and can't go another day without you." He captured her, biting his fingers into the tender flesh of her upper arms, holding on as if he'd never let her go. He kissed her with more power than ever before, not just asking for her surrender, but demanding it. *"Fuck,* Makenna. I love you."

"You…"

"I love you. I've been losing my mind. There's never been anyone like you. From the moment I saw you watching the Hewitts, I knew you were mine."

"It took me a little longer to accept that."

He let her go to run his hand through his hair. "I'm screwing this up."

She placed a hand on his chest, over his heart. "What?"

Then her big powerful alpha lowered himself to one knee.

"Zachary?" She couldn't breathe.

"Will you…?" He reached into his pocket and pulled out a magnificent square-cut diamond ring. It winked in the light, casting its radiance everywhere. "Makenna Helton, will you do me the honor of becoming my bride?"

Emotion swamped over her as her dreams all came true. "Oh my God." She burst into tears.

"Makenna?" He remained where he was. "Put me out of my misery? Tell me you'll marry me."

"Yes, *yes."* Tears ran down her cheeks as he took her hand in his and slid the ring into place. "A million times yes. I love you, Zachary. *I love you."*

He stood and kissed her again, but this time there was a

greater feeling to it. He tasted of promise. Of forever.

"It won't always be easy."

"We've had a glimpse of that."

"But together…? Turn to me, trust in me."

"Always." She raised on tiptoes to kiss him. "And forever."

Makenna stretched out her legs and wiggled her toes, soaking in the warmth. For long minutes, she stared, taking in the stunning blue water of the Caribbean.

Zachary had been impatient and didn't want to wait to get married. Yesterday, just a week after he'd proposed, they'd had a small ceremony at the wedding chapel that she'd toured the day her life was turned upside down.

And he'd surprised her with a trip, booking them a private suite that overlooked the water. The villa's thatched roof added an island flair, and she was in love with the enormous four-poster bed. This morning, she'd been tempted to stay there all day.

But he'd coaxed her out with coffee and breakfast. And now they were lounging near the water and beneath a luxurious cabana that shaded them from the sun.

As an added benefit, they only had to share their server with one other couple.

"Most people call this a honeymoon. I call it a babymoon."

She tipped back the brim of her hat and lowered her sunglasses to look at him. "A babymoon is when a woman is pregnant and the couple takes a vacation before their child is born, like a last-chance getaway before giving birth."

"Well, that might be the traditional definition." He sipped from the fruity drink that had been delivered in a coconut. It had all sorts of fruit on a dagger that crossed the opening, and it was adorned with a festive umbrella.

In any other man's hand, it might look ridiculous. But he was a breathtaking alpha.

"In our case, a babymoon is a trip we take for the express purpose of getting you pregnant."

"You…" Her book fell from her fingers.

He shrugged. "Or have fun trying."

"Are you serious?" Even though he was smiling, it appeared more like a king-of-the- mountain grin than actual humor.

"I am."

They'd talked about children in the abstract, but she hadn't realized that he'd meant now. Today, even.

"Any objection?"

"Uhm… A million, maybe."

"Let's hear them."

"Where will we live?"

"Anywhere you want. If you want a huge yard, we can have one. Doesn't have to be Vegas. We can go to LA or New York, even overseas." He stirred his drink.

"You've thought about this."

"My little innocent, that first night at my condo, I imagined your belly growing with my child. It was the most powerful orgasm of my life."

Her husband took her breath away.

"Next concern? In case you're worried, I'll be cutting back my travel schedule."

"Wait. What? You'll still be gone from time to time, right?"

"I'm offended." He took a long sip of the tropical-rum concoction. Then he raised a hand. "I solemnly swear I will not get in the way of your happy hours."

"Thank goodness." She leaned over and gave him a kiss. "That was my greatest worry."

"I knew it!"

"And…me working?"

"That's your call entirely. We can hire a nanny if needed. Or you can quit work if you want."

Makenna shook her head. "I love my job, and I've spent too long building the business just to walk away."

"Agreed."

"But maybe after we have a baby, I can work remotely sometimes."

"Or hire more staff."

"True." She had considered expanding, and Riley was definitely ready for more responsibility.

"Anything else?"

"That about covers it."

"Good, then we're set. You have a massage this evening. And dinner will be served at a private table for two near the ocean. And then we're going dancing."

"Really?"

"If you remember, once I had you on the dance floor at Cole and Avery's wedding, the band started playing, and I worked myself into your heart."

"That's not exactly true."

"No?"

"It was a little later." She grinned. "You had me at spearmint and eucalyptus."

His answering smile filled her soul. "So I did."

After they finished their drinks, he helped her up from her chaise longue. "How about an afternoon siesta?"

She narrowed her eyes suspiciously. "Why do I get the feeling your suggestion has nothing to do with sleep?"

"You could be right." He pulled her to him. "I love you, Makenna."

"And I love you, my protector, my lover…my Dominant."

He grabbed her rear and squeezed hard, igniting a flame. "Shall we?"

"After you, Sir."

ALL-IN

TITANS: SIN CITY, BOOK THREE

ALL-IN

SIN CITY TITANS

USA TODAY BESTSELLING AUTHOR
SIERRA CARTWRIGHT

CHAPTER ONE

"Hey, boss. You need to have a look at this."

Lorenzo Carrington stopped on his way out of the security command center and strode back to the console where Enrico, one of his most trusted deputies, was seated. "What's up, Rico?"

Dozens of monitors supplied real-time video of Lorenzo's entire Bella Rosa resort, from the casino's numerous tables, to the hotel elevators, restaurants, nightclubs, food court, workout space, spa, even the numerous pool decks.

Rico selected one of the feeds, showing Excess, the nightclub.

The area was bathed in its signature purple light, and scores of Las Vegas's trendiest and richest were crowded onto the dance floor. The most expensive DJ in town spun tunes, and frenetic energy thumped through the place.

"Right here, boss."

Lorenzo studied one of the monitors. A group of four people were being shown to their VIP table. "What am I looking at?" Or rather, *who?* After all, his team knew to inform him if certain guests entered the premises.

Rico zoomed in.

Fuck.

Even though she was faced away from him, and the long brunette sweep of her hair curtained around her in a glorious waterfall of distraction, Lorenzo knew her. His dick had cataloged her every sinful curve. Every primal instinct was on fire with the need to possess her.

Zara Davis.

What the hell was she thinking, venturing into the lethal grip of his lair? *Tempting fate?*

The rational part of his brain recognized that she was allowed to be here with anyone she wanted. He snarled. There'd never been anything rational about his reaction to the daughter of a man who was indebted to him.

After everyone was seated on the black leather couches, Zara's companion said something to her. She turned and gifted him with a smile so big and bright it would make ordinary men forget their names. And in this case, the lucky recipient was Maverick Rothschild, the spoiled son of one of America's wealthiest families. Unaccountably the fact that she was clearly dazzling the prick pissed Lorenzo the fuck off. "Shut it down."

"Sure, boss." Rico clicked a couple of buttons.

Throughout the day and evening, Lorenzo made regular sweeps through the public areas of his property—to see and be seen. Which meant there was nothing unusual about leaving the resort's security room with Mario—his ever-present deputy—following close behind him.

Mario pressed his thumb to the unobtrusive pad that served as the private elevator's call button. This particular car existed solely for Lorenzo and his crew to move through the main tower without the inconvenience of delay.

They bypassed the line of people waiting behind the

velvet ropes to enter the nightclub and made their way through the throngs of revelers.

From the day the property opened, Excess had become one of Sin City's hottest spots. In that respect, it was no wonder Zara was here. Though she was an heiress, she'd distanced herself from her father and brothers and was charting her own path as a social media influencer. Her clients paid her big money to show up and be photographed at their events. But he'd never had any interest in being one of her clients.

He wanted much, much more from her.

Though he stopped to converse with a group of regulars, Lorenzo kept his eye on the VIP section. Zara was posed on the arm of the settee, head tipped back. The light caught the burnished copper and blonde highlights in her hair, giving her an ethereal princess-like glow. The camera loved her. And maybe he did too.

He shook his head to clear it. *What the fuck?* Once again, there was nothing remotely logical about his thought process —and hadn't been from the first time he set eyes on her.

Their server arrived with a bottle of whiskey and cocktails, sliding them onto the glass-topped table.

The Rothschild spawn took her wrist and tugged her down onto the cushion next to him.

Leashing his possessive anger, Lorenzo threaded his way toward their table. No doubt she knew he'd had eyes on her since she walked through the building's main entrance. But he wanted her to know how closely he was watching.

Their other guests headed out to the dance floor, leaving her alone with Rothschild. While she reached into her purse for a tube of lipstick, fucking Rothschild tipped a powder into her drink. When she faced him again, he picked up the martini glass and offered it to her.

Fury flamed. "Move in."

Behind him, Mario cued his comms and began issuing instructions to the security staff.

Predator to prey, hands clenched at his sides, Lorenzo devoured the remaining distance. To her, he snapped, "Put down that goddamn glass." Then he yanked Rothschild to his feet.

"Lorenzo!"

His fury focused, he landed a satisfying uppercut to the little fucker's jaw, sending him reeling back onto the couch. Mario moved in closer, and another team of men arrived to block sightlines and provide their boss with the protection he needed.

When Lorenzo's vision cleared, Zara was standing there, hands on her hips, eyes blazing with regal indignation. "What the hell are you doing, Lorenzo?"

"Saving your ass."

"I'm capable of taking care of myself."

The fuck you are. "Get him out of here."

Mario hauled Rothschild to his feet again. Unsteady, he rubbed his jaw.

Lorenzo got in the man's face and smelled the putrid stench of fear. "Either walk under your own power like the man you pretend to be, or you'll be carried out of here on a gurney."

"The hell is wrong with you? I didn't do anything." A lock of hair fell forward, making him look like a petulant toddler.

"If she took even one sip, they'll never find your worthless body."

Rothschild's remaining color fled, and he might have crumpled if Mario hadn't been behind him.

"This time your daddy isn't going to be able to save you, you sorry motherfucker."

Zara grabbed Lorenzo's forearm. "Stop being a Neanderthal." Then, shaking her head, she looked at her date again. "Maverick? Are you okay?"

"He has nothing to say to you." Or wouldn't, if he was smart. Lorenzo angled his head toward Mario. "Save a piece of him for me. Move."

"Lorenzo!" She squeezed his arm tighter. "You can't do this."

"If you know what's good for you, *principessa*, keep your mouth shut."

"This is outrageous, and I will not be told what—"

"Oh yes." He leaned in closer, breathing in the life-giving scent of her, innocence mixed with feminine allure. "You will."

Without anyone being aware of what was happening, his men escorted Rothschild through an unseen exit. He'd have plenty of time to think before Lorenzo arrived to deliver the rest of his punishment.

Then he turned his full attention on Zara. "You're with me."

As she released her grip, she shook her head, her eyes spiking with hard daggers. "Who the hell do you think you are?"

"The lord and master of all I survey." He raked his gaze down her body. *Jesus fucking Christ.* Her nipples were hard, pressing against her short silver formfitting dress, which meant she didn't have a bra on. *And what about panties?*

If he didn't get her out of here in the next few seconds, he'd lose what was left of his composure. "Let's go, Zara."

"Absolutely not." She shook her head. "We came with friends, and I'm not leaving without Mav."

"You can see what's left of him tomorrow." It was a lie. After tonight, Maverick Rothschild would never look at—or talk to—her again.

"I mean it, Lorenzo."

He picked up her purse, zipped it open, then pulled out her cell phone. "What's your password?"

"Screw you."

With a slight shrug, he offered the device to one of his team. "Break in."

"Wait!"

Lorenzo regarded her.

"It's biometric."

He reached for her hand and pressed her fingertip to the scanner. Once the screen showed an array of apps, he glanced at her again. "Who are you here with?"

"Elias Henry." She gritted her teeth. "A client who is paying me big money, and the woman he's trying to impress."

"I'll ensure they enjoy their evening." He typed in a message and then dropped the device back into her purse.

The server passed by, and he stopped her. "Let Mr. Henry know his bill is comped and that there's a table available for him at the steak house at his convenience."

Zara's mouth fell open, and the sight was satisfying.

He crooked a finger toward one of the security team members. "Get these drinks analyzed, and tell Rico we're gonna need the security footage."

"Yes, sir, Mr. Carrington."

Next, Lorenzo instructed the server to bring a fresh bottle and another cocktail for Elias's date.

"Anything else, sir?"

He shook his head, and she hurried away. Patrons who'd been staring returned to their own conversations, and all the remaining security operatives returned to work. Except for Mario's unobtrusive presence, he was alone with Zara. Around them, purple light pulsed, and electronic music thumped, arousing sexual tension. "Ms. Davis, you're with me."

Zara's eyes spat fire and fury as she stood her ground. "What the hell did you say to my client?"

He admired her defiance, as useless as it was. "That you had an emergency and you hoped he'd accept your apology, in the form of a penthouse suite for the rest of the weekend."

She blinked. "But the hotel is sold out for months."

"It is." He tilted his head in acknowledgment. "Fortunately you were able to pull some strings with the owner."

Inclining his head, Mario turned his back to make the arrangements his boss required.

"Any other objections"—he leaned ever closer to her, and they breathed the same air—"Zara?"

She took a shaky step away from him, rocking back and forth on her mile-high heels. Her lack of composure set fire to a flame of pure masculine satisfaction.

"You can't…"

He raised an eyebrow in response to the helpless frustration swimming in her eyes. "I can't what?"

"Rough up Mav."

He planned to do more than that. Much, much more.

"Or make me come anywhere with you." She tilted her chin. "I'm going to call someone."

Daddy? One of her four older brothers? "I'm not open to discussion or compromise." Lorenzo crowded her space a little more. Oh so satisfyingly, she froze, a beautiful butterfly ensnared in his net. "You can come with me willingly, or I'll toss you over my shoulder." Did she have any fucking clue how much his inner alpha male wanted to goad her into taking the second option? "What will people say when they see pictures of your ass in the air?" Especially since his hand would be on it.

Color drained from her face, and she wobbled. He had a certain reputation, and she knew it. "Lorenzo—"

"Choose, principessa. And do it now."

CHAPTER TWO

TEN YEARS AGO...
Despite her age, Zara was sipping champagne as she mingled with the crowd at her father's annual Christmas party, held in their spacious home near Las Vegas's Billionaire's Row. He'd asked her to serve as his hostess, and Zara had been thrilled by the grownup honor.

Lorenzo Carrington, with his man behind him, strode through the front door uninvited and sought out one of her brothers and issued a nonnegotiable demand to see her father.

From across the room, she frowned. Her beloved and strong father paled when he turned to face the newcomer.

Even though she was young and lacked experience, something deep inside her recognized Lorenzo's ruthlessness.

Responding to the warning flares her intuition was shooting off, she excused herself from the old, boring man she'd been talking to and rushed to her father's side. "Is everything okay, Daddy?"

"I'll be back in a moment." He patted her hand, and his touch was not reassuring.

Lorenzo met her eyes, and rockets of awareness shot through her. "We haven't met."

Rather than introducing them, her father shook his head. "Please, Zara. See to our guests. I'm counting on you."

His voice was strong, but as he turned and headed down the hallway toward his study, his shoulders slumped. He seemed to have aged a dozen years.

Her two oldest brothers followed, as did Lorenzo and his man.

Before he entered her father's office, Lorenzo looked back. At his predatory glance, a chill whispered through her.

Then he severed their gazes, and the moment was over. The door closed behind them, and the *click* reached her, despite the instrumental version of *Greensleeves* that spilled from the living room speakers.

For a moment, she remained frozen in place.

Then one of her brothers beckoned her to join them near the fireplace. For ambience, the gas flames danced beneath the draping of festive greenery.

Unsettled, but determined not to show it—after all, she was Joseph Davis's daughter—she pasted on a false smile. After sliding her flute onto a nearby ornamental table, she moved deeper into the living room, resolved to be the hostess her father needed.

Time dragged. Despite her resolve, she couldn't help but dart occasional nervous glances back toward the hallway.

Sometime later, she walked through the French doors leading to her father's art gallery to join a group of people gathered there. Matching the theme of the room, a brightly lit twelve-foot Christmas tree stood in the corner, decorated in hammered tin stars, small rope lassos, and ornaments crafted to look like horses, cacti, cowboy hats and boots, even some metal spurs.

She answered a few questions about one of the artists renowned for her landscapes of the American West.

When they exited, Zara remained where she was, soaking in the peace found in momentary solitude.

A minute later, footsteps echoed off the polished marble floor, and she turned around, wearing a practiced smile as Jeffrey Berto, one of her father's clients, strolled in and closed the door behind him.

"I've been looking for you." He adjusted one of his lapels.

"Hello, Mr. Berto."

"You're all grown up, Zara. Please call me Jeffrey."

I'd rather not. He'd been coming to the house for several years, and she'd never liked the creepy way he looked at her.

He took another step, and she automatically retreated before stopping herself. "Enjoy the gallery. I need to return to my guests. If you'll excuse me…"

As she brushed past him, he grabbed her elbow, painfully preventing her escape.

"No, actually, I won't."

Appalled at his tactics—no man had ever touched her before—she glanced at his whitened knuckles before looking at his face. "Release me this instant."

"We're not done here."

"My father is expecting me."

"He's busy with the motherfucking nephew of Marco La Rosa."

Zara scowled in confusion.

"You didn't know, did you? Dear old daddy owes money to the mob."

Rather than giving him the satisfaction of a reply, she clamped her mouth shut.

"That's why I'm in here." With his free hand, he traced the outline of her pendant, a platinum heart that her father had given her mom on the day they married. It had been Zara's sixteenth birthday gift—one she cherished as a connection between her and the mother she'd never met.

Berto fisted her pendant and tugged on it even as his fingers bit deeper into her elbow.

The sonofabitch was hurting her, but she refused to show it.

"But you're going to be the Davis family savior, aren't you?" He licked his lips, and the glistening spit—garish in the flashing lights from the Christmas tree—held her horrifyingly mesmerized. "He hasn't told you."

She lifted her hand, trying to pry her jewelry from his grip so she could escape. It didn't matter if her arm was bruised for a week, but he couldn't have the only gift that came from her mother.

"You're going to be my wife." He twitched his nose; then it froze in place as he leaned in closer. "Sold to give your father the money to get the La Rosas off his back."

Frantically she shook her head. "No." Her daddy wouldn't do that to her. *Never.* "You're a filthy liar."

"And you're a spoiled child who will be taught a lesson." He grinned lecherously. "I deserve to sample the goods. A little taste to keep me going as I wait for your next birthday."

He lowered his head toward her, but instead of kissing her, he changed the angle and bit the side of her neck.

Revulsion rocked through her, and she slapped at him, barely missing his face.

He growled like a pissed-off animal. "You need to learn some manners, little bitch." Then, with a snarl, he yanked, severing the chain of her necklace.

"Give it back." Frantically she grabbed for the memento.

"It'll be your wedding present." He shook her. "Providing you behave." He dropped his prize into his pants pocket.

He grinned lecherously. His cock was swollen and pressed out the front of his trousers, repulsing her. "Go ahead, Zara. Slide your hand right inside." His voice was low and taunting. "You can keep it if you can get it out."

"*Fuck you.*" Fury consumed her, and she reached for the tree, grabbing blindly for anything she could use as a weapon.

He shook her hard again, and she brought forward her arm, slamming it into the side of his face and dragging it down, gouging him with the spikes of a metal spur.

"Ungrateful little bitch!" Leaning forward, spittle staining the side of his mouth, he yanked her dress strap down. The material tore, and her breast spilled free.

Humiliation swirling with anger, she slammed her stiletto heel on his foot.

His eyes narrowed as he slapped her across the face. The room exploded into a million shards. Her ears rang, drowning out any other sound.

And then he was yanked away from her. As she blinked, Lorenzo smashed his fist into Berto's face, leaving him in a crumpled heap on the marble floor.

Lorenzo curled his fist at his side before flexing his fingers a couple of times. "Principessa." He bowed. "At your service." He gathered the jagged edge of her dress and lifted it to cover her, his touch unbelievably gentle for a man so big and powerful.

When he lowered his hand, she reached for the spot he'd covered. "I…" She gulped. "Thank you."

"Let's get you out of here."

Berto stirred, and Lorenzo's man placed his polished shoe on the attacker's back to ensure he stayed down.

Never in her life had she experienced anything like this violence. Her father adored her, as did most of her brothers. The two closest in age resented that her birth caused their mother's death, but even they treated her with the respect their father demanded.

A passerby peered into the gallery. With a gasp, the woman hurried away.

Lorenzo shrugged off his suit coat and draped it over Zara's shoulders. The garment smelled of him, spice and power, protection and risk.

Moments later, two of her brothers strode in, followed by her father.

"Daddy!" Her heart thundering, seeking safe harbor, Zara hurried to him. Shockingly he ignored her, leaving her standing there, shaking, disheveled, more lost than she ever remembered being.

"What's the meaning of this, Carrington?" His voice dripped venom.

"This piece of shit—" He lifted his chin in Berto's direction. "Assaulted your daughter."

When the man groaned, then tried to push himself upright, Lorenzo's man exerted even more pressure.

"Get him off me!" Berto's pathetic plea was followed by a cough.

Lorenzo flicked his gaze to her. Compassion, along with something she couldn't name, flared in his eyes. Just as quickly, it vanished, and he severed their connection to level a cold stare at her father. "Your office, Davis. Two minutes." After crooking a finger in the direction of his deputy, Lorenzo used the toe of his shoe to turn over Berto's body. Then he crouched to fist the man's tie and lift his upper body from the ground. "You get within one hundred feet of Ms. Davis again, I'll slit your fucking throat. Am I clear?"

Berto's eyes widened, and sweat poured down his face. When Lorenzo pulled the man up farther, he frantically nodded.

Lorenzo abruptly released Berto, and he slammed back to the floor.

As he stood, Lorenzo adjusted one of his cuffs.

ALL-IN

The room thundered with tension.

Lorenzo stepped over Berto's inert body and crossed to her. "Ms. Davis." His voice was gentle, lacking the awful threat it had contained when he addressed her attacker. "Allow me."

With equal measures of power and command, he inserted his body between her and her father and turned her away from the scene to draw her out of the gallery. Shortening his stride to match hers, he led her toward the bottom of the stairs. "I'm sorry you were treated that way."

But he never apologized for his actions or threats. "What do you want to talk to my father about?"

Rather than answer, he changed the topic entirely. "I'm sure you need a moment to compose yourself."

Since she didn't know what to say next, she settled for nodding. He was an enigma who'd changed her world.

Her mind swimming, she climbed the stairs. At the top, she paused to glance over her shoulder. He was standing there, looking up, following her every move.

Disturbed on so many levels—from Berto's unexpected attack to her ridiculous reaction to the stranger—she continued to her bedroom and closed the door. She leaned against it, trying to put the last bizarre few minutes into perspective.

Jarringly the party continued. Faint strands from a jazz version of *Have Yourself a Merry Little Christmas* floated on the air, mixed with laughter and tinkling glasses.

Outside a car engine roared to life, and tires spun on concrete. *Berto leaving?*

Driven by curiosity and an insatiable urge to see Lorenzo again, she dropped his jacket onto the edge of her bed.

In the mirror, she studied herself. Long strands of hair had escaped the elegant chignon her stylist had spent an hour on.

Just then the torn piece of her dress slid down, exposing a light purple bruise just above her breast.

Anger spurring her on, she yanked off the gown and discarded it in the trashcan before changing into a black dress with cap sleeves.

After applying a fresh coat of red lipstick, she touched up her mascara, then pulled the pins out of her hair, allowing the locks to spill over her shoulders and down her back.

Zara picked up Lorenzo's jacket and draped it over her arm. The spicy scent of him clung to the fabric, enveloping her with reassurance.

With her shoulders squared, she descended the staircase. She entered the living room and caught a glimpse of him outside, on the patio, looking out at the swimming pool.

A polite smile in place, she joined him, placing his jacket on the railing next to him.

He turned his gaze to her.

"I wanted to thank you."

"Women are to be treasured and honored."

Is that how you see me?

"Are you all right?"

Am I? "I will be." After all, as she'd heard her entire life, she was Franklin Davis's daughter. "Did you mean it back there?"

He quirked one of his stark, formidable eyebrows.

"When you said..." His words had been crude, making her falter. "About killing him?"

"Every word."

Morbidly fascinated, she turned her back to the railing, hoping she could more easily read his expression. And then she realized that wasn't possible. His eyes were opaque, his expression inscrutable. No doubt he revealed only what he chose. "Who are you, Lorenzo...?"

"Carrington." He shrugged. "I'm a businessman."

"Or superhero."

A small smile danced at the corner of his lips.

"Rescuer? Savior, perhaps? Defender of honor?"

"Not everyone's."

That now familiar glint of intensity was back in his eyes, the same one she'd witnessed in the gallery. She was too inexperienced to define it, yet on a deeply feminine level, she recognized the primal power he held over her.

"You should avoid dangerous men, Ms. Davis."

"Does that include you?"

"Especially me." He stroked her cheek, igniting heat deep inside her. "No doubt your survival instincts are warning you to stay away. Heed them."

He asked the impossible.

"Boss?"

Lorenzo glanced over his shoulder. "I'll be right with you."

"So this is goodbye?" she asked.

Before answering, he hesitated. "For now."

Lorenzo shrugged into his jacket. The expensive tailored fabric hugged his massive shoulders and fit perfectly against his trim waist.

"Before I forget." He reached into his pocket and pulled out her necklace. Then he fastened his suit coat button before striding away without another word, leaving her clutching the pendant in her palm, bereft, forever changed.

PRESENT DAY

Zara tipped back her head to meet Lorenzo's chilling, calculating gray eyes. They were narrowed with purposeful intent, and his jaw was set in a formidable line, leaving no doubt he meant everything he said. The man wasn't just dangerous; he was terrifying. Just like the first time she'd met —and fallen for him—ten years prior.

A lack of oxygen burned her lungs.

Even though it had been years since they interacted, she'd never forgotten the cold blackness in his eyes when he'd knocked Berto to the ground. And that same dangerous expression lurked in their depths now. "Look, Lorenzo—"

"I'm offering you a choice, and you're almost out of time. Walk under your own power, or I'll toss you over my shoulder." His words were clipped and carefully enunciated.

If she didn't yield, the bastard would make good on his threat. He wouldn't give a flying fuck about the humiliation he inflicted. Such things were beneath him.

She shot a quick glance toward his man, the same one who'd been his silent companion the night they'd met. Behind his dark glasses, his expression was unreadable, but he folded his arms, proving she'd find no sympathy there.

"You're out of time." Without waiting, Lorenzo moved to strike.

Pulse galloping, with music clashing and lights pulsing around them, she held up a hand. "Wait!"

Bare inches from her, he stopped.

"I'll walk."

He gave a brief nod. "I thought you might."

Possessively he rested his fingertips against the small of her back. A security guard walked in front of them to create a path through the crowd, while his loyal deputy fell in behind them. With inexorable force, Lorenzo moved her through the nightclub to a rear exit that she'd never noticed.

They left the noise and disorienting light behind them, emerging into a wide-open area where staff hurried about.

Next to an elevator, the deputy placed his thumb on a pad, and the doors immediately parted.

"For your personal use only?"

He nodded.

Of course.

Lorenzo nudged her into the compartment. *Am I stupid for going?* But what choice had he given her?

The security guard nodded, then vanished as Lorenzo's deputy stepped in and pressed a button marked OS. *Owner's Suite?*

She was forced to bend her knees for stability as the car rocketed up.

Lorenzo's gaze was focused forward, and his man's back was to them.

In the years since Lorenzo had blazed into her life with a storm of fury, she'd studied him.

The accusation Jeffrey Berto had leveled all those years ago was true—Lorenzo Carrington was the nephew of a Mafia don, and reportedly, they were close. Still, she hadn't found any reports that proved Lorenzo himself was an actual mobster. After the way he'd calmly threatened Jeffrey, she wouldn't have been surprised.

He was rumored to be a Titan, a member of the Zetas, a secret society filled with billionaires, scientists, creatives, world leaders, even criminals. Since nothing existed tying him to any wrongdoing, the rumor and speculation could be fantastical stories concocted about one of Las Vegas's most renowned casino owners. The fact that he was blessed with Latin-lover good looks made him a target of endless media speculation. And hers too, if she was honest with herself.

The elevator whooshed to a stop so fast that she was left dizzy. "You don't like to waste time, do you?"

"Every minute is precious."

She expected the car to open directly into his living space, but it didn't. Instead, there was another layer of security between him and the world.

A set of double doors was emblazoned with a crest of

sorts. Lorenzo crossed the space to stand in front of a scanner that unlocked the entrance.

His man turned his back to stand sentry as they entered his suite.

Suite was an absurd understatement.

The entrance was enormous, with a spiral staircase leading to a second level. Massive windows offered breathtaking city views, and she couldn't help her reaction. "This is spectacular."

"I'm glad you're pleased. You're welcome to leave your purse on the table."

Facing him, she angled her chin. "I won't be staying."

His slight smile was set somewhere between smug and resolute. "On the contrary. You'll be my guest until I say otherwise."

She darted around him and lunged for the door. Surprising her, he didn't try to stop her.

Zara turned the knob, but nothing happened.

"You might as well enjoy my hospitality."

Eyes narrowed, she swung back to face him. "You've gone too far. This whole thing is outrageous." Why had she expected anything else? This man got what he wanted, when he wanted. "I demand you let me go."

"Or?"

She snatched her phone from her pocketbook to call... *Who?*

No one would get past his security. Except, maybe, the police. And she definitely didn't want to involve them.

He keyed a mic she hadn't noticed he'd been wearing. "Send the video to my office." Then he lowered his hand, and the two emeralds in his ring winked in the overhead light. Looking at her, he added, "I think you'll want to see this. Then make your decision."

If she were in real danger, she'd consider calling for help.

But experience had taught her that he might be ruthless, but he was also trustworthy. This situation, no matter how annoying, was an inconvenience, nothing more.

Equal parts curious and reluctant, she put her cell phone back, then placed her purse on the table and followed him.

"Would you like a tour?"

"As I said, I won't be here long enough for it to be necessary."

She soon learned his question had been rhetorical.

No doubt his home would be featured in an architectural magazine, if it hadn't already been. While it could have been considered stark because of the size and sparsity of the furnishings, personal touches were everywhere. He was reading a biography, judging by the hardback lying on the couch, a business card stuck in it as a bookmark. Photos, in mismatched frames, adorned the mantelpiece. And a vase filled with enormous pink roses dominated the coffee table.

She followed him through to the kitchen. With its marble countertops and high-end appliances, it was a chef's delight. Since he lived in a resort recognized for its cuisine, and he employed one of the largest catering staffs in the city, she was surprised by the massive space. "Do you cook?"

"Yes."

She gawked. "Seriously?"

"My mother made sure I knew how. Every breakfast, and dinner on Sunday. I have my most trusted people with me. It's a tradition."

"Does that include your shadow?"

"Mario?"

"Is that his name? The one standing outside?" The same man who'd backed Lorenzo at her father's Christmas party.

"Yes. He's invaluable to me."

"A…"

Folding his arms, he waited.

"Lieutenant?"

A grin toyed with his mouth. "What do you think you know of my world, principessa?"

Nothing. Except it alternately terrified and fascinated her. "I've done some reading."

"Gossip." He waved a dismissive hand, his ring once again capturing the light. "Nothing more."

"So you're not a Titan?"

Although he angled his head to one side, he didn't respond.

"And you're not Marco La Rosa's nephew?"

"I'm guessing you already know the answer. My mother is his sister, yes."

His clipped response didn't invite further questions, but she couldn't help herself. "You're close to him?"

"Against my mother's wishes, yes."

"Isn't he…?" She trailed off. In person, calling his uncle a Mafia don seemed preposterous. And yet conjecture swirled around the family and had for years—generations, even.

"A successful businessman? Owner of a casino? Investor in my resort? Yes."

The La Rosa patriarch had never granted an interview, and though charges had been brought against him, he'd never been found guilty. Evidence against him had an interesting way of disappearing, and informants never showed up in court. "You're going to admit to nothing?"

"Opening the Bella Rosa has kept me too busy to read scandal rags." He turned up a corner of his lip. In judgment of her?

"I haven't—"

"Clearly you have."

Before she could open her mouth again, he turned his back on her and walked past the fully stocked bar.

With a sigh, annoyed with herself for sounding

accusatory—and equally frustrated that he'd dismissed her questions—she followed him through a frosted glass door. She missed a step when she entered his version of a wonderland.

The area was gigantic, a glass-covered playground. He had a large swimming pool, complete with a swim-up bar. Around it was a grassy area and running track, along with a high-tech workout system attached to the wall. Numerous tables with umbrellas were scattered about, alongside lounge chairs. Potted palms stood sentry in the corners. In keeping with the resort's theme, he also had dozens of pink rose bushes.

She struggled to take it in. Fairy lights were strung everywhere, and their reflection danced off the water, creating a fanciful air. She imagined herself spending a relaxing afternoon here. "It's…magnificent."

"The roof retracts in case you want fresh air."

Why am I not surprised?

Rather than turning back to the exit, he continued along the length of the pool deck, pointing out where towels and accessories were stored.

Her favorite was the inflatable floating flamingo, complete with cupholder.

She'd grown up around a fair amount of wealth, but she never imagined anything like this existed.

At the far end of his private playground was a spa. "And my workout room."

But he didn't mention anything about the final door, so she assumed it was for pool operations. "This"—she swept her hand around—"it's ridiculous. You know that."

"I spend a lot of time here. And I like to entertain."

"Women?" *Jesus. Where did that come from?* She wasn't jealous—had no reason to be.

"Once again, principessa, you know nothing about me."

He closed the distance between them and captured her shoulders in his powerful grip. While he could have easily hurt her, he didn't. Like the first time they'd met, his touch offered both promise and reassurance.

And that completely unsettled her.

He took in a breath, deep, as if memorizing her. "If you only knew…"

Tell me.

Holding her gaze, he leaned toward her. For a terrifying moment that made the world tilt on its axis, she thought he might kiss her. She wanted it. Wanted *him.*

Then he released her, ending the moment. In frustration, she sighed, though she should have been drinking in relief. He might fulfil her fantasies, but he wasn't the type of man who would ever offer her a future.

Gossip sites were filled with rumors of the women he dated, and over the years, he'd left a long trail of broken hearts behind him. At some point, she needed to separate her hero worship from the very real, complicated man in front of her.

After he released her, the furrow between his eyebrows vanished. It seemed he'd harnessed his emotions, but his unfinished sentence charged the air between them.

Without a word, he pivoted, then led her back to the main part of the home and his office that was protected by more biometrics.

A bank of monitors hung from the wall. The feeds featured various parts of the resort and casino floor. He ignored the chair in favor of standing as he moved his fingers over the nearby keyboard, so quickly she couldn't have memorized his security passcode if she'd tried.

The picture on one of the screens changed, displaying an image of the nightclub. For several seconds, it showed her and her group arriving at their table and getting settled. In the next segment, the server arrived. Then the camera zoomed in on Zara. "You were watching me?"

He looked over his shoulder, seared her with the intensity in his arresting green eyes. "I would have expected you would know that."

I'd hoped. Zara shivered. For the past decade, he'd starred in her dreams, and she'd compared every man to him. Maybe unsurprisingly, she'd found them lacking.

As part of her job, she frequented the Bella Rosa's martini bar. Most often, a pair of security guards intentionally passed her table, acknowledging her by name as they did so. All that had made her wonder if Lorenzo ever saw her for who she was. Or was she still just someone who needed rescuing?

By the time she found her voice, he'd returned his attention to the task in front of him, fast forwarding to the moment their server had slid beverages onto the table.

While she'd been at the nightclub, nothing had seemed odd. She'd laughed with her client, ensuring he was enjoying his evening. But now, with the thumping music filtered out and watching through the dispassionate lens of a camera, Zara noted the determined gleam in Maverick's eyes when he'd grabbed her wrist and possessively pulled her down onto the couch beside him.

The next few minutes passed normally as their foursome clinked the rims of their glasses together.

Impatience gnawed at her as nothing happened. "I think you overreacted, Lorenzo."

His face was set in impassive lines, and he ignored her sigh.

After saying they were going to dance, her client and the woman he was trying to impress stood and walked away, leaving Zara and Maverick alone. She took the opportunity to grab her favorite lipstick from her bag and used the mirror on the end of the tube to swipe on a layer of the new Kiss Me red color.

Since she was concentrating on what she was doing, she hadn't realized what happened next.

Maverick turned away slightly, reached into his jacket pocket, pulled out a vial, and then dumped the contents into her martini.

She blinked, unable to fathom what she was seeing.

Lorenzo froze the frame and turned toward her.

Her stomach roiling, she protectively wrapped her arms around her middle.

With another strike of a key, the video continued. Maverick picked up her drink and offered it to her.

"Oh my God." The horror splintered her mind.

Lorenzo killed the feed, and the monitor went blank, but the image was burned into her memory.

"We're having it analyzed."

"He..." The world spun, and Lorenzo was there immediately, pulling back the chair and helping her into it. Maverick—a man she considered a friend—had tried to drug her. *Would he have raped me?*

Cold sweat chased down her spine.

Lorenzo curled a reassuring hand around her shoulder.

Once again—as always—he was her savior. She gripped the edge of his desk as she drew several breaths to steady herself. After Berto's attack when she was seventeen, she'd taken self-defense classes, vowing no man would ever manhandle her that way ever again.

But this...? She preferred to hang out with a group of friends rather than actually dating. When she did spend time with the opposite sex, she enjoyed scening with Dominants at a club or play party, where the rules were agreed to and she consented to everything that happened. On the rare occasions she had dinner with someone, she selected true gentlemen who wouldn't push for sex. All of that had left her completely unprepared for something like she'd just witnessed.

Lorenzo reached past her to continue so they could watch the next couple of minutes.

Of course, he'd arrived before she'd taken a sip of the tainted beverage.

"You're safe here, principessa."

Despite his reassurance, the realization of how close she'd come to danger shook her, and her body was now chilled. She'd promised herself she'd never be vulnerable to a predator again, and if it hadn't been for Lorenzo, the evening's outcome could have been unthinkable.

"You'll be staying here while I deal with the situation."

"I'd rather go home."

"That's not an option."

Once again—or, as always—he was dictatorial. Her automatic instinct was to rail against his high-handedness and insist on her independence.

When he spoke again, his voice was softer. Unsurprisingly, however, steel was hammered beneath it. "You've had a shock."

"Look, Lorenzo..." She straightened her spine. "You can't keep me here as your prisoner."

"I assure you, Ms. Davis, I can. And I will."

Despite her protests, he was right. The evening's events had unnerved her. "What are you planning to do to Maverick?"

"I have a zero-tolerance policy for that type of behavior at my resort." Gently he turned her to face him, and he leaned forward to place his hands on the arms of the chair, bringing them oh so close together. "Even less when it comes to you."

"Thank you." Her gratitude was a little late. But the evening's events had sent her mind a thousand different directions. "For everything." Not just taking care of her, but ensuring her clients had a nice evening, something Maverick had tried to sabotage.

"Make yourself at home. There's food in the refrigerator, or you're welcome to order room service." He gave a sharp nod. "There will be a security guard outside the door. If you'll excuse me."

With that, he exited, leaving her trapped in his gilded cage.

CHAPTER THREE

The minutes crawled by, turning into hours, and frustration warred with temper. Finally, around midnight, she strode to his bar area, opened the wine fridge, and pulled out a very nice bottle of champagne. The first delicious glass in hand, she accepted his offer to make herself at home.

She wandered to the pool area where she crouched to trail her fingertips through the water. It was warmer than she imagined, and wonderfully inviting. *Should I?* Since she may never again have the opportunity to enjoy this experience, she succumbed to the temptation—she stripped, then made herself comfortable in the flamingo inflatable. With a smile, she floated around and sipped from her flute of bubbles. If she was going to be his prisoner, she might as well make the most of it.

She must have spent an hour with her head tipped back, looking out through the glass roof as clouds sauntered across the sky. At times, stars vanished, only to reemerge, a twinkling promise for the future.

No matter how hard she tried to shove away thoughts of Lorenzo, she failed.

When her client hired her, she'd immediately suggested they spend the evening at Excess. As the city's hottest nightclub, it was the place to be seen. But there'd been more to it. In the back of her mind, she'd hoped that Lorenzo would seek her out.

But nothing had turned out the way she planned. Maverick's awful behavior was a betrayal of the worst kind. At this point, she didn't care what happened to him, as long as he never bothered her again. If her guess was correct, Lorenzo would make sure of it, just like he had with Jeffrey at the Christmas party all those years ago. Numerous times, she'd asked her father what had happened that night. He always said it wasn't worth discussing.

In the distance, a grandfather clock chimed three times.

What kind of hours did Lorenzo keep?

Zara made her way to the pool's steps, then sought out a towel and wrapped herself in it before picking up her clothes and climbing the spiral staircase to the home's second level. Only one door was open, and a soft light beckoned to her.

From the way it seared her senses, this had to be Lorenzo's room. The massive bed, with a black duvet cover offset by numerous white pillows, was the focal point. The nightstands were made from glass and chrome. A fabulous wingback chair with matching ottoman was angled beneath a reading lamp. Not surprising her, a hardback book—this one a history of Las Vegas—sat on the seat cushion.

Slowly, the tile cool beneath her feet, Zara walked deeper into the space. Lorenzo's masculine scent hung in the air, intoxicating her. No man had ever possessed the power to unsettle her as he did.

And yet she instinctively trusted him and sought his strength.

Knowing she was trespassing but rationalizing that he had to have expected that when he locked her up and didn't return, she made her way to the spa-like bathroom.

It was every bit as spectacular as she'd expected with the soaker tub in front of a massive window. From here she was on top of the world. And since there were no other buildings nearby, she had complete privacy, even with the shades open.

Wanting to wash off the chlorine from the pool, she stepped into his steam shower and adjusted the knobs until she figured out how it worked. The water and warmth soothed her nerves as well as her body.

Though she didn't use it, she picked up his soap. Gray lines swirled through the bar, and the spicy, citrusy scent of bergamot hit her.

She inhaled deeply, then imagined him working the bar into a lather before rubbing the creaminess over his fit, naked body. Her hand trembled, and she instantly placed the soap back where it belonged.

After her shower, she reached for a big fluffy white towel that was big enough to wrap around her body more than once. Since she had no extra clothes with her, she padded to his closet. The space was larger than her bedroom at home, and fastidiously organized. Dozens of pairs of polished shoes were placed next to each other with military precision.

His suits were organized by color. Drawers contained ties in individual little compartments, also arranged by color. Along one wall was exercise gear, with athletic sneakers placed beneath. He also had numerous bathrobes, some terrycloth, others a black, sexy silk.

Unless she was missing something, he had few casual clothes. Did that mean he spent most of his time overseeing his empire?

She pulled a snowy-white dress shirt from a hanger and wiggled into it. The sleeves were ridiculously long. As she rolled up the cuffs, she noticed they were embroidered with his initials.

Now that she was warm and safe, exhaustion hit her. It wasn't just the lateness or the champagne and shower, but also the events of the evening. Her body demanded sleep.

In the distance, the clock marked the passing of another hour.

Since she didn't intend to sleep on a couch, she pulled back the covers on his bed and crawled between his crisp sheets.

And now, with the first rays of sun filtering through the window, Zara blinked, trying to orient herself.

When she opened her eyes all the way, reality pressed down on her.

Dragging the covers with her, she sat up in his bed, then stifled a gasp.

Her jailer was back, sitting in the chair, feet propped on the ottoman. While he was still dressed, he'd discarded his jacket, loosened his tie, and unfastened his top few buttons.

With an untamed lock of dark hair falling across his forehead, he was overwhelmingly handsome. But as he slept, his defenses had dropped a little—she wasn't stupid enough to think they'd disappeared entirely—making him less formidable.

As if sensing her scrutiny, he lifted his head to meet her gaze.

His eyes were dark with smoky intent. "Principessa." He wrapped the word in a husky purr.

She drew a frantic breath, unsure of what to say to the man whose bed she occupied.

"I trust you had an enjoyable night?"

"No."

He raised an eyebrow. *In disbelief? Or just in question?*

"I don't like being held against my will while other people take action in my life."

"The thousand-dollar bottle of champagne didn't help?"

She winced. Had it really cost that much?

"Or a shower?"

Belatedly she remembered the clothing she'd left in his bathroom.

"Or my bed?"

She shrugged off his question. "You told me to make myself comfortable."

He tipped his head to one side in silent agreement.

"What happened last night? With Maverick?"

"He's currently a guest of the city."

"Jail?" She gaped.

"As I said, I don't tolerate bad behavior in my house."

"You called the police on him?"

"Most assuredly."

She narrowed her gaze. "And what else happened?"

"We had a…fruitful conversation about how to treat ladies."

"And what was the nature of your *conversation?*"

"Nothing extraordinary." Lorenzo dropped his feet to the floor, then stood. "I'll drive you home when you're ready."

"No need. I have a driver on call, and he's always—"

"It wasn't a suggestion."

She momentarily pressed her hands against her face. This arrogant specimen of masculinity frustrated her at every turn. "Look. Lorenzo. I appreciate what you've done, but I can take care of myself from here."

With a few fast strides, he was at the bedside, and she scooted against the headboard, instinctively retreating.

"Principessa, you're my obligation."

"No." She shook her head. "I'm not."

He leaned toward her. "You are—have been for ten years."

They breathed the same air, and in the closeness, she was captivated by the purposeful intent in his gaze.

Her heartbeat reverberated in her ears.

"You feel it."

Frantically she shook her head, lying to them both. Her reaction to him—screaming, visceral need—terrified her. If she gave in, she'd be lost in him, maybe forever.

He closed in, just a fraction of an inch more.

Zara was powerless, and her body betrayed her with the truth. "Yes." Unable to help herself, she reached toward him, placing two fingers on his jawline.

"Be careful." The warning was harsh. "You have no idea what you're getting into."

"Maybe I do."

With a rough laugh, he shook his head. "I have certain tastes."

She'd heard whispers that he occasionally attended BDSM play parties at the sprawling, impressive home of the city's legal eagles, Diana and Alcott Hewitt. But she doubted he realized that she visited as well. "I know."

His slight laugh was rough. "My demands may terrify you."

His air of danger drew her. She could escape his web, but she no longer wanted to. "They won't." He couldn't know that she'd never found anyone who intrigued her the way he did.

Lorenzo didn't kiss her. Instead, he claimed her, capturing her lips with his.

He tasted of danger and promise, and he plundered her mouth.

This wasn't a polite dance of seduction—it was the explosion of a pent-up demand, bending her to his indomitable will.

He curled his fingers into her shoulders. With inexorable

force, he drew her onto her knees, and she was helpless to resist. She wrapped her arms around his neck and offered herself to him. Like a greedy man, he accepted, consuming her.

When her lips were bruised and her body shook from the intensity of his domination, he tore his lips from hers. *"Fuck."*

Still kneeling, she touched her swollen mouth.

"You need to get dressed before I throw you beneath me, tie you up, and take what I want." With a last hard look, his eyes feral, he crossed the room, distancing himself from her.

"Lorenzo…" How did she admit she wanted that?

He left, slamming the door behind him.

When she managed to draw a breath, Zara changed positions, sitting with her knees to her chest. Had he meant that? That he was as hungry for her as she was for him? If so, why had he walked away? *Your misplaced sense of obligation?*

God, the man was confounding.

He'd given them both some space, and no doubt it was in her best interest to get out of here.

Her clothes weren't in the bathroom. Instead, they were in his closet. He'd hung her dress next to his suits. Her shoes were tucked alongside his. Heat chased across her cheeks when she noticed her panties were draped over the hamper.

In the light of day, the sight scandalized her.

He'd taken care of the items she'd discarded, and the fact that he'd handled her lingerie scandalized her.

Hurriedly, she removed his shirt, then pulled on her dress, wishing it were several inches longer. As for her underwear, she would place them in her purse.

With her hand on the banister for stability, she descended the stairs to the foyer. She tucked away her panties, kicked off her shoes and left them beneath the hall table, then wandered barefoot to the kitchen where she found him.

The coffeemaker hissed and spluttered as it finished its brew cycle.

Though she hadn't made a sound, he turned to face her.

Lorenzo, relaxed in his environment, disarmed her. His sleeves were rolled up, exposing his forearms. And he now stood mere inches away from her. His top few buttons were still open, and she noticed the alluring smattering of hair on his chest. His ultramasculinity appealed to all her feminine instincts.

Pretending this was an ordinary experience, she smiled. "Is there enough to share?"

"The coffee? It's all for you."

She frowned. "You don't consume caffeine?" *Are you superhuman?*

"I prefer a protein smoothie before my workout." He poured her a cup, then mentioned that various creamers were in the refrigerator.

"That surprises me."

"I keep them for my crew."

"You're a thoughtful host."

He quirked his lips. "That's a step up from prison guard, I suppose."

As far as being held against her will, maybe it hadn't been too bad. The thousand-dollar bottle of bubbles had certainly helped.

She added a splash of cream to her beverage while she watched him scoop a green powder into a blender. He followed it with almond milk, some beets, kale, and aloe juice. When he was done pulsing the thing into oblivion, it was as thin as water and smelled completely unappetizing. "You're really going to drink that?"

"Every day."

After pouring the concoction into a glass, he downed it in three swallows.

It might help keep him trim and focused, but for her, it would be much too high a price to pay.

"Would you like me to make you something to eat?"

She shuddered. "Not if anything like that is on the menu."

"Eggs and bacon? Pancakes?"

"Seriously?"

"I like to take care of people. And that means fulfilling their every need."

The cup halfway to her mouth, Zara froze. Then telling herself she was reading too much into his words, she returned to his question. "I usually skip breakfast and grab something on my way to the office." A bagel maybe. At times, a donut or croissant. Chocolate, at any rate.

He nodded. "Give me five minutes to change."

While she crossed into the living room to finish her coffee near the window, he jogged up the stairs.

The past twelve hours had been surreal, and it was impossible to believe she'd slept in Lorenzo Carrington's bed. And how she wished it had been under different circumstances.

She shook her head to clear it as he descended toward her.

Lorenzo in a suit was breathtaking. But in a long-sleeved form-hugging dove-gray shirt and high-tech black shorts, he was devastating. His upper body was exquisite, from his broad shoulders and massive chest to his honed biceps. His leg muscles were chiseled, no doubt from weight training as much as cardio.

Even though she cleared her throat, she couldn't find her voice.

"Ready?"

Now that it was a new day, and he'd kissed her senseless, he wanted her to return to her normal life? *Fine by me.*

Setting her chin, she followed him to the foyer, where she snagged her purse.

He opened the door, and as always, Mario was on duty. Did no one ever rest?

Together with Lorenzo's ever-present companion, they entered the waiting elevator and were whisked to a level where a sleek yellow sports car waited.

"What?" She blinked. "No limo?"

"There are times I prefer to drive myself."

But as he accelerated onto the empty street, a glance in the mirror showed another vehicle trailing them.

What kind of world do you live in? The speculation he'd dismissed earlier now seemed more believable to her.

"You still live with your father?"

Zara nodded. Maybe she should have moved out, but she didn't see the point. The house was massive, and now that most of her brothers had left, she had a wing to herself. Her grandmother had willed her a generous inheritance, and Zara had used it to get her start in business. She wanted to be judicious with her funds, and honestly, even though her father was imperfect, she loved him.

During the short drive, Lorenzo made conversation, asking about her job.

"I didn't want to go into the family business, and I found some success with being a social media influencer." She shifted uncomfortably on the luxurious leather seat.

"A lot of success."

She turned slightly toward him, looking for hints of sarcasm, but found none. "It's not something everyone understands."

"They don't have to. You get people the coverage they want and access into the places they want to be. You have over two million followers, if I remember correctly?"

"You've researched me?"

"You're not the only one who does some reading in their spare time."

"Touché."

After a quick grin, he went on. "With those kinds of numbers, you'll get the attention of numerous places and brands, and that creates its own opportunities."

His knowledge of her job exceeded that of anyone she'd ever talked to. She received plenty of support from her friends Makenna and Avery, whom she'd met through a Women in Business group, but even then, she'd had to explain—in detail—what she did and how she made her money.

"You're evidently working with a major cosmetic manufacturer on your own line of makeup?"

"That was supposed to be a secret."

"I have excellent sources."

"So you did more than a cursory internet search?" She didn't expect an answer. And he didn't provide one. But it made her wonder how much he did know about her.

"Venues around town no doubt pay you nice sums to host parties and post photos."

In her case, a picture wasn't just worth a thousand words—it could generate a thousand, or more, dollars. "Is the Bella Rosa interested in contracting me?"

"I'll put you in touch with my marketing team."

His offer was casual, making her wonder if he meant it. "You've received plenty of free publicity from me already."

"We appreciate it."

"You've noticed?"

"Every post. Every mention. Every one of your visits."

Despite the early-morning warmth, she shivered. He *had* been watching her—which was no doubt how he'd managed to snatch away her martini before she took a drink. Still, his team was always likely on the lookout for that kind of behavior. He definitely didn't want his resort to earn a reputation as a place where women's drinks were spiked with date-rape drugs.

When they reached her father's home, he rounded the car to open her door, then walked her up the path to the porch. *Old-world manners*. Which made him even more appealing.

Once there, she hesitated. Unsure what to say, she settled for thanking him.

"I will always keep you safe." He tucked a strand of her hair behind her ear. "Have dinner with me tonight?"

She wanted nothing more "I have to work."

"Afterward, then."

"I..."

With his thumb, he lifted her chin, then once again staked his claim on her mouth. She was his, and his hot, plundering possession erased any doubt.

"I look forward to seeing you." With the pad of his thumb, he traced her lips that were now more bruised than ever.

Zara watched him leave.

If she accepted his offer, her life would change forever. Did she have the courage to get involved with a man potentially associated with the Mafia? What scared her most was the terrible realization that she might not have the conviction to stay away.

CHAPTER FOUR

During the afternoon, Zara's cell phone rang, and the display showed the name of her friend Makenna. Even though she was in the middle of composing her social media posts for the rest of the week, Zara answered the call.

Makenna skipped her normal greeting and dived straight in. "Is everything okay?"

She blinked. "Why wouldn't it be?"

"I just saw breaking news on *Scandalicious*."

Breath rushed out of Zara's lungs, and her heart raced. The respected paparazzi site was known for reporting the juiciest gossip before any other outlet. Before she could ask what her friend was talking about, Makenna supplied the missing information.

"It was about Maverick. He looks like he went a few rounds in a cage match."

She struggled to find her voice.

"You went out with him last night, right?"

"Yes."

"You didn't know?" Makenna exhaled. "So you weren't together when he got in the fight? I was worried."

"I..." It was too complicated to explain in a quick phone call. "We went our separate ways early."

"You'll give me all the details later?"

Since she already had a date scheduled with Makenna and Avery that afternoon at the Royal Sterling teahouse, she made the promise—not that she'd ever be able to escape Makenna's interrogation. "Swear."

"I'm glad you're okay."

So was she—more than anyone realized.

After she put down her phone, Zara opened the *Scandalicious* site and scrolled to the article with a click-baity title. BAD HEIR DAY.

A large grainy picture showed Maverick entering his car. A second shot zoomed in on his face. She gasped at the black eye he sported. His jaw was swollen, and there was an open cut on his upper lip.

The breath she was holding burned her lungs.

She hadn't known how Lorenzo would deal with the predator, but she shouldn't have been surprised. He was complicated in many ways. She'd seen firsthand the way he'd dealt with Jeffrey. Yet with her, he'd shown extraordinary tenderness. More than once, he could have taken advantage of her, but he never had.

His complexities confounded her. Any relationship with him would not be easy...or ordinary.

The next few hours passed in a blur. She was preoccupied with thoughts of Lorenzo and everything they'd shared, and she never finished editing her posts.

Her assistant knocked on her office door, then entered without waiting for an invitation. "Your plans are confirmed for tonight."

"Thank you." At least one of them was thinking straight.

"Anything else you need?"

She shook her head. Elise was a godsend, and today she

was doubly on top of things. "I'll be in late tomorrow. And I'm leaving soon."

"Tea with Makenna and Avery." Elise looked at her watch. "In less than twenty minutes."

"Seriously?" Zara blinked and glanced at the clock on the wall.

"Head down to the lobby, I'll call Bryan and have him meet you out front."

Bryan was her semiprivate driver. At times, Vegas lines for cabs or rideshares was ridiculous. No way could she afford a private chauffeur, so this arrangement worked out well. He kept his client list manageable, and he stayed in the immediate area. "I couldn't do this without you."

"I'll remind you of this at my annual review."

"I'm sure you will."

They both grinned.

Bryan pulled up within a few minutes. Zara arrived at the Royal Sterling to find her friends were already there. They immediately stood to hug her; then Makenna swept a careful gaze over Zara. "I know you said you were okay, but I had to see for myself."

Grateful for the support, she smiled.

"I hope you don't mind, I brought Avery up to speed."

"Thank you."

After they were seated, their server approached, highlighting the day's features, and Zara opted for a pot of Earl Grey. After all, it would be hours until dinner, and it promised to be a long night.

"Okay," Makenna began when they were alone. "Tell us what happened last night with Maverick."

Though there were no tables nearby, she leaned forward. A few months ago, Makenna had had a terrible experience with the paparazzi. And since Maverick had been photographed by what was presumably a long-range lens, Zara wanted to be certain they weren't overheard.

She gave a brief recap, starting with their arrival at Excess and then Maverick spiking her drink while she was distracted. "It was..." She gave herself a mental shake. "I was lucky. Lorenzo saw it happen on video and intervened."

"Lorenzo?" Makenna echoed.

Their group knew him, and he'd attended Avery's recent wedding.

"The owner himself came to deal with it?"

"Yeah. I'm sure it wouldn't have been good for the Rose's reputation."

Even though the casino and resort had only been open for a matter of months, it had already earned the nickname the Rose among the area's locals.

"What happened then?" Avery asked.

"He, uhm... His security team escorted Maverick out."

"Escorted?" Makenna raised a skeptical eyebrow.

"According to Cole, Lorenzo is definitely not the type to put up with that crap." Cole was Avery's husband, a security expert who'd worked directly with the Bella Rosa's staff.

"So, that's why Mav looks like he's in training to be an MMA fighter?"

Zara shrugged. "I'm sure Lorenzo would deny anything happened."

"Well, I think Maverick deserved much worse." Avery's face scrunched in a ferocious scowl.

"From what I've seen on the gossip sites, his reputation is wrecked." Makenna smiled. "I hate what he tried to do to you, and I wouldn't be surprised if it has happened before. His daddy has enough money to make legal charges vanish, and records can be sealed. But this? He won't forget it. And maybe he'll think twice in the future. I'm sure he's banned from the Bella Rosa and probably some other places in town."

Lorenzo's uncle's resort, for certain.

"So where were you during this whole thing?"

Makenna's question made Zara squirm. "Lorenzo's suite."

Avery's eyes widened. "Seriously?"

"Okay." Makenna leaned back. "You have to tell us more."

She shook her head. "There's not much to say."

"I was blown away the first time I saw Zachary's place."

Makenna's husband owned a penthouse at the resort, and the couple were living there temporarily. Makenna wanted a house with a yard, while he preferred something that had very little maintenance.

"So I can't imagine what Lorenzo's place is like. I have heard rumors, though. Does he really have a pool of his own?"

"And a retractable roof."

"You'd never be able to get me to leave." Avery fanned herself.

If Zara gave in to temptation, she'd be back there in a matter of hours.

The server returned with pots of tea and lots of delectable treats.

Once she'd settled again, Zara changed the subject. Though she basked in the spotlight, she didn't make a habit of sharing the most intimate details of her life. "Enough about me. How is married life treating you both?"

Avery grinned as she set down her cup of chamomile tea. "I have news."

"Oh?" Zara asked.

"Tell us!" Makenna demanded with a grin.

"I'm expecting."

Full of excitement, they both stood to hug their friend.

"Details," Makenna prompted a few minutes later.

"I'm tired. And…"

"And?" Zara prompted.

"We just found out we're having twins."

"Twins?" Zara demanded.

"Twins?" Makenna echoed.

"My husband doesn't do anything by half measures." With a sigh, Avery grinned. "Or waste any time."

A few minutes later, Makenna, in her customary planning mode, got down to business. "Since twins sometimes come early, we'll need to set a date, sooner rather than later, for your shower."

"I haven't been able to think about much other than how to work from home most of the time. My energy level is zapped."

"Don't worry. I'll handle the details. With Zara's help."

She held up a hand in protest. "Babies aren't my expertise."

"But venues are. Somewhere kind of intimate. With excellent food." Makenna grabbed her phone and opened an app. Stylus in hand, she looked at Avery. "How many people? And are you wanting something co-ed?"

At the suggestion, Avery's eyes lit up. "Cole hates to be left out of anything. And I definitely want to watch him try to win a doll-diapering competition."

Though Zara grinned at the idea, her heart ground to a halt. Of course she would attend the event, but not having a date might be a little uncomfortable.

Unbidden, thoughts of Lorenzo plundered her mind, and she wondered if he'd ever thought of having children. What kind of father would he make?

"Zara?"

Realizing Makenna had asked her something, she shook her head. "Sorry."

"What do you think? A private room at a restaurant as a venue?"

"Unless we want to do it at someone's home."

"Great suggestion. What do you think, Avery? I'd offer to host, but I'm not sure if we'll move before then."

"Let's have it at a restaurant." Avery nodded, decision made. "Maybe here at the Sterling. That way it's easy for Aunt Scarlett."

"Perfect." Makenna nodded. "I'll get on it tomorrow."

"Now it's your turn," Avery told Makenna. "How's married life treating you?"

She grinned. "I had no idea how demanding Zachary could be. I've never been more exhausted... Or happier."

"Good." Genuinely happy for her friends, Zara smiled.

For the next half hour, they discussed business, bouncing ideas off each other.

The server returned to ask if they needed anything.

Avery shook her head. "As much as I'd like to stay, I want to see Aunt Scarlett before she goes onstage."

At eighty-something, the woman was a Las Vegas phenomenon. She still choreographed and danced in her own burlesque show almost every night of the week. At last report, she was juggling no less than three boyfriends, one of whom was an A-list actor a third of her age.

Zara nodded her agreement. "I have to work tonight, so I need to get ready."

"In that case, just the check, please." Makenna pulled out her credit card. "I'll take it."

"I think it's my turn," Zara protested.

"Are you kidding? Since we're baby shower planning, it's a business expense."

Twenty minutes later, Zara was back at her office, changing for the evening's event with an up-and-coming singer, and his entourage—libations at a grand opening of a newly renovated club on the Strip. A lot of press would be in attendance, and no doubt the outing would be covered by *Scandalicious.*

As she was slipping into an outrageously tall pair of sandals, she sighed. Generally she loved her job and gained energy from socializing. Tonight, however, she'd have preferred to have accepted Lorenzo's invitation so they could discuss what had happened to Maverick.

Still, she had obligations, and she'd be the perfect socialite, ensuring everyone had a good time, and no one would guess she had any turmoil.

Finally ready, she headed out and texted the club's owner that she was on her way. The place had a back entrance, but she opted to meet him out front, where he escorted her to the front of the line. As expected, tons of pictures were snapped, and she posed with a couple of women for a selfie—ensuring the club's name was captured in the shot.

Once they were inside the thumping, strobe-filled room, the owner shook her hand. "Thanks for coming out."

"Bobby is looking forward to the chance to get onstage later."

"We'll make it happen."

The manager joined them, introduced himself, and showed her to the section he'd reserved for her group. "Marlene will be your server. Let me know if there's anything else you need."

Instead of shouting to be heard, she nodded and smiled.

By the time Bobby Keyes and his entourage arrived, she had bottles of champagne, whiskey, and vodka waiting, along with all the appropriate mixers. Of course, the club boasted excellent cocktails, if anyone wanted them.

Keyes—real name unknown—was younger than expected, and easier to work with than most. He was tall and lanky, and thin to the point of gaunt. To complete his rockstar image, he'd poured himself into skintight leather pants, then only bothered to fasten the bottom two buttons on his shirt.

The group filmed tons of videos, and when he took to the stage, numerous people went live on various social media platforms. His voice was remarkably good, and the original tune captivating. He hadn't settled for performing a cover. He'd gone straight for the gold. She admired his style.

He signed autographs on anything imaginable—receipts, cocktail napkins, clothing people were still wearing, even the top of a woman's ass when she tugged up her skirt.

After the band had finished their set and announced a break, Keyes shook her hand and leaned forward to be heard over the din of the piped-in electronic music. "Marvie job. I mean it."

"I'm going to head out. I'll get some more posts up in the coming hours and days to keep the excitement humming. When you hit number one, come back to Vegas."

With that, he grinned.

A woman sidled up next to him, and he draped an arm around her shoulder. The man was easygoing and charismatic. And he worked the publicity machine nonstop, leaving her with little doubt he would achieve his goals.

She made her exit, this time through the back door, where her driver was waiting.

"Where to?"

Home would be smart. The past twenty-four hours had taken an emotional toll, and yet she hungered for Lorenzo. "The Bella Rosa. And I won't need you anymore this evening."

He met her gaze in the rearview mirror. "I can hang around for a couple of hours."

She was fortunate to have Bryan. He took his job seriously and always looked out for her. "Thank you. I'll be okay."

"If you need me, just call."

Even though it was after midnight, Bryan still had to take his turn behind a long line of limousines and expensive cars. Finally, he pulled beneath the brightly lit pink brick porte cochere.

A hotel employee opened her car door.

As she walked toward the entrance, she pulled her shoulders back and pushed through the heavy revolving door.

Now what?

She hadn't thought this through. Lorenzo hadn't given her his contact information, and she'd never confirmed that she would be here this evening. If what he said was true, however, he would soon know she was in the house.

Because the Rose's Martini Bar was her favorite hotspot, she decided to grab a drink there. The drinks were arguably the best in Vegas, and at this time of the night—or more technically, the morning—it shouldn't be so crowded that she couldn't get a table or a seat at the bar.

If he didn't seek her out by the time she was finished, she'd ask her server or the bartender for help in locating him.

Zara hadn't taken more than two dozen steps inside the air-conditioned resort when Mario appeared in front of her.

Startled, she stopped and clutched her pocketbook.

"Ms. Davis." He nodded.

She gave him a half smile. "Mario."

"If you'll follow me, please."

"I was going to grab a martini."

"The boss wishes you to join him."

When she remained where she was, scowling, he relented. "I'll have one sent to you."

She sighed. Lorenzo's world was so completely different from hers.

"What's your preference?"

Though their chocolate martinis were amazing, she generally stuck with their signature drink: the Rose, complete with a petal floating on the top, from the resort's flower gardens.

After telling him what she wanted, he repeated the order into his microphone, then extended his hand, pointed in front of him, silently indicating she should walk with him. As if she had a choice?

This time, she wasn't surprised when they entered the private elevator.

Instead of pushing the button for Lorenzo's apartment, Mario selected one that was marked T. As she expected, they were whisked upward, and the car drew to a disorienting stop in mere seconds.

They exited into a foyer and moved toward a frosted glass door that was opened for them.

Mario didn't follow her inside, and from the back of the space, Lorenzo walked forward to greet her.

The moment she saw him, every upset, every hesitation disappeared as if they'd never existed. He stopped a couple of feet away and swept his gaze over her as if she were the most important woman in the world. By slow measures, he smiled, transforming his features.

"Principessa." He took her hand and raised it to his lips.

Her pulse fluttered, and her thoughts splintered into disarray. The appealing scent of him wrapped around her.

The last time she'd seen him, he'd been dressed to pump iron. Now he was back in a tailored suit, with an eye-catching red tie. Even if she hadn't known who he was, she would have instinctively recognized his power and authority. *And been attracted to it.*

"The gods have indeed bestowed a blessing on me this evening. I wasn't sure you'd come."

"Where am I?"

"A members-only retreat."

The lobby-type area had comfortable seating and a bar. Along one wall were numerous other rooms, with seating for no more than four people. They had doors for privacy, and a few were closed. "This would be fabulous for private discussions or business meetings."

He nodded his agreement. "Food and beverage service is available."

"I didn't know it existed. I'd love to do a shoot here."

"We prefer to keep it secret."

"If you change your mind..."

"Then you'll be the first person I notify."

"Knowing the owner has its perks."

He leaned toward her.

The atmosphere heated, matching the burst of awareness that flooded her. "And its obligations."

Like what? She was too scared to ask the question.

Then he spoke, and the moment was over. "Join me?"

She followed him all the way to the back of the space; then he indicated she should precede him through a doorway.

This room was larger than the others. Breath rushed from her lungs at the spectacular skyscape. "This... It's stunning. How high are we?"

"Fifty-third floor."

Top of the world. Lord and master of all he surveyed...as he'd told her before "Your uncle's property is on the north side, right?"

"It is."

He pulled back a chair and then scooted it in when she sat.

After she was situated, he took his place across from her,

steepling his hands together. The jewels in his ring caught the light, refracting off the wall.

"What do you use this place for?"

"Conversation. Reflection." He grinned, quick and seductive. "Planning. Of all sorts."

A shudder ghosted up her spine.

Moments later, someone knocked on the door.

"Accedere."

The woman who'd been tending bar entered, carrying Zara's rose martini. "Wow." The beverage was picture-perfect, and she couldn't resist grabbing her phone from her purse. "Thank you."

"Of course." Then she looked at Lorenzo. "Is that all, sir?"

He gave a tight nod.

When the woman left, Zara snapped a photo. "I can't believe how fast this was."

"I will meet all your needs, principessa."

To cover the way his bold statement shook her, she took a sip of the beverage. "This is divine."

He nodded. Of course he demanded perfection.

After a second taste, she placed the gorgeous Z-shaped glass back onto the black cocktail napkin bearing the resort's gold logo.

She met his gaze. He was regarding her over his palms, his whiskey glass sitting to one side untouched.

"There was an article in *Scandalicious* about Maverick."

"Who?"

Zara frowned. "Pictures as well. He looked as if he'd been beat up."

"How unfortunate for him."

"You had nothing to do with it?"

"Principessa." He leaned forward. "I take care of what's mine."

"But—"

"Deny it."

How could she? She'd been his since he saw her at her father's Christmas party. "Why?"

"You tell me."

"You protected me." *And still do.*

"It's more than an obligation. I saw your innocence."

But had never corrupted it.

"Admired your belief in your father."

He hadn't mentioned the overwhelming attraction that had singed her nerve endings. "And now?"

"And now, principessa? I've waited long enough."

"What does that mean?"

"You're mine. And I intend to have you."

Her pulse careened out of control.

"You want it also." He captured her shoulders and pulled her toward him, and she couldn't deny him. "Are you brave enough to pay the price?"

CHAPTER FIVE

Zara wasn't convinced she'd ever get accustomed to the speed of his private elevator. Once again, she bent her knees for stability when they arrived at his floor. No doubt the experience was heightened by the desire spiraling through her.

Lorenzo nodded to his man. "You're off duty, Mario."

"I'll stay till the kid arrives to relieve me." Then he inclined his head in her direction. "Evening, Ms. Davis."

"Thank you, Mario."

She followed Lorenzo into his apartment, and he shut the door behind them. Then he beckoned to her.

"May I have your hand?"

She frowned.

"Nothing nefarious. I want to program the apartment so you're free to come and go as you please. Even the elevator will respond."

"So you're not keeping me prisoner ever again?"

"As long as you avoid men who need pummeling." His face was expressionless, and she had no idea whether he was serious or not.

After placing her purse on the table, she extended her hand, and he pressed her fingertip against the pad on the wall.

"Hold still for about five seconds."

A moment later, a green light above the sensor flashed, and a cultured, disembodied female voice filled the foyer. *"Fingerprint accepted, Mr. Carrington."*

"Thank you, Sally."

Stunned by the interaction, Zara asked, "Sally?"

"My whole-house computer. Designed by Julien Bonds, fueled by AI."

"There's nothing artificial about my intelligence, Mr. Carrington." The disembodied voice held an offended note.

Zara smiled. "A computer that talks back? I like that."

"I prefer the word assistant, ma'am."

"Of course." She grinned while Lorenzo sighed.

"Sally, please say hello to Ms. Davis."

"I'm at your service."

Sally enchanted her. "Thank you." Then she frowned. "Am I supposed to thank a computer?"

"Not necessary."

"Yes."

"The programming is as glitchy as Bonds's personality." Lorenzo shook his head. "She responds better to positive interaction."

Suppressing a grin, Zara glanced at him through her eyelashes. "Something we both have in common."

"Touché."

"Would you like a drink? I can prepare a martini, but it won't compare to the one you just had." He loosened his tie. "Or I may have another bottle of your favorite champagne." He opened the top button on his shirt, then leveled a hard look at her. "However, for what I have in mind for you, I'd prefer you didn't drink anymore."

Swept up in him, she shivered. "In that case, no. Thank you."

With purposeful intent, he walked toward her and captured her face between his palms, holding her steady while he ravaged her mouth.

When they were both breathless, he ended the kiss, and she grabbed hold of his wrists for support.

"We have a few things to discuss before I completely lose myself in you."

Though she wanted nothing more than to surrender to the moment and think later, she nodded. At least one of them was using their brain.

He pivoted and put several feet of distance between them before turning to face her again. "I want to make love to you."

Finally. She ached to touch him. "Me too."

"I have condoms."

"I'm on the pill."

His eyes burned with intensity. "I will still use a condom if you want."

"You've proven yourself to be an honorable man. If you tell me you don't need one, I will believe you."

"I promise, principessa, you are always safe with me."

She nodded. "You mentioned that you have particular tastes."

Patiently he waited for her to go on.

Everything inside her shimmered with awareness. "I have certain desires of my own."

He grinned in a way that told her he suspected—or knew—that information already.

Still, she went on. "I attend BDSM play parties at Diana and Alcott's home."

"We are well suited."

She'd never doubted that.

"What are your hard limits?"

Since this part was easy for her, she was able to pretend he was an ordinary man. "No extreme pain."

"Canes?"

"A hard pass. I'm more into the sensuality, the psychological aspects of it—but no humiliation."

"Understood. And a safe word?"

"I'm not terribly creative. Red for stop. Yellow for slow down."

He continued to regard her. "And how about collars?"

"I've never worn one." *Because I've been waiting for you.* "Until now."

"In that case, I'm honored." In an incredibly masculine move, he folded his arms behind him. "Is there anything you need me to be aware of?"

She tipped her head back to meet his gaze. In addition to being confounding and frustrating, he possessed a very dark side. As long as she lived, she'd never forget the way he'd handled Jeffrey. Maybe she was foolish, but... "I trust you."

"I will do my best to deserve you." Time stretched, and when she didn't speak, he crossed to her. "I had a collar made for you. It's on the nightstand in my bedroom. When you're ready, please fetch it."

Shock paralyzed her. Obviously he'd had no doubts that she'd submit to him. After a few seconds, she managed to gather her wits and left the room, climbing the staircase on shaky legs.

The diamond-studded choker was nestled in a velvet-lined box. The stunning piece of jewelry stole her breath. It was beautiful enough to have been designed for royalty, and it was a fantasy come true.

Though she'd scened before, she'd never been with a man whose entire focus was on her pleasure.

Reverently she picked up the collar—*her collar*—then headed down the stairs.

He stood with his back to the window, feet planted shoulder-width apart. He'd discarded his tie and turned back his shirtsleeves.

She misstepped, then froze.

This was a new side of him—a Dominant one that made her reel.

Her blood heated, and her thought process slowed.

A pillow was at his feet, and she knew it was meant for her. He was very deliberate with the way he exerted his will, and it wove an inescapable spell around her.

He didn't order her to come to him. Rather, he waited.

Uncertain of her actions in a way she hadn't been at any other time in her life, she walked forward, feeding on the approval in his eyes.

She lowered herself to her knees, recognizing the next logical step, the only one she was capable of taking. Struggling to school her breathing, she lowered her head and offered the stunning piece to him.

"Exquisite. I've waited a lifetime for you, principessa."

The same was true for her.

"Will you lift your hair for me?"

Her heart rate slowed. It was as if every part of her knew that this was right.

When she did as he asked, he crouched in front of her and compelled her to meet his gaze.

"You do know that I may never let you go?"

"Yes," she whispered.

With a deft touch, he fastened the collar into place. Next, he gently moved her hands so that her hair fell over her shoulders and down her back.

"Perfect." He stood. "Exactly as I imagined."

Zara accepted the hand up that he offered.

"I want you naked. Would you like to remove your dress? Or would you prefer I do it for you?"

She almost answered but then caught herself. "Whichever you prefer, Lorenzo."

"Perfect answer." His pleasure, in his smile and his voice, electrified her.

In a deft, smooth move, he scooped up the hem of her dress and drew it upward. Because it was formfitting, she wiggled a little, helping him remove the garment.

He continued, pulling it up and off before draping it over the back of the couch.

Mostly naked, she fought an instinctive moment of embarrassment. From the moment they first met, he'd known she was blessed with curves, and he'd always seemed to approve.

"You're even more beautiful than I imagined."

His appreciation poured through her, giving her confidence.

"Please remove your bra."

Because she was entering a more submissive mindset, her movements slowed. She fumbled with the clasp several times until it finally released. When she shrugged, the straps fell over her shoulders, and her breasts spilled from the lacy lingerie.

He inhaled sharply. "Your breasts are magnificent. Your nipples…dusky and already so hard. I could suck on them for hours. And I will."

Nervous anticipation danced through her. *Yes, please.*

He extended his hand for her bra, and she offered it to him.

"Now your panties."

She gulped hard before easing them over her hips and down her thighs.

"Principessa, you'll be lucky if I ever allow you to wear clothes again." He placed all her garments in the same pile. "I love the way your legs look in those shoes. Are you comfortable enough in them?"

She nodded.

"Good. In that case, I'd like you to walk to the pool area."

Puzzled, but not questioning him, she moved through his apartment, hyperaware of the sway of her hips and his scrutiny.

"Keep going."

Toward the room he hadn't shown her.

When they arrived, he pressed his thumb to the pad on the wall. The door opened with a soft snick.

Once she entered his dungeon, she froze, rooted to the spot. The rest of his apartment was spectacular, and this was no exception.

The room boasted floor-to-ceiling windows. And because no buildings were nearby, they had complete privacy.

One wall was lined with glass doors, displaying every impact toy imaginable. A set of matching drawers—with chrome pull handles—held other equipment. Nipple clamps, plugs, cuffs, rope, vibrators, blindfolds, gags, even a few things she didn't immediately recognize.

He had a small refrigerator as well as a countertop and sink.

But the focal point was a beautifully supple white leather swing that hung from the ceiling near the center of the room.

The room also contained a chrome St. Andrew's cross and a red leather spanking bench.

"All for you, principessa."

She took it all in—or tried to.

A massive television was mounted to a wall, and he also had a leather chair and an oversize loveseat.

"You never have to leave." She faced him.

"My point exactly." He folded his arms in a commanding

manner. As always, lord of his domain. "Where shall we begin?"

No doubt he didn't expect an answer. And yet she couldn't resist. "Everywhere."

"That's the answer I wanted." His footfalls loud on the tile, he crossed to her.

Drowning in anticipation, aware of her nudity, she held her breath.

He cupped her breasts, then lightly kneaded them.

Warmth and dampness swirled through her as he caressed a nipple between his thumb and forefinger.

As he watched her, he pulled on the hardened nub, elongating it. For support she grabbed hold of him.

He shook his head. "I want you helpless."

Lorenzo captured her hands and imprisoned them behind her. She moaned both from pleasure and in protest, and she longed to touch him.

"This moment is mine."

He tugged upward, forcing her onto her tiptoes, mad with desire. He tightened his grip on her nipple, leaving her breathless, unable to think, as he took what he wanted, but giving her oh so much more in return.

Delirious, she tipped back her head and closed her eyes, offering more.

Greedily he took it, releasing her nipple to relentlessly squeeze her breast. "Lorenzo, I can't…"

When she was convinced she couldn't take it one moment longer, he slowly released her.

Her reprieve was short lived as he immediately moved on to her other breast. This time, he lowered his head to draw her nipple into his mouth. He used his teeth, biting with exquisite tenderness, making her scream his name.

"I've never heard anything as sweet."

He slid his hand between her thighs. Responding to his unspoken command, she spread her legs.

His touch demanding, inflaming, he stroked between her folds, teasing her clit, making her wet. Caught up in the moment, she moved in unison with him. Within a minute, she was on the edge of an orgasm.

"There's nothing I desire more than to have you shatter in my arms."

"Yes."

"But I want you to hold on a bit longer. Can you do that for me?

Frantically she shook her head. She knew he expected her obedience, but she had waited, fantasized, for so many years. "Lorenzo, please."

"Don't make me stop, principessa. Don't make me punish your neediness." His words were a serrated knife edge wrapped in silk.

Relentlessly he drove her forward, sliding one of his fingers inside her damp channel. "So ready. Tight."

He changed the angle to find her G-spot while he pressed his thumb hard against her clitoris.

"My God, Lorenzo. I'm going to come."

He bent his head. "Open your mouth for me."

As if she had any choice. Zara surrendered. Everything she had, everything she was, she offered to him.

He'd kissed her before, but never like this, with emotion and promise.

Time stretched, morphed, as she swirled into bliss, and suddenly she didn't know where he ended and she began.

Even though he'd ordered her not to orgasm, he relentlessly drove her to the precipice. His grip on her wrists intensified, every bit as unyielding as handcuffs would have been.

Her back was arched, and her body aflame. Lorenzo

deepened the kiss as he exerted more pressure on her pleasure spots.

A million pinpricks of light filled her vision as an orgasm overtook her. She screamed, and her whole body shook.

But as always, Lorenzo was there, holding her, supporting her, providing what she needed.

Without her being aware of it, he somehow ended the kiss.

By slow measures, her breathing returned to normal, and she blinked and met his gaze. He wore a satisfied grin, and one of his eyebrows was raised as he looked at her. "You're spectacular."

"That was the best orgasm I've ever had."

"Your responses are so honest, pleasing." He kissed her forehead. "But you came without my permission."

Mutinously she set her chin. "That's not fair. You didn't give me a choice."

"Hmm." His voice contained no sympathy. "Still, there's a price to pay for your disobedience."

Her heart plummeted as devilment danced in his dark, merciless eyes.

Still holding her captive, he licked her essence from his fingertips. Then he released her wrists. "Come with me."

Her stilettos tapped on the tile floor, keeping rhythm with her thumping heart as she followed him to the closet where he stored his impact toys.

"Tonight, as it's your first time, I'll allow you to select which implement we use."

She glanced at him, searching his features.

"Pain, mixed with pleasure. I'd like you to select how I mark you."

Arousal crashed into her.

She was turning over her body to him, and soon, it would bear the proof of his Domination.

Her mouth dried, both from a touch of fear and the heady knowledge that they'd reached a turning point they could never go back from.

She surveyed the implements and considered the tiny bites they'd leave behind. She loved surrendering to a flogging. When her stress level was high, a paddling or tawsing could soothe her.

For a moment, she considered the single tail. But she wanted to experience his touch everywhere.

Finally, after surveying all the tantalizing possibilities, she turned back toward him.

"Decision made?"

She nodded. "I'd like you to use your hands."

He folded his arms across his chest. "Interesting choice."

"It's the intimacy." She swallowed, then offered honesty she'd never given anyone else. "I want you to own me."

"So brave."

"Foolish?"

"Yes. Perhaps."

She'd expected his reassurance. That he hadn't offered it ignited a flare of anticipation inside her. With him she was bolder than she had been with any other person. It was as if he unlocked all the fire she'd been keeping pent-up inside, just for him.

"Come with me, principessa."

CHAPTER SIX

Lorenzo led her to the corner of the room, to an overhead bar with a massive O-ring attached to it. He left her for a moment to fetch two lengths of silken white rope.

With practiced ease, he bound her wrists and then secured them above her head.

Being in this position, bound and helpless, heightened her already powerful response to him.

Next, he crossed to one of the glass drawers and selected a thick blindfold.

"I want you a little disoriented, not knowing what to expect."

The thought terrified her, but since she wanted the experience, she nodded.

Within seconds, he'd secured it in place. "How's that?"

"Fine."

Then he touched his thumb pad to the fast, throbbing beat of her heart in her throat. "How are your bonds? Not too restrictive?"

Even though she assured him they were perfect, he checked for himself.

"Can you keep your legs apart for me?"

He was right about the effects of the blindfold. She turned her head to the side, trying to ascertain where he was standing.

"Or would a spreader bar help you to follow orders better?"

"I've never used one before."

"In that case, it's a delicious night for first experiences."

Intently she listened to the sound of his footsteps. Some were loud, others softer and farther away.

"I love the way you look. Helpless. Waiting on my pleasure."

She gulped a shallow breath but couldn't respond.

Jolting her, Lorenzo placed his hands on her hips. She hadn't realized he was so close.

With his knuckles, he brushed her hair back over her shoulders, then whispered a kiss across the side of her neck.

"Your nipples are hard again." He captured both.

Slowly—agonizingly so—he twisted them before exerting even more pressure.

"I need you, Lorenzo. Make love to me."

"In time."

While she writhed, arching her back toward him, he captured her breasts, then pushed them together. Driving her wild, he sucked on her nipples in turn, gently biting before laving the swollen tips.

His skillful handling of her body brought her to the edge of another orgasm, but each time she whimpered, he pulled away, denying her any relief.

"Lorenzo!"

He laughed, an awful, mirthless sound that proved that he knew exactly what he was doing.

"In time, precious." He trailed his fingertips down her sides, pausing at her hips before continuing across her belly, then lower, to her pubis. For a long, dizzying moment she thought perhaps he would touch her pussy.

But he continued, igniting a firestorm of response in her, until he tapped her ankle.

"I'd like your legs as far apart as you can get them."

As she complied with his command, he gripped her waist to help keep her steady.

"Good." He fastened the bar in place. "Now you truly are my captive."

She ached to make eye contact, to read what was on his mind. But she was helpless, lost inside her own head.

He placed a hand between her legs, then tenderly stroked, soothing her, lulling her deeper into her surrender.

Then he cupped her pussy. She gasped, not from the miniscule pain, but from the shock.

"You wanted an intimate punishment. That's what you shall receive."

Because of the confounding blindfold, she had no idea what to expect, but wanting more, she strained against her bonds only for him to flick her nipples, making them harder still.

Overwhelmed by the pleasure, the pain, she whimpered.

But he was persistent. Now that her pussy burned and her nipples hurt, he pinched the inside of one of her thighs, then her calf. He was bringing her entire body alive, and her brain responded, flooding her with endorphins.

With short, harsh spanks, he made his way up the insides of her legs only to lay dozens more against her pussy, leaving her dizzy. No matter how hard she twisted and strained, she couldn't escape his focused determination.

Her most sensitive flesh was on fire, leaving her hungry. When she thought the torture would never end, he moved to stand behind her, then pulled her back against his body. Once again, he palmed her breasts, biting his fingers into them. From this angle, his grip was even stronger, terrible and thrilling.

When she'd asked him to punish her intimately, she'd had no idea what she was asking for. Or how magnificently wonderful it would be.

The room spun beneath her, and he stopped the beautiful torment to slide his powerful forearm against the softness of her belly.

He skimmed his fingertips over her buttocks and the backs of her thighs. Fearing what would happen next, she instinctively tightened her muscles.

"Relax as much as you can." Gradually he increased the tempo, moving from a gentle touch to light spanks before increasing the force to bring blood flow to the area.

"Don't deny me." He pressed his palm against her pussy, then dragged his fingers backward across her already swollen flesh.

Crying out, she arched forward, desperate to escape, despite his harsh demand.

Once again, he adjusted his position, and he plumped her buttocks.

Damn. He was masterful. The moment she was tempted to admit she couldn't endure any more, he changed up what he was doing.

When she was certain his fingertips would leave tiny bruises on her skin, he resumed his gentle, measured spanks on both her ass cheeks. The pleasure was divine, greater than anything she'd ever known.

Beneath his ministrations, she relaxed, and her insides turned molten with desire.

Suddenly he blazed a hand across the fleshiest part of her

buttocks. Her breath rushed out in a startled, strangled gasp. "Lorenzo!"

"That's it. Take what I give you."

This was what she'd asked for, what she wanted, and it was so much more than she'd imagined possible.

Ruthlessly he scorched her body. He dug his grip into her everywhere, keeping her inflamed.

"You're wearing the marks of my possession."

"Yes."

He sank his teeth into that tender space between her shoulder and her neck. Twisting, she tried to escape him, but her efforts were futile. His arm was still in place, and he effortlessly dragged her back for more.

His touch was everywhere all at once, pinching and spanking until she was crying out his name and sweat drenched her body. But rather than wanting it to end, she thrust her hips back, a silent entreaty for more.

"You were made for me."

She couldn't deny his truth. Whatever he gave, she wanted.

He continued to make her his, leaving no part of her body unexplored. "You're so fucking sexy, principessa."

Zara was lost in darkness, flying in a world that he created.

He moved a hand between her legs. "You've got fifteen seconds to get yourself off before I change my mind."

"Are you serious?" Surely he couldn't be so cruel.

"Try me."

Being unable to read his expression left her foundering.

"Ten seconds remaining." He continued masturbating her, and she was desperate to climax.

Frantic and hampered by the spreader bar and her hands being immobilized, she began to undulate her body, seeking the relief he'd promised.

"Five seconds."

"Please. Lorenzo, please!" She wasn't sure she could survive if she didn't manage to climax.

He entered her, burying two fingers deep inside her.

Even though she was past his time limit, he kept going. And she was grateful, helpless and surrendered.

"That's it. Keep working it. Fuck my hand."

His filthy words freed her. Trusting he would support her and keep her safe, she moved faster and faster. "I'm going to—"

Shockingly, he slapped the underside of her buttocks, bringing his free hand quickly and with more force than before, pitching her forward. The depth of him inside her combined with the blazing explosion against her ass sent her splintering into an abyss of completion—satiated, floating in a place she'd never known existed.

"Such a perfect submissive."

From a vast distance, his rough voice reached her.

"You're everything I imagined, principessa."

Limply, she allowed the ropes to support her.

Talking in soothing words and with gentle movements, taking care not to snag her hair, he removed her blindfold.

Dizzy, she blinked the world back into focus.

Words failed her when she looked into the richness in his eyes. They were darker than normal, filled with emotion and something else. *Reverence, maybe?* Whatever had happened to her, he had also experienced it.

"My darling principessa." Lorenzo traced a fingertip down the column of her throat and paused at the hollow there. "You complete me."

Overwhelmed by his words and with her reaction to their scene, she squeezed her eyes shut. Her knees buckled. If her bonds hadn't been so perfect, she might have fallen. "I can't wait any longer. I need you inside me."

In less than two minutes, he unshackled her ankles and released her wrists. "Stay where you are." The perfect Dominant, he rubbed the circulation back into her hands and shoulders. "How's that?"

After shrugging, she slowly lowered her arms.

Then, stealing the breath from her lungs, he swept her from the floor and strode back through his dungeon and onto the pool deck.

She expected him to put her down, but he continued into the main part of the house. "Where are we going?"

"To my bedroom."

"Are you kidding?" Zara braced a palm on his chest and pushed herself away so she could look into his eyes. "You can't carry me up the stairs!"

"I assure you I can."

Shaking her head, she curled into him, wrapping an arm around his neck for stability.

Without even breathing hard, he climbed the narrow winding staircase. Then he continued across the room and placed her on his bed.

She sat with her knees upturned and shamelessly stared as he began unbuttoning his shirt, revealing a faint amount of chest hair that arrowed straight down.

Even though she'd seen him in his athletic gear, she wasn't prepared for the mouthwatering sight of his chiseled abdomen or his wide shoulders and well-defined biceps.

He placed his shirt on the back of the chair he'd slept in last night before toeing off his shoes and pulling off his socks. Then he unfastened his trousers and stepped out of them, revealing his trim waist. Shamelessly she continued to drink in the sight of his gorgeous body.

The man must be relentless in all his pursuits, including working out.

But as he removed his boxer briefs, all her attention was focused on his enormous cock and heavy, full balls.

Obviously enjoying her intensity, he grinned. "Dominating you turns me on."

As she continued to watch, he stroked himself. His pleasure fed her own. Joining with him would be unlike anything she'd ever known.

Still fisting himself, he strode toward her, filling her vision until nothing existed in her life except him. "I'm a little nervous, I have to admit."

"Oh, you'll take me."

She shook her head. He was enormously endowed, in both length and girth.

When he reached the edge of the bed, he caught her gaze and crooked his finger. "Come here."

Unsure what to expect, she crawled to him.

"Take my cockhead in your mouth."

Nervously she licked a drop of precum from the glistening slit.

"That's right." He ensnared one of her hands and placed it on his shaft where his had been. "Take the whole head."

Trying to be brave, she drew the tip of him into her mouth.

"Good." With a groan, he dug his hands into her, holding her steady. "Now more." He pumped his hips slightly, forcing his shaft deeper. *"Fuck."*

Her eyes watered, but she continued to take more until he eventually pulled out.

With lightning-fast movements, he had her flat on her back; then he tugged her to the edge of the mattress. "Now lift your legs."

"Uhm, my ass will be hanging off the edge of the bed."

"Did I ask for your opinion on the mechanics?"

ALL-IN

She blinked. "No. But..." She cleared her throat. "I'm not going to be able to take you from that angle."

"Trust me."

Still skeptical, she did as he said.

With iron strength, he imprisoned her ankles. "Bend your knees."

He slid a finger inside her, driving her mad, reigniting all the nerve endings that had been so recently aroused. All her protests vanished beneath a clawing layer of need.

When she was wet and ready, he slid his cock back and forth between her feminine folds, slapping her pussy with his shaft until they were both slick from her arousal.

Then he moved between her legs. "I want you to keep your eyes open. I want you to see me as I make love to you."

But before he entered her, he played with her breasts once again, kneading, sucking the tips into his mouth, rocketing desire straight through her.

She reached for him. "Don't make me wait any longer."

Instead of claiming her with a single thrust, he took his time, easing in, then pulling back, using short, purposeful strokes. As her body accommodated his massive length, he went deeper.

"So tight." Impatience tinged his words.

Wanting to be his in every way possible, she spread her legs wider. "Fuck me, Lorenzo."

With a guttural groan, he accepted her invitation.

Once he was fully inside her, Zara was completed in a way she never imagined, as if she'd found the missing piece of her heart.

"My precious Zara." He captured her mouth and moved inside her.

She surrendered to the primal pulse that connected them.

For a moment, he lifted himself a little, enough to finger

her clit. The touch sent her spiraling, as all her nerve endings flooded with desire. "God. Lorenzo…"

"Come anytime."

Despite his earlier order, she closed her eyes and turned herself over to the incredible sensation of him filling her—taking and simultaneously giving.

He flicked her clit. A climax tore through her, and she came hard, calling his name, lifting her body, seeking more.

"Take it. Take all of me." Tiny drops of exertion dotted his forehead, and she realized he was forcibly holding back his orgasm.

"Come in me, Lorenzo."

"Fuuuuuuck." Teeth gritted, he tipped back his head.

Impossibly his cock became even thicker. Time froze as he went rigid. A fraction of a moment later, he climaxed, spilling himself deep inside her.

She threaded her hands into his hair, marveling at their union.

When he stopped pulsing long moments later, he shook his head. "Goddamn."

With a rough exhalation, he moved quickly, rolling to one side and pulling her against him. "You were worth the wait. Every year, every month, every moment." He dropped the gentlest of kisses on her forehead.

She sighed into him, more relaxed, feeling safer than she ever had in her entire life.

Her lover, her Dominant, held her until their breathing returned to normal. Then he suggested a shower. She was too tired and overwhelmed to say much of anything, but she enjoyed his tender ministrations as he washed her with a bar of lavender soap that hadn't been there last night.

When he was finished, she looked up at him. "My turn."

"Of course." Impossibly his cock was still half-hard and became thicker as she lathered his chest.

"See what you do to me?"

She gave him a wicked grin. "I think that's only fair given what you do to me."

He turned so she could wash his back, and she paused when she noticed a massive tattoo on his right shoulder blade. "Is this the same one that is on your door?"

"It is. A representation of my family. And my fealty to it."

She shivered.

He turned to her. "Scared?"

"Maybe." It was his first stark admission of who he was. "Everything I've heard about you? It's true?"

"Some of it is surely exaggerated."

"And your ring?"

He lifted his hand so she could garner a closer look—an owl, framed by laurel leaves. "The Zeta Society really exists."

"I won't deny it."

"And your uncle…?"

His silence was his admission.

"My life is not for everyone. And you have a decision to make."

"You've trusted me with your secrets."

"With my life."

She exhaled, not knowing what the future held, and the risks and threats that surrounded him. "I think I made my decision the moment I walked through the revolving glass door this evening."

His eyes smoldered as he captured her mouth. Then he lifted her, pinning her against the tile wall. Even though she was tender and not quite ready for him, he sank his massive cock inside her.

"I'm never letting you go."

Their gazes locked.

"We'll be married as soon as I can get it arranged."

What? Her head spun. How was this even possible? "Married?"

"Say yes, Zara." He traced the delicate line of her collar. "Tell me you'll be beside me for the rest of our lives."

Laughing, crying, happier than she'd ever been, lost in him, she nodded. "Yes."

He fucked her hard, proving just how completely she belonged to him, and then he took her to bed and made love to her once more, sealing their heartfelt promise to each other.

CHAPTER SEVEN

Zara awakened late the next morning to the scent of coffee. Because of the thrilling night she had shared with Lorenzo, it might be the only thing that would entice her out of bed.

Even after their hot shower sex, he'd repeatedly made love to her. Each time, he'd snuggled her close and held her as they drifted back to sleep. And honestly, she didn't recall her body ever being more tender than it was right now.

Then a memory filtered back, making her warm. *He asked me to marry him.*

Grinning, she rolled onto her tummy and propped her chin into her upturned hands. Ever since she'd set eyes on him, Lorenzo had been the man of her dreams.

He knew how to make her body respond. And he pulled on all her heartstrings. Life couldn't get any better.

"Principessa! Get your sweet little ass down here before I come and paddle it."

"Yes, Sir!" she shouted back, giggling as she did so.

Then devilment enticed her. The idea of starting her day with his strong hand on her buttocks was utterly enticing.

She stayed where she was, disobeying him and waiting for the consequences.

In less than a minute he stood in the doorway, an eyebrow arched. "So that's how it is?"

Her future husband could not be any sexier. He wore only a pair of loose-fitting pants, leaving the rest of him bare. Goose bumps prickled her arms at the sight of his honed body.

He took a step into the room, and the force of his energy supercharged the atmosphere.

"I guess your coffee can wait while I deal with you."

Her mouth dried. With half a dozen purposeful steps, he crossed to her. Too late, she noticed the wooden spoon he'd hidden behind his back.

"No! No, no! I'll behave."

"Too late."

Ignoring her protests and promises, he scooped up her wiggling body from the bed. He carried her to the chair and sat in it before turning her over his knee.

Frantically she kicked. But her attempted escape failed when he trapped her legs between his much more powerful ones.

Then he bounced his knee, pitching her forward and adjusting her position so that her hair brushed the floor and her behind was positioned upward, inviting his punishment. Relentless, he slid his fingers between her legs. "Be careful what you ask for, my future bride."

His warning thrilled her. *A lifetime of this?* She refused to pinch herself. If this was a fantasy, she never wanted to wake up.

He inserted a finger inside her. "You're wet. Should we start every day with a spanking? Would it help keep you in line?" He skimmed his touch across her upper thighs and her buttocks. "You have a few red marks left over from last night, and I think it's fitting that we add a few more."

Without warming her up, he seared her skin with his palm. Gasping from the unexpected force, she kicked her legs in earnest.

"Heed my warnings, principessa." With a fingertip, he traced the path he'd just blazed.

Then after a few more swats, he eased off, only to rub her vigorously. Though she knew he was preparing for further spanks, she couldn't help but purr. Lorenzo was already an expert at making her respond.

Before she was ready, he smacked her bottom with the wooden spoon.

"Oww!" She reached back to cool the hot spot on her ass.

"Put your fingertips on the floor, unless you want me to cuff your hands."

The mood he was in this morning, she wouldn't put it past him.

To hurry her along, he gave her another taste of the spoon. "That thing hurts, Sir!"

"Hmm. Perhaps in future you'll think twice before disobeying me."

Probably not. Still, this time, she placed her hands where he instructed. If she didn't, balancing would be even more difficult.

Despite the way the implement burned, arousal began to unfurl. Suddenly it didn't matter how sore she was. She wanted to make love with him again.

He used the kitchen tool several more times in quick succession, and she wiggled ferociously to avoid it. But he was stronger, leaving her helpless to his will.

With determination, he continued. "Is this what you wanted?"

Because of her position, she couldn't draw enough breath to answer him.

"Are you ready to be finished?"

Wondering if the upside-down position was affecting her thought process, she shook her head.

"Your wish is my command." Discarding the spoon, he spanked her with his open hand, setting a rhythmic pace.

With a deep sigh, she gave herself over to it, to him.

When he was done, he rubbed her tenderly and brushed her pussy with his fingers. She relaxed even more, waiting for him to enter her. But he didn't.

Instead, he released her legs, then took her waist and helped her to stand up.

"Are you...?" Flabbergasted, she blinked. "I mean, you're not...we're not going to have sex?"

"You think I should reward your disobedience?" In his frustratingly calm way, he arched his diabolical eyebrow.

"But...you made me horny."

"And you can spend the rest of the day suffering."

"What?" Even more stunned, she searched his features, looking for any sign that he was joking.

"You're forbidden from masturbating until I give permission."

This was a part of BDSM she'd never explored, having a full-time Dominant rather than someone she walked away from at the end of the evening. She had told him she liked the psychological aspects the most. She just hadn't expected him to exploit his power in this way.

"Unless you'd like to wear a chastity device when we're apart?"

"You wouldn't!"

"On the contrary, principessa." His lips were set in an uncompromising line. "The idea of locking up your cunt and pocketing the key holds tremendous appeal. Heed my warning and don't push me."

His expression chilled her. He meant every word. Lorenzo might be a careful lover, but he was a steely Dominant.

"Understand?"

Unable to find her voice, she nodded.

"I need the words." He hadn't moved, hadn't changed the timbre of his voice, but his intent was clear. In this, he wouldn't be denied.

"Yes, Lorenzo. I promise I won't get myself off today."

"You have no idea how much I enjoy the idea of you being miserable while we're apart. And how easily you'll come for me later."

Uncomfortably she squirmed. His harshness made her even wetter.

He stood, then leaned forward to tap the inside of her right thigh. Following his wordless command, she spread her legs.

"This"—he cupped his hand over her pussy and squeezed, making a point, stopping just short of being painful—"is mine."

She was rooted to the spot, her heart thumping. "Yes, Lorenzo." What he didn't know was that it always had been.

"Good." Slowly he released her, and she sucked in a relieved breath. "When you come downstairs, we need to talk about you moving in."

The way he switched topics left her reeling.

"Your coffee is waiting." He paused. "Unless you'd like another taste of this?" He picked up the wooden spoon and bounced it off his open palm.

"No, Sir."

"I'm sorry?"

"I mean... No, Sir. Thank you." Not only would it hurt her

bruised rear end, but he'd be so deliberate with the way he used it that she'd be even more desperate for an orgasm. "And what about this?" She touched the collar.

"We'll remove it for now. Later we'll discuss you wearing one permanently."

She nodded. But when it was gone, her skin tingled, and she missed its weight.

"Join me downstairs."

The air conditioner turned on, and the cold air swept over her damp body, sending a chill through her. She hurried to the closet for one of his shirts. Once she stepped inside the space, she shook her head, unable to believe what she saw.

He'd hung up the gown she'd worn last night…next to an array of gowns and casual clothes. She flipped through the hangers that were filled with blouses, skirts, shorts, slacks, sundresses. All the pieces were things she would have selected for herself.

On the floor, next to her stilettos, were a few pairs of sandals, some dress shoes, and a pair of sneakers. Hanging from a hook was a short robe with embroidering on the lapel. As she pulled it down and wrapped herself in it, she realized it wasn't the Bella Rosa's logo. Instead, it was Lorenzo's family insignia—a serious message that she acknowledged.

When she joined him in the kitchen, he looked up from what he was doing. "The robe is perfect on you."

"This waffle weave material is wonderful." So light and cozy. "You bought me a bunch of clothes."

"I want you to be comfortable." He narrowed his gaze. "And not have any excuses to shorten the amount of time we have together."

"Thank you. You made excellent choices." She accepted the coffee he'd already poured for her.

"I hope I got the amount of creamer right."

Propping her hips on the counter, she took a sip. "It's wonderful." Lorenzo may not always operate on the correct side of the law, and at times his ferocity was frightening, but he knew how to take care of her. "Thank you."

She watched him finish making his smoothie. "I'll marry you as long as you promise that I never have to drink one of those."

"You might like it."

She wrinkled her nose. "That's a hard pass from me."

He blended the drink, then addressed her. "About the wedding…"

"I still haven't gotten over the fact that you proposed."

"Are you working Saturday afternoon?"

"No. I have an engagement in the evening, but I'm free until seven o'clock."

"I'll make an appointment with the jeweler for your ring."

He was making it so real, so fast.

"Do you have a wedding planner you'd like to use?"

This decision was easy. "My friend Makenna. She organized Avery and Cole's wedding."

"Please set up an appointment for us either at the end of this week, or the beginning of next. Let me know when, and I'll clear my schedule."

"You meant it when you said you'd like to be married in a matter of months?"

"We're wasting time. I intend for you to be my wife. And I'd like for us to have children."

"Children?"

"Six."

Her mouth dropped open "You…you can't be serious." Though she came from a large family, she'd never considered the idea of having more than one or two.

"No." He grinned. "A couple, maybe three or four. But I'll happily spend the rest of my life trying to get you pregnant."

We could get started right now. She was still so turned on that she was edgy.

"As I was asking upstairs, is there any reason that you can't move in immediately?

There wasn't, except for the fact that it was just so fast. But there again she wasn't sure she wanted to spend one more day without him.

"I have extra rooms upstairs. You're welcome to use one as an office or retreat. The Rose's designer is at your disposal. And I know you'll want to put your stamp on the rest of the apartment. I'll trust your judgment."

When his mind was made up, he was a force to be reckoned with.

"I can arrange for movers."

She nodded. "How about after I've met with the designer?"

"The sooner, the better."

"Agreed."

"When you're ready, I'll take you home. Though I'd prefer you never leave."

Together, they went upstairs. She chose one of the sundresses while he changed into workout gear. "Do you exercise every day?"

"It helps me stay focused."

"And look like a god."

"In that case, I'll never skip another session." He grinned. "When I have a decision to make, I'll indulge in a long swim. My form of meditation, I suppose."

"So the pool isn't just for casual purposes?"

"No. But it's certainly good for that as well. If you like, this weekend we can spend some time relaxing."

Floating in her flamingo sounded perfect.

"You're also free to schedule a massage at any time. Just tell Sally to arrange it." He shot her a wicked grin. "I need your body to be in prime shape for what I have in mind for your future."

Anticipation collided with nerves and tap-danced through her tummy.

When they left the apartment, Mario was on duty, standing next to the waiting elevator.

Their greetings weren't even finished when the doors opened on the floor where Lorenzo's car was running, pointed toward the exit.

Because it was already midmorning, he sifted through moderate traffic to her father's mansion. Today, however, instead of kissing her when they were on the porch, he took the key from her and turned the lock, letting her inside, then following her.

Dressed for work, her father was walking down the stairs, and he froze when he noticed Lorenzo, knuckles whitening on the banister. "What the fuck are you doing here?" A nasty tic throbbed in his temple, and Zara stared at him in stunned silence.

"Daddy?"

Ignoring her, he leveled an icy gaze at Lorenzo. "I told you never again to enter my house."

"As a matter of respect, I wanted you to be the first to know."

"Know what?" Nostrils flaring, he descended the rest of the stairs.

"Zara has agreed to be my wife."

"Not until I rot in hell." Her father's face mottled with fury. Then he rounded on her. "He's a piece of shit, Zara, and I forbid it."

Stupefied, she looked between the two men like she had all those years ago.

With a snarl, he glared at Lorenzo. "Did you tell her?"

"Tell me what?"

Silence ricocheted from the ceiling.

"Tell me *what?*"

"You didn't, did you?" Her father sneered. "How did you get her to agree?"

"Tread carefully." Lorenzo's words were coated with calm, deadly in their intent.

"I don't know what game he thinks he's playing. He owns us, Zara. The business, the house. Bleeding us dry, month after month."

The room spun. With her father's words echoing damningly, she faced Lorenzo.

But her father wasn't done. "He's a fucking vulture, waiting to pick our carcasses. When he has you, there'll be nothing to stop him from pushing me and your brothers out. He doesn't love you, Zara, and you can't believe he does."

Her father's words broke her. She and Lorenzo had shared so very much, talked of the future and babies, but he'd never once admitted he loved her.

"You're nothing more than an amusing little bauble he intends to crush."

Legs shaking as emotion threatened to overwhelm her, she looked into the dark eyes of the man she'd promised to marry. "Tell me it's a lie. Please. *Please.*"

He captured her chin. "Principessa—"

"Tell me!"

"Let me explain—"

On the verge of cracking, she frantically swatted away his hand as she pulled back from him. A sob caught in her throat. "Tell me he's lying."

"It's not what you think."

"What do you expect from a Mafia cockroach?" her father demanded. "You know how they are. Marry a good woman, have heirs to continue the line and their crooked ways, then take a mistress on the side. You'll be lucky if he doesn't flaunt it in your face."

Say it's not true. "Lorenzo…" She gave him one last chance.

His silence condemned him.

"You can have everything you want, but you can't have my daughter."

Fury and devastation collided in her, and she squared her shoulders as she held onto the tattered remnants of her pride. "Get out."

"Zara. Principessa, allow me to explain…"

She fled upstairs to her room, and once she was there with the door closed, she collapsed, drowning in her devastation.

CHAPTER EIGHT

It had been over a week since Zara vanquished Lorenzo from her life. Since then, she hadn't slept more than a couple of hours at a time. She'd fallen behind on her work, and because her appetite was ruined, she'd lost several pounds.

No matter how hard she tried to harness her thoughts, she couldn't stop replaying events they'd shared—making love, wearing his collar. Surely it had been real. At least some of it had to have been.

She'd been tempted to cancel today's meeting with Avery and Makenna, but Elise had kicked her out of the office, saying a change of scenery would do her good.

When Zara arrived at the Royal Sterling's teahouse, she'd ordered green tea, and now she was on her second pot.

"Zara?"

Interrupted from her reverie, she shook her head and gave Makenna a small, forced smile. "Sorry."

"I have news."

"Do tell."

"I'm going to promote Riley so that I have more time to travel with Zachary."

"That's wonderful!" Zara exclaimed.

Makenna turned to Avery. "Are you accepting new clients?"

"I've always got room for you." Avery had recently started her own accounting firm, and it was growing rapidly.

"I'll be hiring more staff to help with the workload, but I'm planning to oversee things from home, even when I'm on maternity leave."

"Uhm…" Makenna winced. "Should I ask about your rates?"

Avery waved a hand. "Be prepared. They're outrageous. But I'll keep you out of trouble, and that makes me worth every penny."

"Having that worry off my mind is worth it."

The conversation moved on to Avery's baby shower.

"Did you receive the save-the-date invitation?" Avery asked Zara.

"I did, thank you. I added it to my calendar, and if it's okay, you can consider this my RSVP."

Makenna opened an app on her phone and entered the information.

"I just hope I'm not waddling by then. I swear to God these babies feel enormous, even though the doctor promises they're not."

"You're the world's most beautiful pregnant woman," Makenna insisted.

"More like the most exhausted."

As her friends discussed some final baby shower details, Zara blinked, recalling Lorenzo teasing her that he wanted to have six children, or at least keep trying for that many.

Was he now planning to have them with some other woman?

That thought arrowed a knife straight through her heart.

"Zara? Is everything okay?"

Realizing Makenna had been talking to her yet again, Zara refocused her attention. "I missed the question."

"I was asking how business is."

Without thinking, she responded honestly. "I've been a little off my game."

"Do you want to talk about it?" Avery asked.

Though her heart was broken, she needed the support of her friends.

Makenna refreshed her cup. "You've always been there for us."

Though she left out Lorenzo's rumored Mafia affiliation, she outlined what had happened, beginning with her father's financial mess and ending with the confrontation between the two men. "I should be grateful that I found out before we got married." She pressed her lips together to hold back the ever-present grief. "But I'm not."

She expected her friends to jump in and tell her that she should move on and forget him. But they didn't.

Instead, Avery leaned forward. "I'm confused. How did Lorenzo know about the debt to begin with?" Trust Avery and her financial mind for zeroing in on that question.

Zara frowned. "I have no idea." She recalled him attending the Christmas party, and her father being shaken by Lorenzo's presence. Since then, he'd never dropped by. Until last week.

After waiting for a moment, Makenna spoke. "I don't know Lorenzo well, but Zachary considers him a friend."

Avery nodded agreement. "So does Cole."

"Which makes me want to give him the benefit of the doubt."

Intrigued, Zara encouraged Makenna to go on.

"I think you need more information. Certain things aren't

adding up for you. You say you should let it go, but how can you with so many questions?"

"Kenna's right," Avery stated. "I'm not jumping in to defend Lorenzo, and I care about you. But that night with Maverick, he protected you."

And it wasn't the first time.

Then Makenna made a promise. "Whatever you decide, we're going to support you."

"If you need to talk, call me or Kenna."

The server brought a plate of petit fours to the table. "I shouldn't. But..." Shrugging, Avery reached for one.

Since she'd lost weight, Zara did too.

A few minutes later, the conversation wound down.

After everyone had gone their separate ways, Zara debated what to do, and she decided Makenna was right. Before she could put Lorenzo out of her head forever, Zara needed more information, and she knew where to get it.

For one of the first evenings in memory, she didn't have an event lined up, and when she exited the Royal Sterling, she asked Bryan to drop her off at her father's office.

She found him sitting behind his desk, staring morosely into a glass of scotch.

"Since when do you drink at work?" Without waiting for an invitation, she took a seat across from him.

"To what do I owe this honor?"

"I want answers."

He finished his drink in a single swallow, then put down the glass with a distinct clatter.

"How did Lorenzo come to own us?"

"Bad decisions."

"Look Dad. I'm not backing down." Taking a breath, she stared at the man she'd worshipped and admired her whole life. "If you don't tell me the truth, I'll find it on my own."

Anger flashed in his eyes.

"Fine." She pushed back a chair and stood. "I'll hire an investigator."

"Wait." He held up a hand.

Doubtful he'd be forthcoming enough to change her mind, she resumed her seat.

He swiveled to grab the decanter from his credenza. After pouring himself at least three fingers' worth of the alcohol, he faced her. His features were haggard. "You mean the world to me, Zara. Even though your mother never met you, she loved you completely." He took a breath.

"Dad—"

"Things looked bad. She begged and pleaded for the doctors to save you."

"I have no idea why you're telling me all of this."

"Your mother always saw the best in people. In me. I was lost after she died. Drinking. Gambling."

Zara closed her eyes against the horror of the picture he painted. But all those years ago, Jeffrey Berto made a horrible accusation. She had to know if it was true. "You owed money to Marco La Rosa."

His shoulders slumped forward.

No doubt the mob charged usurious rates on the debt, with no way out. And the more he bet, the worse it had gotten.

This conversation was awful, but she intended to press forward. "And how does Berto fit it?"

His eyes were stricken, and that told her everything.

It's true. All of it. Her heart twisted with the sick reality of her past and the blind love she'd given her father.

"I would have never let him hurt you."

"If Lorenzo hadn't saved me, he would have." Her father's betrayal was worse than anything else she'd ever endured.

He downed the scotch in a few gulps.

"Why was he there that day?"

"To collect money. A fucking goon sent to break my legs if I didn't pay up. It was our goddamn holiday party."

While she couldn't excuse Lorenzo, her father was the one who'd bet money he didn't have. "None of that explains why he owns us."

"After he saw what happened with Berto, Lorenzo bought the debt from his uncle. He told me he'd kill me if anything happened to you."

And it never had, because he'd been watching, for ten years.

"He owns a significant part of the business and the house. It's his *graciousness*"—he spat the word—"that allows us to stay here."

At any time, even now, Lorenzo could have destroyed her family.

"I swear to you by everything that is holy... I've been tormented every day of my life."

"Not as much as I have." Vibrating with anger, she stood and smacked her palms on his desk and leaned forward. "That's why Grandmother left me money, isn't it? Because she knew what you'd done." When he didn't answer, she sighed. "You will never mess around in my life again." Pivoting, she strode from the room.

Bryan was waiting for her downstairs, and she asked him to drive her to the office.

Elise had long since left, but when Zara flipped on the light, she noticed a manila envelope in the middle of her desk. Her name was scrawled on the front, and the return address was Lorenzo's.

Frowning, she snatched it up, then pulled out a sheaf of papers.

It took a second to recognize what the documents were, and when it hit her, she sank onto the edge of her desk.

The deed to her family's house, in her name.

A scrawled note on a sticky piece of yellow paper leaped out at her.

Do with it as you will.
L

It was then that she recognized the date on the first page. The same day he'd saved her from Maverick's attempt to drug her.

Which meant he'd intended to give her the home even before they'd made love.

Nerves and adrenaline racing through her, she called Bryan and asked when he'd be available again.

"Is half an hour all right, Ms. Davis?"

"Perfect."

She used the time to change into her shortest dress with a plunging scooped back and cleavage-revealing front.

After slipping into her highest heels, she brushed her hair, refreshed her makeup, and carefully applied a coat of her signature Kiss Me lipstick.

When Bryan texted that he'd arrived, she rode the elevator to the ground floor, then slid into the backseat.

"Where to?"

"The Bella Rosa, please."

"Hey, boss."

Lorenzo pressed the button that would connect him to Rico.

"Ms. Davis is in the house."

As expected. Despite his anger at the way she'd handled the situation with her father, Lorenzo couldn't prevent the surge of raw hunger that pulsed through him. "Have Mario bring her up. But take your time."

"Sure, boss."

He entered his home office and pulled up video, scrolling until he zeroed in on her, walking to the Martini Bar.

Fuck me.

The back of her gown swooped down to her ass, and he had no idea how her luscious breasts didn't spill from the front.

For a moment, he zoomed in on her beautiful, inviting lips.

Damn it. Every man with a pulse was going to fall at her feet. He growled. She was his, and soon he would goddamn well make sure the whole world knew it.

He kept a camera trained on her as she was seated at a round table designed for cozy get togethers.

With a snarl, he keyed Enrico. "No one better join her."

"Sure, boss."

On the table, her phone lit up. She read a message, then placed it back where it had been, facedown.

Moments later, her drink was delivered, and a young, stupid pup approached her. To her credit, she shook her head, denying the interloper, just seconds before his security team passed her table.

Then, as if knowing he was watching, she turned toward the camera and lifted her glass in a mock toast.

With more than a week's worth of agitation gnawing at him, Lorenzo turned off the camera and strode to the living room where he paced in front of the window until the elevator bell dinged.

Then he folded his arms behind his back, waiting, wondering.

Mario opened the door, then stepped aside while she entered. "Thank you," she said to his most loyal man.

Without a word, Mario left, sealing her inside Lorenzo's domain.

In the bar, she'd been a bit more confident than she was now. Instead of placing her small handbag on the table, she clutched it in front of her.

"Something to say, principessa?"

"I..." Her voice trembled, but he made no move toward her, did nothing to help her out.

Being married to him wouldn't be easy, and he'd warned her of that fact. And still, she'd failed the first test she'd endured.

"I don't deserve it, but I hope you can forgive me."

"Go on."

She closed her eyes, as if she'd hoped that was enough to undo all the damage that she'd caused. Her lower lip quivered, but he refused to be swayed.

"May I come in?"

"Only if you strip off your clothes and drop to your knees as you beg me to give you the beating you deserve." It was harsh, but her words last week had destroyed him, destroyed them.

"Is that what you want? What you demand?" She brought her chin up. "To punish me in anger? If that's what it takes, I'll submit to you. Do your worst, Lorenzo. Use a cane. I don't care. I deserve it."

Principessa. "Why are you here?"

"You're making this difficult."

"What did you expect? That I'd slit my wrists and open my heart to you again?"

"I'm so sorry for what I said, for what I did."

"And?"

Her knuckles whitened as she gripped her purse harder.

"I received your envelope. And my father texted that he also received one, giving him full ownership of the business again."

"I hope he's learned. It's in better shape than it's ever been. Up to him and your brothers whether or not they fuck it up." Well past caring, he shrugged. "If you've come to thank me, you're welcome."

"Even before that, I'd decided to come here."

"For what purpose?"

"To apologize."

"I'm listening. Which is far more grace than you showed me." Without inviting her to join him, he took a seat and continued to regard her.

She tipped her head to the side, acknowledging what he'd said. "It took me some time, and my friends, to help me see where things didn't make sense. So I went to see my father today."

"And?"

"He was my daddy, my whole world. I knew he wasn't perfect, but I had no idea…" She shook her head, sending her hair swaying across her back.

He gave her the room to continue at her own pace.

"I understand you bought his debt from your uncle."

So Davis had revealed more than Lorenzo might have expected him to.

"Why did you do it?"

"Do you have to ask?"

"For me?"

"Yeah. Berto is lucky I didn't kill him with my bare hands that night. And your father is also fortunate that he escaped my wrath for what he tried to do to you."

At the harshness of his words, her shoulders shook.

"I vowed no one would ever touch you again. Even me. You were too fucking young, thought you were grown up.

And I wanted to make sure you gained some experience before coming to me."

"You knew that I worshipped you."

He nodded. "Being with a man like me means you have to make some difficult choices."

"I understand now. You expect your wife to stand by you. Asking questions instead of jumping to conclusions."

"I warned you I'm not perfect. I'm a ruthless sonofabitch who's done things I'm not proud of and will do so again. You should seize this chance and run away."

"Never again." Boldly she met his gaze. "If you'll have me."

"It was never in question."

"I'm sorry it took me so long to see the truth."

And now, having received her heartfelt apology, he softened. A small part of him admired her loyalty to her father, no matter how misplaced it had been.

"You forgive me?"

He stood and extended a hand toward her. "Come to me."

She did, and he drew her against his body, holding her tight. He kissed her, possessed her, made sure she'd never forget they belonged together.

Finally, when he was able to pull his mouth away, she looked up at him through her long, damp eyelashes. "Make love to me? Claim me? I need the connection."

And so did he. "Go upstairs and put on your collar, then strip and meet me in the dungeon."

He watched her go, the sweet sway of her hips tantalizing him.

Everything was close to being perfect once again.

Minutes later, he was in their playroom, and he readied the space for her, selecting a crop with a large star-shaped flapper on the end. Tonight, she wouldn't get a choice in what they did.

After discarding his suit coat and tie, he turned back his shirtsleeves.

Wearing only her heels and the collar, so lovely in her submission, she joined him. Without him issuing a single instruction, she sank to her knees and lowered her head.

He offered a hand up. "Tonight, I want you in the swing."

"I've never done anything like this before."

"You'll enjoy it. Or at least I will." He held it steady while she placed her rear in the curved part.

Then he tucked her feet in the stirrups at the end and secured her arms far apart.

"I was worried I might fall out, but there's no way, is there?"

"No." The seat part was so deep that he'd have to help her out of it.

Lorenzo took his time arousing her, stroking her pussy, then leaning over to lick it, teasing her clit.

He slid one finger inside her, followed by a second, making her moan his name. Instantly his cock hardened. He ached to bury himself in her, but first he intended to give her orgasms she wouldn't forget.

"Oh my God, I'm so ready."

He squeezed her breasts and sucked on her nipples, making her writhe.

Then he left her long enough to pick up the crop.

Her eyes widened. "Where do you intend to use it?"

"Where do you think?"

Futilely she fought to close her legs. "That looks like it's going to hurt."

"I'm sure it will." Returning to her, he parted her folds.

"Lorenzo...?"

He moved behind her and slid the star over her clitoris, and she moaned. "See? Not so bad."

Rather than pulling away, she tried to arch toward it.

Over and over, he tapped it against her, until she reddened, and her clit became a hard nub.

Fisting her glorious hair, he spanked between her legs. This time, because she was more aroused, he used slightly harsher strokes. "Can you come from this, darling principessa?"

"No. It's too much."

Willing to bet otherwise, he continued, increasing the intensity.

"Oh *fuck*."

He tugged a little harder on her hair. "Do it."

"It's…it's…"

He pulled back his hand and unleashed his harshest spank yet, blazing the star into her pussy.

Screaming, she came, and he grinned in raw male triumph.

Still not done, he gave her a small kiss before walking away to toss the crop onto the counter. Then, as she watched, eyes wary and intrigued, he selected a medium-size phallus from one of the drawers. "I think you're wet enough that you won't need any lube for this."

Her mouth parted slightly when he began to ease the toy inside her. As he did so, he parted her swollen folds, relentlessly driving her to another two climaxes.

Only then did he stop. "Now I think you're ready for me."

After he'd undressed, he stroked his cock as he looked at her gorgeous, naked body, red from his crop. "I could do this to you every day."

"Yes, Sir." It was as much of a whisper as it was a plea.

He took her, going in deep, enveloped in her feminine heat.

"I needed this."

He fucked her hard, spilling his seed inside her. But the feral beast in him wasn't satisfied. He wanted her again.

But rational thought prevailed. She needed some time to recover. And now that he had her back, he intended to make her his for eternity.

He wanted a future filled with moments like these, with her by his side.

Consumed with tenderness and a gnawing sense of urgency, he brushed back her hair, dropped a kiss on her forehead, then helped her from the swing.

Tamping back his impatience, but wanting to give her time to gather her wits, he took her upstairs and drew her a bath.

"You're spoiling me."

"Forever and ever."

While she soaked, he took a shower.

"Your cock is hard again, Lorenzo."

He glanced at her through the steam-soaked glass. "Still."

"I'm lucky."

Not as much as I am.

After he toweled dry and dressed in a loose-fitting pair of lounge pants, he returned to the bathroom with a robe for her.

"Luxurious. Thank you."

They made their way to the bedroom.

There, in the middle of the floor, with the blinds open to the farthest reaches of Sin City, he took her hand and lowered himself to one knee.

"Lorenzo…?" She blinked in confusion.

"This isn't the way I planned it." He'd wanted an experience she'd never forget—her name in neon lights, a band to serenade them, maybe a gondola in Venice. But he was an impatient man, and maybe every year he'd propose again in some different way. She deserved it. "Zara Davis, I love you. I'm committed to you today and for every day of the rest of my life. I will do my best to make you happy."

Her eyes filled with tears, and then, shockingly, so did his as emotion clawed at him. "Please, do me the honor of being my wife?"

She clasped her hand over her heart. "Yes! A thousand times yes. Yes, yes, *yes.*"

He slipped her custom-designed ring on her finger.

Eyes wide, she stared at it and traced the outline of the square-shaped diamond. "I love it." She smiled at him. "Thank you."

He stood and swept her into a loving embrace, sealing their commitment with a long, soulful kiss before carrying her to bed.

"Champagne?"

"The thousand-dollar-a-bottle kind?"

"Nothing but the best for you."

"Yes."

He grabbed the bottle and a couple of glasses, then told Sally to turn off all the household lights, except for the one in the bedroom that he wanted at fifty percent brightness. "Enable do-not-disturb mode until nine a.m."

"Seriously, Mr. Carrington?"

"Seriously, Sally." It was a first for him. "Please inform Mario as well."

"Of course, sir. Good night."

In the bedroom, he uncorked the bubbly and filled their flutes. He offered Zara a toast to their future, then touched his rim to hers.

They snuggled in the bed, sipping the champagne, and she admired the way her diamond caught the light. "The ring is stunning, but how is it even possible that you have it? We were supposed to go shopping for it together."

"I kept the appointment with the jeweler. I couldn't wait a moment longer to propose properly. If it's not to your taste, we can get you a different one."

"No. It's…" Blinking back tears, she tried again. "It's exactly the one I would have chosen."

"I'm delighted. In that case, we'll get married tomorrow."

"I thought… But…? What about the big wedding you want?"

"I told you I've waited long enough. We can have a second one, if you wish. Or just one of the biggest receptions the city has ever seen."

"A reception sounds perfect."

He plucked the glass from her hand and placed it alongside his on the nightstand. Then he traced her collar. "I've loved you since the moment you walked out onto your father's balcony, holding my jacket."

"And I've loved you since you saved me and returned my mother's necklace."

He rolled her beneath him and sank inside her in a single thrust. *"Mine."*

"Mine." She dug her hands into his hair.

Her fierce possession made his dick even harder. "I want you to stop taking the pill as soon as you're ready."

A smile played with the corners of her mouth. "How about tomorrow?"

He froze. Children would be the one thing that would make their lives complete. He wasn't foolish enough to believe it would be easy or even possible. But her willingness to try was the thing that mattered the most. "You're ready?"

"Yes. I want to create a future with you."

They made sweet love and drifted off to sleep with whispered promises of love between them—promises made, promises that would be kept. Forever and ever.

BONUS EPILOGUE

From where he stood on the far end of Avery and Cole Stewart's living room, Lorenzo swept his gaze over his new wife. *Zara.* In her little black dress and sky-high heels, she took his breath away. It wasn't just her beauty with long blonde tresses flowing over her shoulders and her signature Kiss Me lipstick making her mouth look even more enticing. Kiss Me? It should be renamed Fuck Me.

He gave a wry smile. The truth was, no matter what she wore, she inflamed his desire. He craved her. And for the first time in his life, the attraction was as emotional and intellectual as it was physical.

They'd worked together seamlessly on their wedding and to establish their new life as a couple. She filled in the jagged pieces of his soul that he hadn't even known were missing.

As lovely as this holiday open house was and as much as he enjoyed being with their friends, he wanted to spend the rest of Christmas Eve with his new bride.

Perhaps sensing his perusal, she glanced up to meet his gaze.

Even though they were separated, he imagined he heard

her breath catch. He inclined his head toward the front door. With a half-smile, she nodded.

After giving her enough time to finish her conversation, he closed the distance between them and placed a possessive palm against the small of her back. As naturally as she breathed, she leaned into him, offering her trust and simultaneously deepening their connection.

"If you'll excuse us, ladies…" He grinned and gave a helpless shrug. "We're newlyweds."

His words were met with knowing glances and approving smiles.

"Merry Christmas." Zara gave each of the women a hug.

Together he and Zara sought out their hosts.

"Thank you for inviting us." Lorenzo shook Cole's hand while Zara and Avery embraced.

"Are we still meeting this week?" Avery asked her friend.

"Absolutely." Zara nodded. "If you're up for it."

"I need to destress."

"The Royal Sterling's teahouse? Tuesday? Four o'clock."

"I'll let Makenna know. She was hoping we wouldn't have to cancel because of the holidays."

The trio had met at a businesswomen's group and had formed a tight bond.

"I want to do our year-end review and discuss goals." Avery patted her enormous stomach. "Once the girls arrive, it will be a little late for planning. I want to be sure everything is in place."

A few moments later Lorenzo and Zara made their way to the front door.

Outside, his man and loyal lieutenant, Mario, detached himself from the shadows and fell in step behind them.

When the valet returned with the car, Lorenzo assisted his wife into the low-slung seat before taking his place behind the wheel and driving away from the Stewart estate.

A quick check in the rearview mirror confirmed Mario was in the car behind them.

Zara scanned their surroundings. "It doesn't feel like Christmas."

She was right. The Las Vegas evening was unseasonably warm, and the last rays of sunlight painted the sky a watery, golden hue. "Are you up for a surprise?"

She turned toward him. "What do you have in mind?"

"I think you'll like it." Six weeks ago, they'd purchased a second home. While they still lived in the owner's suite at his Bella Rosa resort, they'd also wanted a place off the Strip where they could relax.

Instead of taking her to the house where they planned to spend the next few days, he drove to her favorite coffee shop.

"What are we doing here?"

"Getting hot chocolate so we can enjoy some of the holiday lights."

Her face lit up.

Before they'd gotten married, Lorenzo informed her he wanted a big family. Sooner rather than later. So he intended to establish traditions that his new family might enjoy.

Since the drive-through lane was packed, he slid into a parking space. "I'll be right back."

"Are you kidding me? You hate lines."

"Yeah." He grinned. "But I love you."

Once Mario was also parked, Lorenzo braved the crowd that seemed to have the same idea he did.

Fifteen minutes later he emerged carrying three of the largest size cups.

Mario rolled down the driver's side window when Lorenzo approached. "I got you a hot chocolate."

Mario frowned at the sight of the festive red cup. "What am I supposed to do with it?"

"You drink it and enjoy the holidays."

"Yeah. Sure, boss."

With obvious reluctance, the man accepted the offering. Then he quickly pushed the button to raise the window as if afraid Lorenzo may foist a cookie on him.

Grinning, Lorenzo walked to his car and placed the cups on the roof while he opened the door. "For you, *principessa*. One-hundred eighty degrees. Extra whipping cream." He leaned into the passenger compartment.

"And sprinkles?"

"And sprinkles." Before turning over the treat, he stole a kiss. That would have to last him for a while. Suddenly he was debating the wisdom of driving around the city.

While he got settled, she took the lid off her cup and flicked out her tongue to scoop up some of the whipped cream. Even in the twilight, he noted the unholy gleam in her eyes. "You'll pay for that, Mrs. Carrington."

Her grin was as adorable as it was sassy. "I was counting on it, Sir."

For the next hour, they took in some amazing displays. More than once, she asked him to stop so she could take pictures.

"Ready to go home and spend the first night at our new house?"

"I can't wait."

He'd saved the best for last.

As they turned on to their street, Zara gasped. "Lorenzo!"

"Just for you, principessa." Getting everything perfect for her had required its own Christmas miracle.

A full-size sleigh and lifelike Santa Claus dominated the front yard. Every inch of the house was covered with lights, and all the palm trees were decorated.

"I'm sure this display can be seen from the space station."

"I like to make you happy."

"Being your wife is the only gift I need."

Clouds parted, and stars appeared as he opened the ornate gates to park in the driveway.

Mario continued past him to the guest house.

Lorenzo had offered him time off, but since he had no other family, Mario had opted to work. Lorenzo intended to cook dinner tomorrow for Zara and his most loyal men. This year, his uncle would also be joining them. And it would be Zara's first time meeting the notorious don.

He grabbed their bags before opening the front door. Every light in the house was on, including those on the twenty-foot tree next to the hearth.

"My God, Lorenzo. When did you have time to do all this?"

"I figured we can run the air conditioner so that we can turn on the fireplace."

"That seems a bit extravagant."

"It *is* Christmas Eve."

She moved closer to the tree. "These ornaments!"

He grinned.

"The Bella Rosa?"

"And my uncle's resort." It was fitting. The two casinos bookended the Strip.

"They're stunning. So detailed, and the colors are perfect."

He nodded, pleased with the job the artist had done in crafting the detailed glass collectibles. "Would you like your gift this evening? Or on Christmas morning?"

"You've already done too much."

Nothing would repay the hope and joy she'd brought into his life. "Now? Or tomorrow?"

"Usually I like Christmas morning. But…"

"But?"

"I'm curious."

"Tonight it is." He crossed to his bag and pulled out a jewelry box.

Frowning, she opened it. Then she gasped. "These... They're stunning!"

He'd bought her earrings to go along with her other signature pieces. Diamonds. "Beautiful and indestructible. Like our love."

"You're so thoughtful." After replacing the holiday-themed ones she'd worn to Cole and Avery's house, she raised on her toes to kiss him. "Thank you."

His cock hardening, he wrapped his arms around her.

With a laugh she pushed him back. "I have something for you first."

She wiggled away from him and unzipped her bag, then handed him a package wrapped in satiny red paper adorned with a silver bow.

It had been a very long time since he'd received a present, and her thoughtfulness made him ridiculously happy.

With more excitement than he imagined possible, he ripped apart the paper. "A drone?"

"You mentioned you wanted one."

It had been in passing, but he appreciated knowing she heard his every word.

"You can take pictures of our Christmas lights."

Though he intended to do just that, he wouldn't share them publicly. He'd made enemies in his short life, and his wife's safety and privacy were paramount.

"Or you can do them from our rooftop at the Bella Rosa to remind yourself you're King of Sin City."

He wasn't there quite yet, but perhaps he would be with her at his side.

After placing the gift on the counter, he kissed her in gratitude and promise.

In her perfect and submissive way, she leaned into him, wrapping her arms around his neck in surrender.

She tasted of cocoa, cream, and a promise for the future.

"I have another gift for you." Through the impossibly long fringe of her eyelashes, she glanced up at him as she smiled.

With his gaze he devoured her. "I already know."

"You…?" She frowned. "What?"

"I've been wondering when you would tell me." He captured the hem of her little black dress and tugged it up and off.

Then he kissed that sensuous, inviting place where her neck curved into her creamy shoulder. "We're going to have a baby."

She blinked. "You can't possibly know that."

"Principessa." *My darling. My precious.* "I know everything about you. I've seen the radiant changes in your body. Your breasts are fuller." He unfastened her bra, then lowered his head to suck on one of her pebbled nipples.

She gasped.

"And you're more sensitive than ever."

"But I only found out today."

"I've been sure for two weeks." Lorenzo skimmed his fingers over her belly. "You taste different. Sweeter. And there's a bond between us that is more profound than it ever was." He brushed aside the gusset of her panties to tease her clit.

She was wet, already drenched for him.

"I can't get enough of you." He dropped to his knees to tease her sex with his mouth. "I could do this every day."

"As I get bigger, we're going to have to be creative about how we make love."

"I look forward to that." Then he regarded her seriously. "In the future, I'd like to go to doctor's appointments with you."

"You're a busy man, Lorenzo."

"It wasn't a request."

She shivered a little. "Yes, Sir."

"We will go through this together. This is my baby, and I will be there for his or her mother every single day and in every way."

"Make love to me."

Nothing would please him more.

Effortlessly he scooped her up and carried her to their bed.

After he stripped off her panties, she took his cock in hand, watching him, stroking him until he throbbed.

Generally he liked to give her several orgasms before he came. Tonight, however, he wanted them to climax together in celebration.

With his mouth and hands, he aroused her before sliding into her feminine heat. "Wait for me, principessa."

Pressing her lips together, she nodded.

Lorenzo held back as long as he could, but his desire for her consumed him.

He threaded his fingers into her hair, holding her tight. "Come for me."

"Yes. *Yes!*" She screamed his name, and he kissed her deeply.

He held her tight as they rode out their pleasure.

Eventually sated, arms shaky, he captured her gaze. "I love you, Zara."

"And I love you. More today than I did yesterday."

For a few moments they lay together, limbs entwined, enjoying the quiet of the evening.

Then, anxious to show her his final Christmas gift, he fetched a warm, wet cloth from the adjoining bathroom. After cleansing her gently, he offered her a robe. "I have one more surprise for you."

"Are you serious?"

He took her hand, helped her from the bed, then guided her down the hallway to a closed door. "After you."

She turned the knob and walked inside, missing a step.

Instinctively he cupped her elbow to steady her.

"A nursery?"

"I asked Avery for a recommendation on a decorator."

"It's…everything." Her eyes filled with tears.

The room was warm and welcoming with a luxurious rocking chair, a crib, and the millions of things he'd been told a baby needed.

Through her smile, she took in a steadying breath. "You're the best husband ever."

She placed a hand on his chest and then eased lower.

He growled. "Be sure you know what you're doing, principessa."

"Awakening the beast?"

For the last few minutes, he'd been half-hard, and now her confident touch made his erection throb. "In that case, I'm taking you back to bed."

He did just that, and they made sweet, gentle love together.

Hours later, the distant grandfather clock struck midnight. "Merry Christmas, Mrs. Carrington."

"Merry Christmas, Sir."

He cradled her in the protection of his arms. "Thank you for the gift of your love and a baby."

She smiled at him. "Thank *you*."

"This is forever, Zara."

With a happy sigh, she snuggled in closer. "I couldn't wish for anything better."

Outside a star winked in the black, endless sky.

Christmas, and their future, was beginning…

ABOUT THE AUTHOR

I invite you to be the very first to know all the news by subscribing to my very special **VIP Reader newsletter**! You'll find exclusive excerpts, bonus reads, and insider information.

For tons of fun and to join with other awesome people like you, join my Facebook reader group: **Sierra's Super Stars**

And for a current booklist, please visit my **website**.
www.sierracartwright.com

USA Today bestselling author Sierra Cartwright was born in England, and she spent her early childhood traipsing through castles and dreaming of happily-ever afters. She has two wonderful kids and four amazing grand-kitties. She now calls Galveston, Texas home and loves to connect with her readers. Please do drop her a note.

ALSO BY SIERRA CARTWRIGHT

Titans

Sexiest Billionaire

Billionaire's Matchmaker

Billionaire's Christmas

Determined Billionaire

Scandalous Billionaire

Ruthless Billionaire

Titans Quarter

His to Claim

His to Love

His to Cherish

Titans Sin City

Hard Hand

Slow Burn

All-In

Titans: Reserve

Tease Me

Titans Captivated

Theirs to Hold

Hawkeye

Come to Me

Trust in Me

Meant For Me

Hold On To Me

Believe in Me

Hawkeye: Denver

Initiation

Determination

Temptation

Bonds

Crave

Claim

Command

Donovan Dynasty

Bind

Brand

Boss

Mastered

With This Collar

On His Terms

Over The Line

In His Cuffs

For The Sub

In The Den

Collections

Titans Series

Titans Billionaires: Firsts

Titans Billionaires: Volume 1

Risking It All: Titans: Sin City Boxset

Hawkeye Series

Here for Me: Volume One

Beg For Me: Volume Two

Printed in Great Britain
by Amazon